Eloise
and the
GRUMP
NEXT DOOR

**EMMA
ST. CLAIR**

**JENNY
PROCTOR**

To all the readers who make our words come alive, and to everyone who knows to wear pink on Wednesdays.

(But even if you don't, you can still sit with us.)

ONE

Lo

AS FAR AS BIRTHDAYS GO, this one isn't the worst.

And by that, I mean the worst in the entire world. For me *personally*, this birthday takes the cake.

Except it doesn't! Because I don't even have cake. I have a glass of merlot. My second of the night and—true confession time!—my second glass of wine ever.

The problem with being a rule-follower, you see, is all the rules. And until today, I wasn't legal.

"The big twenty-one," Ned the bartender remarks, raising his bushy white brows, which perfectly match his mustache. "And you're celebrating *here?*"

I glance around the bar, which is what I'd call piratecore. Like the popular cottagecore aesthetic trend ... but with pirates. Wood, wood, and more wood, with a lot of swords and ropes. There are fake skulls everywhere, old kegs of rum, and even a wooden mermaid carving that looks like it's been cut straight from the bow of a ship. Based on the mermaid's, um, assets and the flimsy clothes covering them, the ship might have been named *Hooters of the Sea*.

Next to her, a wooden cage houses a parrot I thought was stuffed until he quoted Macbeth. I almost fell off my stool.

His name is Bard the bird, according to Ned, who explained that Bard only speaks lines from classic literature. Because of *course* he does. I've been waiting for a *Treasure Island* quote, but so far, the only ones I've recognized are from Shakespeare, Jane Austen, and the Bronte sisters. It's odd, but oddly fitting given my recently completed bachelor's in English.

"What's wrong with here?" I ask.

Ned chuckles. "Plenty of things are wrong. I should know; I own the place."

"Well, I happen to like the vibe."

I really *do*. The bar is more kitschy than touristy. If I weren't taking a brief hiatus from Instagram, I'd have taken a lot of photos. Ned's Place fits the quirky feel of Oakley Island I remember from my childhood summers. Unlike some of the more popular, touristy barrier islands stretching from North Carolina to Georgia, Oakley feels more like a small town that happens to be located on a beautiful beachy island.

Though a lot has changed since I last visited. The owner of the bed and breakfast where I'm staying was quick to inform me of all the new restaurants and shops that have opened up on Main Street. And I passed a gorgeous and tastefully understated inn on my way into town that I know didn't exist when I was younger.

Ned's voice gentles. "But you're here on your birthday … alone?"

I straighten on my stool, smoothing down the skirt of my favorite dress. It's light turquoise with a pineapple

2

print, and though I can't compete with the wooden mermaid, I like to think it does nice things for my figure. I thought I might as well dress for the party I wish I were having.

"I don't exactly know anyone on the island," I say, glancing around again. *Not anymore.*

"If you don't know anyone, what brings you here?"

"I'm here for my grandmother's funeral," I say quietly, looking down at my glass.

The island is small enough I know Ned had to know Gran. How *well* he knew her, I'm not sure. I glance up and see Ned wearing a soft expression.

"I didn't recognize you," he says. "Not without the pigtails. Eloise?"

I nod. "People call me Lo now. You remember me?"

"You and your sisters." He grins. "Three little terrors."

I slap my palm on the bar, even though I know he's teasing. "We were not!"

"No, you weren't." Ned chuckles. "Not any more than any of the other island kids, anyway. Mine included. I'm sorry about your grandma. Genevieve was a good soul."

"She was." I wait to feel something—*anything*—but just as it's been since I heard the news, my emotions are log jammed somewhere deep inside me.

The pause feels like a paperweight dropped right in the middle of our conversation. I take a sip of wine and wrinkle my nose. I wish I liked the taste more. I think I prefer grape juice.

"Shouldn't your sisters be with you?" Ned asks. "Or your dad?"

I give my head a quick shake. "Not yet. They'll be here tomorrow."

He pulls a few empty glasses off the bar and wipes up a

spill. "Are you planning to stick around? Enjoy the island for a bit?"

The door bangs open just then, ushering in a loud group dressed in suits and dresses, most looking to be in their mid-thirties or early forties. I suddenly feel immensely childish with my pineapple dress and a light buzz from a glass and a half of merlot.

Regardless, I'm grateful for their arrival because it means I don't have to answer Ned's question. He's already moving down the bar taking orders.

I actually *can't* answer his question. Or any other questions about my future plans. Not just the long-term future stuff. We're talking day-after-tomorrow future. It's all a great big question mark, written in pencil.

Five days ago, I walked across a stage, accepting my college diploma and smiling for photographs my mom and sisters were taking.

Four days ago, my family members flew back to their respective homes scattered across three states, and I finished packing up my apartment to move back to Arizona with Mom and the stepfather I barely know. Because when you only apply to one grad school and don't get in, home is the only choice you have.

I know. I've got this adulting thing *down*.

Two days ago, I set out for the drive from North-western and got word six hours into my trip that my grandmother had died. I changed routes and headed straight here, stopping for one night in a motel that smelled like dirty feet and looked twice as bad as it smelled.

This morning, I finally arrived on Oakley Island, thankful the bed and breakfast where I'm staying smells like blueberry muffins and not even a little like feet.

Tomorrow, I'll reunite with my sisters and the father we barely know and his … fourth—fifth?—wife.

But tonight, I'm *alone*. In a pirate bar. On my birthday.

I chug down the last of my wine and wipe a drop from the corner of my mouth. I think wine is supposed to be sipped and enjoyed, not gulped. But who's here to judge me? No one, that's who.

Is it too much to wish, once everyone learned of the funeral, that Sadie and Merritt might have come a night early for my birthday? My sisters are only four and five years older than me, respectively, but it feels like an uncrossable impasse sometimes. They have Real Jobs and Adult Lives. Both already took off work this week for my graduation, and now they're doing it again to be here, so I can't truly begrudge their absence. I will, however, allow myself a very small, very solitary pity party. I think I'm at least entitled to that much.

A pity party instead of a birthday party.

A funeral instead of grad school. This all feels very on trend for my life right now.

While my sisters have been adulting like responsible humans, I've been caught up earning a completely pointless bachelor's degree and hanging all my hopes on a grad program that, in the end, decided they didn't want me.

Hic. I slap a hand over my mouth as a hiccup escapes me.

"'Happiness in marriage is entirely a matter of chance,'" Bard the bird squawks.

That's Jane Austen. *Pride and Prejudice*, I believe. I giggle, grateful for the comedic relief eclipsing my somber thoughts. My giggling is interrupted by another hiccup, this one louder than the first.

Okay, is it just me, or did the wine suddenly go RIGHT to my head? *Hic.*

Ned returns, handing me a glass of water, which I gulp

down like I'm on mile twenty-three of a marathon. Actually, for me, it would be more like mile two. That would be my own personal record as far as running goes.

"Thank you," I say, then promptly hiccup again.

"Another merlot?" Ned asks, and even though I've just met him tonight, I recognize the hesitation in his eyes.

"Better not," I say. *Hic.* "I'm a bit of a lightweight."

Come to think of it, I'm so light that I'm starting to feel like I might float right off this stool.

Ned scratches his chin. "Have you had anything to eat tonight?"

Another customer pulls Ned's attention away while I try and figure out whether I'm hungry. I don't remember eating anything. Which, based on the seriousness of Ned's question, seems like reason for concern. Alcohol on an empty stomach is bad, right?

I startle as a man in a dark gray suit sits down beside me on the last open stool in the bar. I guess Ned's Place really comes alive after nine o'clock. Unlike me. I yawn, then hiccup again. Nine o'clock is usually when I turn into a pineapple. Er—Pumpkin. That's how the fairy tale goes, right?

Without being too obvious, I check out my new bar-neighbor. Yowza! His presence is definitely bringing the temperature up in here. Dark hair, broad shoulders, and eyes whose color I can't make out. Great lashes, though. Why do men always get those? Ugh. Unfair.

He's hunched over his drink, which is one of those very adult-looking amber liquids very adult-looking people toss back in movies. Scotch or bourbon or malt something or other.

This guy, though, he's just staring into his glass, a frown etched on his handsome face. Which I suspect would be

6

even handsomer—more handsome? Handsomier?—if he smiled.

I swivel on my stool to face him. "What can I do to"—*hic*—"turn that frown upside down?"

Smooth, Lo. Real smooth. The hiccup in the middle really helped seal the deal. And also—who says that kind of thing to a grown man? Or at ALL?

So slowly I wonder if he's part sloth, the man turns and—oh my! He is definitely more handsomey from the front. Frownier too. I expect a greeting, perhaps a question, but the only sound is another stupid hiccup from me.

"Sorry," I say, feeling dizzy under his intense gray glare. I didn't think gray eyes were a thing, but they absolutely are, and his are mesmerizing. Or maybe more vaporizing considering the way he's looking at me. "You just look so ... sad."

"I'm fine."

Hic. I wince when his glare intensifies. How does one get rid of hiccups? I can't remember the last time I had them. When I was, like, ten? That's about how old I feel next to Mr. Frowny Face, whose square jaw and dark stubble make him seem years older than the fumbling college boys I've been dating. This guy is all man.

As if to illustrate this point, he turns back to his glass of Very Adult Beverage, emptying it in one swallow. Just like the movies! But it's so much sexier up close—the way his Adam's apple bobs when he swallows, the lush curve of his mouth, the confident way he sets down his glass. The stubble on his jaw calls me like a dark beacon, waving me in. And the way he smells! I don't realize I'm leaning closer to sniff him until I almost fall off my stool.

His hand steadies me, warm on the bare skin of my arm. This gives me a much better chance to smell him. Thousands of acres of smoky woodland forest were sacrificed at the altar of some perfume-maker to create whatever cologne he's wearing. I want to roll around in it. I mean, I would want to if that weren't totally weird.

It shouldn't be weird! Normalize wanting to cloak oneself in men's cologne!

Okay—the wine has definitely taken effect. Or maybe it's him? My thoughts are both fast and slow, my heart working overtime, my face blazing hot.

The man's dark brow furrows with suspicion as he rights me on the stool. To my utter disappointment, he lets go right away. Hopefully, he didn't catch me sniffing him. But the look on his face says he totally saw me. So, I do the best thing ever when caught.

"I didn't just smell you," I lie. *Hic.*

"You didn't." It's half statement, half question, and his single raised brow has me biting back a laugh.

"Nope."

I yawn, suddenly overwhelmed as a wave of drowsiness sweeps over me. Have my eyelids always been this heavy? And my head! Holding this thing up is a full-time job. I just need a tiny rest. I yawn again, hiccup in the middle of it, and lay my head down on the bar. It's a good bar. Not as soft as a pillow, obviously, but decidedly cool against my cheek and not sticky. It's a decent temporary nap area.

I hereby designate it as such! Official TNA.

"I thought you had serving limits, Ned."

That voice! I crack an eye open, giving me a great view of the man's suit jacket, now draped over his arm. The white button-down shirt underneath would be plain on anyone else. But on him, it's totally not plain. So crisp! So white! One button has worked its way almost out of its corresponding hole. If I weren't so tired, I'd lean over and fix it.

But I am way too tired to move. Also, this conversation is might-y interesting, so I need to be still and listen.

"Come on. You know I don't over-serve. She had two glasses of house red. It's her birthday."

"I don't care whose birthday it is. She's so drunk, she passed out on your bar!"

Ha! That's where he's wrong! One—I'm not drunk. Two—I'm not passed out! I'm pretending to sleep so I can eavesdrop.

"I'll get her home." That's Ned.

No offense, Ned. You're not the one I want taking me home.

"You can't leave the bar," the man says. "Plus, I feel responsible."

Why does he feel responsible? I want to ask, though my brain-to-mouth connection is spotty at best. I must make a muffled sound, because a heavy hand comes down on the center of my back, running up and down softly. That's nice. I could get used to this...

There are more words, but I'm too focused on that hand. Up and down. Up, down. His touch is soft and comforting where all other parts of him are sharp and rough. I like the justapo—no, that's not right. The juxtapetition. Juxtaposi-tion! That's the one. I like the juxtaposition of hard and soft. He's a complex man.

I barely hold back a groan of protest when the hand leaves my back. I'm being lifted up, cradled against a broad chest. Shifting my weight slightly, the man manages to drape his jacket over my bare legs. Such a gentleman!

A hot, handsome, and strong gentleman with a great, growly voice and delicious cologne! Can I consider him my birthday present? I vote yes.

He smells even better up close, and, with my cheek pressed to his shirt, I can feel how expensive the fabric is.

"You're expensive," I mumble as he moves through the bar with me cradled to his chest. I feel pleased I'm able to talk now, even if I'm struggling with saying the right words. "I mean, you *smell* expensive. I mean, your shirt feels expensive."

He says nothing, but that's okay. I can handle the strong, silent type. I've got enough words for us both.

"Jake."

A feminine voice interrupts my happy time. Instinct has me tightening my grip on the man—Jake, I guess. At some point, my hands went around his neck. I let my fingers trail into the closely cropped hair. *Hmm.* One more soft thing about him.

His feet slow. "Margo."

I don't know him at all, but Jake doesn't sound pleased. I'm not pleased either, but for different reasons. Namely, territorial ones.

I've already staked my claim, lady! Step aside!

"A little young for you, isn't she?" the woman says.

"It's not what it looks like," Jake says.

"It looks like you're carrying an unconscious young woman out of a bar."

"I'm just getting her home safely."

"Is that who I think it is?"

Does this Margo person know me? Does Jake? He only grunts a response this time, leaving me to wonder.

Jake is moving again, and the movement makes my head feel spinnier.

"Have fun tomorrow!" Margo calls before the door slams.

"She is not nice," I mumble into Jake's chest.

He's quiet, and I hope I didn't offend him. They clearly have some kind of history. She was definitely giving off jilted ex vibes.

"She's not so terrible—on a good day. It hasn't been a good day," Jake says finally.

"It's my birthday."

"So I heard."

I wait for him to wish me a happy birthday, but he doesn't. The walk to the bed and breakfast is short. Too short. I could stay in his arms forever. Except for my spinning head. That part I could do without.

"Which room?"

His voice rumbles through his chest like a purr. He's just a big jungle cat. Maybe if I get him a bowl of milk, I could keep him. No, not milk. Jungle cats eat steak.

Mmm—steak sounds good about now.

"Eloise, which room?" Jake asks again.

"Four," I tell him. "The one with all the anchors."

"Where's your key?"

"In my pocket. My dress has pockets! I got it on sale."

He lets out another grunt—a man of few words, this one —but he shifts around, leaning me against his shoulder while his hand slides into my pocket. I think Jake has four arms. Or ninja skills. His hand is there and gone like a whisper, making goose bumps appear on my arms and bare legs.

"Do you like pineapples?" I ask as he's walking us inside my room.

"Allergic."

"No! That's a tragedy!"

"A tragedy is an event that takes place on a grand scale. It's not me getting hives from a fruit."

"Do you hate my dress?" I whisper. "It has pineapples."

"It ... doesn't give me hives."

"Good. I don't want to give you hives."

This makes me giggle, and then he's laying me down, tucking me into the covers, soft but cool without his warmth.

Grasping for his sleeve, I miss altogether, my hand flopping over the side of the bed. He tucks it back under the covers before I can latch on to him.

"You could stay," I murmur, my eyes squeezed shut.

There is a long pause, and I must start to drift asleep because I jerk awake at the sound of his voice.

"No. I really can't."

I swallow, my tongue feeling thick from emotion or the alcohol or both. I never should have asked. He's just a stranger. A really hot, nice stranger who's allergic to my favorite dress.

He could be an ax murderer! But ax murderers don't usually care about bartenders over-serving—though Ned didn't; it was just my low tolerance and the lack of food in my stomach. Still—I don't know this man, and I've invited him into my room. Alone.

I sit up so suddenly, the whole room lurches. "Are you going to ax murder me?"

Jake turns, again sloth-slow, and blinks at me. "Is that what you think—that I carried you back here when you couldn't walk and tucked you in so I could ax murder you?"

"Ted Bundy was handsome and charming." I cross my arms over my chest.

"You think I'm handsome and charming?"

"Definitely not charming."

When he bites back a smile, I realize what I've said. "And not handsome either! I mean, objectively speaking, yes, sure. But inob—inobjectively—" The word slurs, and I suddenly wish I'd let him leave without trying to say anything else.

"That's not a word. But I think what you're trying to say is that I'm handsome." He looks far too pleased with himself.

"No."

"No, I'm not, or no, that's not what you're trying to say?"

"Ugh—you argue too much. What are you—a lawyer?"

Exhausted, I flop back down and bury my head in the pillow.

He doesn't leave right away. I hear rustling and movement in the bathroom. I can't make myself look even though closing my eyes makes the spinning start again. I don't think merlot likes me.

Well, guess what, merlot? I don't like you either!

I hear him set something on the table next to the bed.

"Water and ibuprofen. You'll want it when you wake up." When he speaks again, he's farther away now, maybe near the door.

"Happy birthday, Eloise."

"My grandma is the only one who called me Eloise."

I manage to force my eyes open the slightest bit, enough to see him pause in the doorway. He doesn't stay long. The door clicks quietly closed, and the darkness spins me to sleep.

TWO

Lo

THE SUN IS AN EVIL, evil orb.

I wake with its dastardly death rays beaming straight into my brain, exacerbating the headache to end all headaches. Somewhere, my phone is vibrating, and it might as well be a whole hive of bees buzzing into a bullhorn.

I groan, sliding a hand over my eyes. Why does everything hurt? Most especially the base of my skull, but also my neck and back. I clearly slept at some kind of inhuman angle and now will pay the price with stiff joints. And my eyelids. *Ugh.* They are resting on my eyes like rough-grit sandpaper.

The phone stops buzzing and for about three seconds, I get blessed silence. Then it starts up again.

Groaning, I reach for the bedside table. Not only do I NOT find my phone, but I knock over a water glass and a small bottle of pills. The noise of everything hitting the floor

14

has me clutching my head in a dramatic—but wholly neces-sary—fashion.

I manage to locate my phone, which is charging on the dresser. Weird. I'm notoriously bad about forgetting to plug in my phone. Sadie is calling. She's the middle sister, the swinging door, the peace treaty between me and Merritt.

"Hello," I whisper.

"You're late!"

I jerk the phone away from my face because not only is it much too loud, but because I've been hit by a sneak attack. My oldest, bossiest, most irritating sister is calling from Sadie's phone.

"Merritt, could you please not shout?" I whisper.

"You are late," Merritt repeats, just as loudly as before. I can hear her seething even as I hold the phone six inches from my face.

There are only two points on which Merritt and I agree. The first is that we both prefer our chocolate without nuts of any kind, and yes, that includes peanut butter. Sadie and Mom like to say this makes us heathens, but it's a hill I'll happily die on. A no-nut, chocolate-covered hill.

The second thing Merritt and I share is that we both abhor tardiness. Which means, despite the tiny men with jackhammers inside my skull, I'm already in motion once I process her words.

"Get over here," Merritt says. "The lawyer charges by the hour, and he looks furious."

"Be there in five."

I hang up before Merritt can get another word in. And I'm sure she has a lot more words for me. Because when I glance at my phone, I'm almost ten minutes late.

I locate the ibuprofen where it rolled under the bed and pop two of them in my mouth, drinking directly from the bathroom faucet to swallow them down. A quick mirror check shows me that last night's eyeliner and mascara have miraculously stayed in place. My pineapple dress is only slightly wrinkled. It will have to do. I spray a puff of perfume in the air, walk through it, and ta-da! I'm all freshened up.

At least on the outside. On the inside, my stomach is clenching and unclenching in disturbing waves while my head throbs. I feel like I'm being fed into a meat grinder.

Which is maybe why, until right now, I have missed some important details.

First—the phone thing. With as bad as I feel now, there's no way I remembered to plug it in last night.

Then there's the ibuprofen and water. I don't remember putting those on my bedside table.

I most definitely didn't line my shoes up neatly by the door, facing the same direction. I'm more of a kick-off-my-heels-at-the-end-of-the-day kind of girl. Same with my bra. More than one morning, I've found it hanging over a lampshade or dangling from the curtains. The underwire digging into my ribs assures me that I didn't remove it last night at all. Another weird fact.

I squint around the room and see nothing but neat order. Even my purse strap is curled neatly around the body of the bag. Housekeeping wouldn't have come through while I was sleeping, right?

Unease swirls through me, and my stomach clenches tightly. Nope—that's not unease. Or not ONLY unease. It's apparently how my digestive system responds to alcohol on an empty stomach. Seriously, though—who gets a hangover from two glasses of wine?

I don't have time to worry about any of this now. I can practically hear Merritt grumbling as she checks her watch. I grab my purse and slip on the heels I wore last night to the bar.

THE BAR.

I almost fall off my heels and grab the wall for support. When I squeeze my eyes closed, it all comes back to me. Well —*most* of it. In pieces, like some kind of horror movie patchwork quilt.

I remember walking half a block to the bar, feeling lonely but keeping a pep in my step because it was my birthday. I drank a glass of wine, feeling guilty and sad about Gran but keeping my emotions under wraps as I talked to the bartender.

What was his name?

The fact I don't remember is terrifying. Forget the sun being evil. Alcohol is the straight-up devil.

Speaking of things I don't remember—I absolutely do not remember the name of the handsome man who sat down next to me. The very manly man whose very presence made me feel childish in my pineapple dress. Though so much of the night exists in patchy pieces, I could paint a picture of that man's lightly stubbled jaw and his glaring gray eyes. I recall a few vague things I said to him between my hiccups. Nothing I would say in a sober state.

And I *smelled* him.

Then I lied about it. Not very well, either. At least this answers the question of the odd things in my room. Nameless hot man carried me back here, plugged my phone in, left water and medicine on my bedside table—oh!

Oh no. *I asked him to stay!* Mortification rubs against me like a wool sweater.

With a groan, I lock the door and narrowly avoid getting hit by a golf cart full of teenage girls in bikinis as I cross the street. I forgot about that—how islanders tend to leave their

17

cars parked and zip around on golf carts instead. The thump of bass from whatever they're listening to combined with the sun has my head pounding double-time.

Wine, you are NOT my friend. Wine, you are my frenemy— making me feel all warm and nice and then letting me make a fool out of myself in front of the hottest man I've ever seen in person.

He WAS hot, wasn't he? I've never understood the meaning of beer goggles, but now I have to wonder if the image in my head is real or some kind of alcohol-induced mirage.

My only saving grace is that it's unlikely I'll ever have to see him again. The island may be small, but I don't plan to stay past tomorrow. Unless I'm needed to help with anything at Gran's. But I assume Dad has a plan in place. Not that he's so great with plans or responsibility—the fact that he's barely maintained contact with the three of us since the divorce is evidence of that. But there's likely money involved with Gran's estate, and not much makes Dad show up and be present like cold, hard cash.

Which feels gross to think about, so I won't.

The list of things I don't want to think about is growing longer by the minute as I walk into the small cottage housing our lawyer's office. With its teal paint, bright white trim, and yellow door, it looks more like a beach rental than a place you go to hear the reading of a will. I push inside, grateful there's no bell over the door and that the interior is lit mostly by natural light. There is no secretary behind the desk in the main room, but I hear the unmistakable sound of Sadie's voice from a door cracked open just down the hall.

Smoothing my hands down my wrinkled dress, I draw in a deep breath. No need to die of humiliation or hangover today. Today is about Gran, and though I'm deeply sad, it will be okay.

18

It has to be.

My shiny optimism lasts until I walk through the door. Both my sisters' heads snap up. They're seated across from the lawyer's desk. Merritt's dark brown hair is in a fancy updo so tight it makes my head throb harder just looking at it. Her navy suit is immaculate, like she just walked out of some board meeting with the CEO. She and Sadie both caught redeyes late last night from their respective homes in New York and D.C., which only makes it more irritating that they both look fresh as a daisy.

I shouldn't be surprised they both look so put together. My sisters are expert adults. Merritt's sole driving focus in life is winning a cutthroat game of corporate Chutes and Ladders while Sadie stays holed up in a cave somewhere— okay, fine, a really nice loft we've heard about but never seen —doing cybersecurity for the government. I'm not sure exactly what her job is, but she likes us to think she's saved the world twice over with her exceptional firewalls.

My gaze flits from one sister to the other.

Funny how even though I slept in a comfortable bed across the street instead of on an airplane, I appear to be the only one wearing yesterday's clothes.

My sisters notice, of course. Oh—they notice.

Sadie lifts one dark brow. "Looks like little Mary Sue is doing a walk of shame. Her first, probably. I love it. It's a good look on you."

Of all the nicknames in the world, Mary Sue is the *worst*. Yes, I follow the rules. No, this does not make me a boring do-gooder.

Okay, maybe I am, just a little bit. And maybe I tattled on my sisters from time to time when we were growing up, but still! Is that something to be insulted over? Made fun of?

Sadie's smirk dies when Merritt elbows her.

"Can you pretend to be professional for at least five minutes?" Merritt hisses.

I resist the urge to either gloat or stick my tongue out at Sadie.

"Sorry," Sadie says, actually looking (mostly) like she means it. She may be the peacemaker between me and Merritt, but this does not make her by any means *peaceful*. She's an instigator as much as she's the one who bridges the gaps.

"I am *not* doing a walk of shame." I take my seat next to Sadie, whipping off my sunglasses in a move I regret instantly as the evil sun pierces my retinas through the big window. I immediately put them back on.

"Well, we're all here now," Merritt says. "Sorry *once again* about the delay."

Ugh. Does she have to be so self-righteous? I finally glance at the lawyer, intending to apologize for being late, but the words die on my lips. I take in broad shoulders, dark stubble, and those gray eyes.

Forget what I said. This is beyond a walk of shame. It's a marathon of shame, one walked in slow motion through a bog while wearing steel-toed boots.

He looks every bit as handsome illuminated by the sun's evil light as he does in my fuzzy memories. He also looks furious. With me, specifically.

"You." The word drops from my lips in a whisper, and my sisters don't miss this either.

His expression doesn't change, even as Sadie chuckles. Merritt leans across to whisper, "Tell me you didn't spend the night with Gran's lawyer."

"It wasn't *all* night," I say, just as he says, "I did *not* spend the night with Eloise."

I remember, suddenly, how he called me Eloise last night,

too. He *knows* me. I'm not sure how or in what context, but he recognized me in the bar. And he said *nothing*. This makes me feel exposed for reasons I can't explain.

The last time I felt this deeply mortified was when I walked through the entire cafeteria in seventh grade with the back of my dress tucked into my underwear. Not my cute underwear either, but the kind that used to be white but then faded to a color one could only describe as dirty dishwater. This current embarrassment even beats that, because it's so much more up close and personal.

I slump in my chair. What further humiliation could possibly await me this fine morning?

Welcome to twenty-one! All of your nightmares will converge in one incredibly awkward morning, making you wish for a total do-over.

Our lawyer, whose name I suddenly remember with striking clarity is Jake, clears his throat. "Could we please get started?"

"Of course," Merritt says.

Sadie is still chuckling softly. I discreetly stomp on her foot, and she grunts.

I cannot look at Jake, though it seems he's waiting for all of us to acknowledge him. I tilt my chin up slightly, keeping my eyes on his shirt, the blue of spring morning skies. His tie is the same bright yellow as the pineapples on my dress.

Jake is allergic to pineapples. This useless bit of trivia comes to me, further proof of a horribly embarrassing night.

"Wait," I say. "Why isn't Dad here?"

"Per your grandmother's request," Jake says, and because I'm trying not to look at his face, I notice the way he presses the corner of the folder on his desk under his fingernail.

A nervous tic? No—Jake seems like the kind of man who doesn't know what nerves are.

"Can you hold all questions until the end?" he asks, his tone all ice.

Sadie nudges me with her elbow, and I nod. "Of course. Sorry."

I keep my gaze on Jake's desk and ONLY on his desk as he explains Grandma's will and its stipulations. I don't look at him even as shock makes my chest feel cold, then hot. I keep my gaze on the desk even as Sadie grabs my hand with frightening strength, even as Merritt interrupts again and again with questions, totally disregarding the request Jake made for us to hold questions until the end. Merritt isn't the kind of person you make wait.

It's only after Jake finishes and Merritt runs out of questions that I allow myself to look him fully in the face. "I'm sorry—could you give me the two-sentence summary? I'm not sure I'm completely getting the basics."

Merritt sighs heavily, but Sadie nods like she needs this too. Jake's eyes flick to me, then quickly back to the papers on his desk. I'm not sure if he can feel my gaze or not, but the slightest flush appears just above his collar.

"Your grandmother left the entirety of her estate to the three of you. Nothing to your father. There is a trust set aside solely for the purpose of renovations designed to turn the property into a bed and breakfast. At the completion of the renovations, you may sell the property"—I don't miss the way he flinches slightly at this—"and split the profits, share the dwelling space and operate the bed and breakfast, or one or more of you may buy the others out. At that time, you will also split any money remaining in the trust and the rest of your inheritance."

"Wait, there's money outside of what's in the trust? Money that wasn't set aside for renovations?" Sadie asks.

She sounds a little callous if you ask me, even if her question is valid.

Jake pauses, again running the corner of the folder under his fingernail. "Your grandmother had a sizable estate. But none of it can be touched until renovations are complete. Until then, one or more of you must be living on the property full-time."

"That's what I was afraid you said," Sadie says with a groan.

"Why afraid?" asks Merritt. "It's a gift, any way you look at it."

"One we don't deserve," I mutter, but my sisters don't seem to hear. Jake's head snaps up because clearly, he misses nothing.

"Feels more like a trap," Sadie says. "Are *you* going to leave your fancy job to come down here, Mer?"

Merritt clamps her mouth shut.

"That's what I thought," Sadie says.

Live here. Someone has to live *here*—one or all of us.

The memories of so many summers here hit me like the slap of a wave. I swear I can smell sunscreen and bug spray, hear the rhythmic buzz of cicadas over the roar of the ocean. I rub a hand over my sternum, but it does nothing to ease the ache.

"You're awfully quiet over there, Lo," Merritt says.

Jake watches me, his expression giving nothing away.

"I'm ... processing."

"Nothing has to be decided today," Jake says. "Though you do need to appoint at least one person to stay at the house."

"Is it livable?" Merritt asks.

He nods. "A lot of it has fallen into disrepair, but your

grandmother was living in the house up until she—" His voice catches here, and he clears his throat. "Until she died. You wouldn't want to live there while renovating, however. There's a carriage house at the back of the property—renovated into a duplex—where your grandmother intended for you to stay. It's completely furnished and ready for one or all three of you."

"Who's going to stay?" I don't know why Sadie even asks, because both of my very employed sisters look at me, the recent college grad who didn't make it into grad school and still hasn't managed to line up a job.

It's a relief, in a way. I had no idea what I was doing next. Moving in with Mom and Craig was a last resort. Now there's a very clear path. Maybe not one I planned for, but the prospect excites me anyway. I always loved it here, and I definitely wasn't looking forward to moving home.

The biggest downside is sitting across the desk from me. I'll have to share the island with Jake and be reminded of my humiliation. There is no way, on an island this small, I won't see him.

"Wait," Merritt says. "You said the carriage house is a duplex? Are both sides for our use?"

Jake shakes his head, tightness forming around his eyes. "Only one. The other is occupied."

"By whom?"

His gaze flicks to me, then darts back to my oldest sister, where it stays. He clears his throat, and I already know what's coming before he says the words.

"By me."

THREE

Jake

THE THREE SISTERS are silent for a few long seconds, staring at me. Merritt's cold blue eyes piercing, Sadie's gray-blue narrowed, Eloise's bright blue hidden behind her huge sunglasses. I try not to blink. No swallowing. Deep, even breaths. Any movement from me, and they look ready to tear me apart.

Then, with almost comedic timing, they turn on each other, all talking at once.

I relax into my chair, steepling my fingers on the desk as I watch them argue. Gennie told me the three weren't very close, something that made her almost as sad as the fact they rarely visited. But they fight—*discuss?*—the way only siblings can, with an innate knowledge of each other. I suspect Gennie would be watching this with amusement. I'm surprised to find myself doing the same.

My feelings toward the Markham sisters are complicated.

They are all younger than I am and only spent summers here, so I met them only in passing years ago. I've gotten to know them a little through Gennie's stories, though she saw them through the rosiest tinted glasses. She never had anything but positive things to say about them. Even in the past ten years when they all but stopped visiting. Sadness lurked behind Gennie's eyes whenever she mentioned their names. But pride, too.

Her love for them never dimmed. She never complained. Never got bitter or felt sorry for herself. Her son, on the other hand, received all of her blame and ire. Deservedly so. Ken wrecked his marriage with multiple affairs, blew through Gennie's money until she cut him off, and essentially abandoned his daughters.

And then they, in turn, abandoned their grandmother. Gennie may not have seen it that way, but it's hard for me NOT to. I never said as much to Gennie, though she may have sensed it.

I'd love to give them all the benefit of the doubt. I would.

But they need to give me a solid reason. Bickering about the enormous gift they've inherited while barely mentioning the amazing woman who gave it to them is not helping.

"It'll have to be you, Lo," Merritt says.

Eloise opens her mouth, but Sadie jumps in first. "I work remotely, but it would take a while for me to move and set up everything I need. I could, but not for a while."

"I get it. You both have big important jobs, while I have …" She spreads her arms wide but doesn't finish her statement.

"Instagram?" Sadie suggests.

"You could do the whole *influencer* thing from here." Merritt's voice is too bright. Like she's offering Eloise a gift.

It would be more believable if Merritt didn't say *influencer* like it was a curse word.

Which, in my mind, it pretty much is. Social media is an inane waste of time at best. A collection of lies and scams at worst. I *have* a Facebook account—one where my profile photo is of the ocean, and I have eighty-seven friend requests I have no intention of responding to. I keep my LinkedIn profile updated because that's not social media. It's business.

The word *influencer* calls to mind Kardashians and photos of kombucha and avocado toast that *no one wants to see.*

I study Eloise for a moment, trying to reconcile the idea in my head with the woman in front of me.

Last night, it took me all of five entire minutes to get an accurate read on Eloise.

I may deal more with contracts than with people, but I've cultivated my ability to take a person's full measure. I don't make snap judgments—I make accurate assessments faster than most people do. And I'm never wrong.

Which is how I know three things about Eloise with utter certainty.

One: she is the only Markham sister who seems to be at all emotionally invested. For this reason, I'm glad she's the one Sadie and Merritt are pushing to stay.

At the same time, and this is observation number two, she is clearly the most inexperienced of the three, and not just because of her age. She is going to be in way over her head, which means she'll likely require a lot of handholding, a prospect I'd rather avoid.

Which leads me to my third and final observation: Eloise Markham is absolutely, unequivocally too young for me.

She was too young for me when she leaned close enough *not* to smell me at the bar, sending traces of her floral scent up my nose.

She was too young for me as I carried her to the bed and breakfast, no matter how easily her head nestled against my shoulder. Or how alluring she looked in her ridiculous pineapple dress.

And she's too young for me now—Eloise the alleged influencer, sitting across from my desk, accepting the weighty responsibility her sisters are dumping on her without ceremony.

Why do I even need this reminder? I can't say. A pretty woman isn't usually enough to set my head spinning, and Eloise definitely falls in the beautiful category. But something about her called to me from the moment I sat down last night at the bar. She's like a loose thread in my thoughts, one I can't stop pulling.

As long as she stays just in my thoughts, that's fine. So long as this loose thread doesn't make me unravel.

After a few more minutes of the sisters debating how long Eloise should expect to handle things on her own, I lift a hand, surprised when they quickly fall silent.

"There is one more point I ought to mention," I say, though I'm half-tempted to save this particular revelation for another time. I haven't gotten the warmest reception from the Markham women. Perhaps they can sense my own wariness of them, though I've been careful to give little away. Sadie and Merritt both seem unduly suspicious of me. Eloise has had trouble meeting my eyes, likely embarrassed and afraid I might tell her older sisters about last night.

I would *never*.

I clear my throat. "Your grandmother appointed an objective third party to act as a resource—an informal overseer, if you will—during the renovations. Someone familiar with the island's unique culture who understands what will and won't be approved."

"Approved by whom?" Merritt scoffs, clearly not very familiar with the idea of needing third-party supervision.

I try to remember how Gennie described her oldest granddaughter. I think she called Merritt driven and doggedly stubborn when it came to getting what she wanted. *If my Merritt demanded it*, Gennie said once with a chuckle, *the earth would start spinning backward.*

"As you may remember, Oakley Island is privately owned," I explain. "The owner has very strict codes and a small preservation society to uphold them. There are a lot of historical structures, including your grandmother's house. You can do whatever you want to the inside, but the outside has to meet certain standards—comply with how buildings were built and decorated in the time they were originally constructed."

"That seems tedious," Sadie says.

I nod. "It can be. Which is why it's helpful to have someone who understands the restrictions and guidelines."

The sisters might be annoyed at the prospect of outside help, but if they had to interact with Benedict Oakley King on their own, it wouldn't take long for them to wish for a go-between. He might be my best friend, but Benedict can be a little obsessive about his ownership of Oakley Island.

Yes. I did say *ownership*. He inherited Oakley from his mother's very wealthy side of the family. Residents own the land they live on, but all the businesses, beaches, and other public-use areas belong to Benedict.

On the surface, Benedict projects more of an easy-going, beach bum kind of vibe, but it's a bit of a mask. He is precise. Particular. And a major history nerd who is dedicated to keeping the old parts of Oakley in pristine historical condition. He chairs the historical preservation society himself, not even caring it only boasts three members, and oversees the preservation standards with laser focus and a bit of an iron hand.

He would eat sweet little Eloise for breakfast. And her pineapples too.

"Let me guess," Eloise says, lifting her sunglasses to narrow her suddenly shrewd gaze on me. "The person overseeing the renovations, the one *familiar* with island culture and historical standards. It's you, isn't it?"

I dip my head the slightest bit, surprised she figured me out. Maybe my original assessment of her didn't quite catch everything.

"I'm more than qualified," I say. "Though, it's less overseeing and more offering support and advice. I grew up on Oakley. And I know the chair of the historical preservation society personally. It will be a benefit to have me involved as an objective third party."

Okay, maybe not completely objective given my relationship with Gennie, my love for her house, and my friendship with Benedict. But objective enough.

"So, an overseer," Merritt says.

"More like over*lord*," Eloise mutters, eliciting a chuckle from Sadie.

This meeting feels about ten seconds and one snarky comment away from devolving into the kind of hot mess I avoid.

"Interesting." Merritt leans forward, assessing me with an eye so critical, I can almost feel her gaze creeping across my skin. "You handled her will. You're overseeing the renovations. *And* you're living in her carriage house." She taps a manicured fingernail to her chin. "How very ... cozy."

"Everything is legal and perfectly legitimate, I promise you that." I might be *from* Oakley, but I passed the Georgia bar exam, same as every other lawyer in the state. And other than the standard fees and the living arrangement, I'm not profiting in any other way. I had absolutely zero to do with these terms, other than writing them up as Gennie requested. "And again, I'm not overseeing. Just providing support if you need it."

Merritt shrugs. "Tomato, to-mah-to."

"It just seems a little … odd," Sadie says. "Is this kind of bequest typical?"

Truth is, the arrangement *is* a little small-town, even a little strange, but it still holds up, legally speaking. When I helped Gennie with her will, she was adamant about the terms but closed-lipped about her reasons. Aside from saying she was too old to renovate the house herself, and she hoped it might be a "fun project" for her granddaughters, she didn't provide much insight on why she didn't leave them the house outright.

Genevieve's house is on two acres of prime real estate in the heart of Oakley Island, right on the beach. Easy walking distance to shops and restaurants. Even without the improvements and renovations the will requires, the house is worth more money than most regular people see in a lifetime.

Did she hope intentional time on the island might convince one or even all of them to stay? Did she think having the three of them work together would help them grow closer? Was she afraid her granddaughters might have inherited some of their father's bad business sense?

After everything was finalized, I vowed I'd follow up, give Gennie the opportunity to talk about her intentions if only so I could understand what they were. But any time I asked, she waved me off and distracted me with home-cooked fried chicken or pie. I told myself I'd push her for answers, but then life got busy, and I never did.

Now it's too late.

"I've seen stranger requests and requirements," I say. "You might be surprised by what people decide when it comes to their final wishes."

"What if we decide, as the *new* owners, that we no longer want a tenant on the property?" Sadie smiles sweetly. "How soon can you pack your bags?"

Gennie's words ring in my ears. *Sadie—now that one is my firecracker. With a mind like a laser and a heaping dose of who-cares attitude, she keeps everyone on their toes. She's quirky and fun—when she remembers she's not too old for it, that is.*

I square my shoulders. Neither Merritt nor Sadie trusts me. Fine. I'm not intimidated. At least there's still Eloise. If me bringing her safely home from the bar last night didn't build trust, I don't know what will.

"That's a valid question. The complete terms of your grandmother's will address my occupancy of the carriage house. As long as your family is in possession of the property, I may, if I so choose, continue to live there and pay rent directly into the monies set aside for renovations of the main house. When renovations are complete, I'll be obligated to either move or sign a new lease agreement with the new owners."

A twinge of discomfort shoots through me at the thought of some outsider owning Genevieve's house. The three outsiders sitting in front of me are bad enough. But they could sell to *anyone*.

"What if we *don't* sell?"

It's all I can do not to beam at Eloise for asking the question. I'm not at all surprised that out of the three, she's the one at least entertaining the possibility of keeping the property.

Sadie scoffs. "Of course we'll sell."

Merritt doesn't even spare her sisters a glance. Her eyes stay trained on me. "You must have really meant something to our grandmother, Mr. Fieldstone. I can't imagine what. Or why. Though I'm sure Eloise will puzzle it out and fill us in. You'll be neighbors, after all."

Eloise snorts from her place across the desk, but I can't make out her expression because of her sunglasses. My confidence wavers.

I have no idea what I did to make such an unfavorable impression on the Markham women. I may not be the friendliest guy around. I'm not the guy who hugs everyone or even waves and says hello. But if you really get to know me, like Genevieve did, I can be nice.

Nice-ish.

I might even smile.

Sometimes.

If there's a really good reason.

And I always do my job. Professionally. With candor, yes, but also with respect. I have ample reason to judge these women—I know their grandmother better than they do, after all—but they don't have reason to judge me. I even *rescued* Eloise, which, I'm just saying, goes far and above a typical attorney/client relationship.

Not that she knew I was her attorney then.

I can't explain why I let Eloise think I was a stranger last night, why I didn't introduce myself or give her any context. Even when I was tucking her into bed. I knew who she was the minute I saw her face. Even though I haven't seen any of the sisters in years, Gennie showed me enough pictures.

"I'm looking forward to our *working* relationship," I manage to say as the sisters get to their feet.

I half-expect Eloise to stay back and talk to me. There was no shortage of words coming out of her mouth last night.

But all I get is an unreadable look tossed over her shoulder, her sunglasses now perched on top of her head. Her eyebrows are raised, two perfect arches over eyes that are the lightest shade of blue I've ever seen on a person. All three Markham sisters have startling blue eyes—just like their grandmother—but Eloise's are the lightest of the three—a shimmery turquoise blue.

The look she's giving me says I shouldn't underestimate her. I'm guessing people do that a lot. She looks sweet. So naive. But the fire in her eyes says there's more to her than what's on the surface.

I don't love anything about this. About losing Genevieve. About handing the house over to whatever stranger bids the highest after the sisters finish renovating.

But I'll begrudgingly admit, I'm glad Eloise is the one staying. Eloise—not Merritt or Sadie—being on the other side of the wall in the carriage house. Eloise on Oakley indefinitely. Eloise with her piercing blue eyes and penchant for pineapple dresses invading my daily life.

I'm a professional. Just their lawyer. Not a friend. Not … anything else. But as I get ready for Gennie's funeral, my mind keeps circling back to the feel of the youngest Markham sister in my arms, the way her head nestled into my chest. I swear, the floral scent of her perfume lingers like a ghost.

FOUR

Jake

I WISH LOCATING the appropriate emotions for a funeral was as easy as slipping on a black suit. Maybe it's because I spent a lot of time this week processing the way I process best—alone. But after the service ends and I'm sitting in the receiving hall at the back of the old chapel, I just feel ... numb.

Observing the Markham family makes for a perfect distraction. Genevieve's son, Ken, whom I communicated with briefly prior to reading the will with his daughters, stands apart from the rest of the family. A very unnatural redhead has had her fingers tangled in the hair at the base of his scalp since the funeral ended. Maybe it's supposed to be comforting, but it reads as possessive.

The woman looks like money with her real pearls and diamond studs—old money classic. This may explain why Ken Markham didn't seem overly concerned that his mother cut him out of her will completely. He told me he expected as much when I called him, and then snarkily wished his daughters well, claiming the last thing he wanted was the headache they just inherited.

The sisters are near the door, smiling graciously as Oakley's old guard shuffle past and offer their condolences. Those closest to Genevieve already had a celebration of life—one more personal and just for islanders—so this service is more just a formality for the family. I'm trying not to silently judge, while silently judging.

Eloise stands to the left of her sisters, a gaping space setting her apart from the others. For reasons that are far from logical, I suddenly want to occupy that empty space. The same urge nearly overwhelmed me when I entered the chapel earlier. She sat on the end of the pew, enough space for one person between her and the aisle. I had to force myself to sit a few rows back next to my father. He tried to hide his surprise that I chose to sit by him, which only made me feel like a jerk. But then, when it comes to Ned, I probably deserve the title.

Eloise has swapped out her pineapples for a black dress, but hers isn't simple like the ones her sisters are wearing. Eloise's dress is covered with tiny red cherries tipped with green leaves. I am *not* allergic to cherries, and that dress is hugging Eloise's curves in all the right places. Not that I should be noticing. Especially given our current location.

Her hair is up, the back of her dress cut low enough to reveal a stretch of—*no*. I'm not noticing anything about her skin. Or her hair. Nothing at all.

Margo sidles up next to me and hooks her arm through mine.

A wave of discomfort—and maybe guilt?—washes over me. But there's no need to feel guilty. We broke up almost a year ago, so I'm free to pay attention to whomever I want.

Though, it should absolutely *not* be Eloise, as I've previously established. I remind myself of all the reasons in quick succession: Client. Too young. Too complicated.

"How are you holding up?" Margo asks, tugging my arm a little closer.

I shift out of her grasp and slide my hands into my pockets.

It's nice that Margo is here. She knows how important Genevieve has always been to me, so I have to appreciate the gesture of her coming.

It's *not* nice that she seems to be touching me every opportunity she gets.

If I had to guess, I'd say she has an ulterior motive that has something to do with luring me back to her father's firm in Savannah. Or maybe just luring me back to her.

Neither prospect is even a remote possibility.

"I'll make it," I manage to say, forcing my gaze to be anywhere but on Eloise Markham. It's bad enough Margo saw me carrying her out of the bar last night.

I take another half step away from Margo, realizing that as much as I don't want her to make assumptions about me and the too-young-for-me Markham sister, I also don't want Eloise to see me with Margo and get the wrong idea.

I ought to be doing the opposite. Encouraging Eloise to make whatever assumptions will keep our relationship impersonal and professional. We'll be in close proximity living side by side. And we'll be in close contact with all the decisions she'll be making about the house, assuming she needs my help. And since she doesn't know anyone on Oakley, she'll absolutely need my help.

That's more than enough *close* for me. I'm already pushing

the lines of attorney/client professionalism, though those lines are admittedly fuzzier in a place like Oakley. Gennie was a client, but she also practically raised me.

"Where's Naomi?" Margo asks. She reaches for my arm again, but when I lean away, she settles for standing *very* close. "She and Liam couldn't make it?"

"Liam had some sort of school celebration. An end-of-the-year thing."

"Ah."

Margo immediately looks disinterested, and a wave of irritation rolls through me. She never liked how much time I spent with my nephew or how much my sister—a single mom—needs my help. Margo tried, for my sake, but it never felt natural. I'd hoped she would eventually warm up to Liam, but she always seemed stiff and uncomfortable whenever Liam hung out with us. It's so clear to me now, it's hard to imagine how I missed the flashing red warning sign it was back then.

Perhaps sensing my discomfort with Margo's closeness, Benedict crosses the room dressed in a black suit so perfectly tailored, I feel shabby in comparison. Margo's hand lifts to her hair, and I fight the urge to roll my eyes. But Benedict has that effect on people. He always has.

He pulls me in for a hug. "Drinks later?" he says, quietly enough that Margo doesn't hear.

She's been pulled into a conversation with Harriett, the owner of Sweet Tea and Toast deli, and, apparently, an admirer of Margo's very expensive-looking shoes. Harriett flips her long white braid over one shoulder as she laughs, and Margo shoots me a look like she wants to be rescued. *Not a chance.*

"Drinks sound good."

Benedict tosses a glance over his shoulder. "Gotten a read on the sisters yet?"

I shrug. "They're . . . not what I expected. And maybe exactly what I expected at the same time? The youngest one is staying."

I don't miss the way Benedict's eyes rove over the Markham sisters, and I hate that I bristle in response.

"How young?" he asks.

"She graduated from college five minutes ago, so young."

"She's gorgeous, at least. Single?"

I can't tell if Benedict is asking for himself or asking because he knows me well enough to catch the interest I should not have for Eloise.

"Who cares? She's only twenty-one."

He rolls his eyes. "And you're thirty, not sixty. You could stand to live a little, Jake."

"I'm thirty-two. And she's temporary." I shrug. "She'll only be around until they sell the place."

"I didn't say marry her. I said *live a little*. And who knows? Maybe she'll stick around. Stranger things have happened."

I shrug. "She wasn't interested in being here before. Why would she be interested now?"

Benedict looks back at the sisters. "What about the one in the middle?"

"Sadie. She works in cybersecurity. Lives up in D.C. or Northern Virginia. The oldest is Merritt, and she lives in New York and works for some big consulting firm."

He nods along while I talk. "Geez, the eyes on all three of them." He gives my shoulder a final clap. "I'll be at The Round Up around nine or so. Don't make me wait for you."

Beside me, Margo finally extricates herself from Harriett's enthusiastic praise and heads for the door, casting me a frustrated look over her shoulder as she goes. Her disdain for

Oakley's residents is a reminder of just how much Margo doesn't fit here. Just like I didn't fit in Savannah when I spent a few years after college working at her father's firm.

Protectiveness rises in me. Harriett is a woman who loves big and loves loud. I get that it might feel overwhelming if you aren't used to the kind of small-town life where everybody knows everybody's business, but Margo never even wanted to *try*.

Harriett steps closer, reaching for both of my hands. "You're not getting back together with that woman, are you, Jake?" she asks, her tone uncharacteristically flat.

I shake my head. "No."

Her expression collapses with relief. "Oh, Lordy, I'm so glad. I about died thinking I might have to pretend to like her for your sake."

I chuckle. "Don't worry. You know my heart belongs to you, Harriett."

"Shoot." She swats my arm. "You big flirt."

I'm not a flirt. Not by any stretch. I don't even like people most of the time. I definitely don't like flirting with them. But Harriett is one of Gennie's best friends and is almost as much of an honorary grandmother to me as Gennie is.

My heart squeezes.

As Genevieve *was*.

I'm still not used to thinking about her in the past tense.

Harriett reaches up and cups her wrinkled hand around my cheek. "You'll take care of Gennie's house, won't you? You won't let her family sell it to a big developer?"

"You know I'll try my best. And you know Benedict won't let some developer get a foothold on Oakley."

"Good boy."

Harriett pinches my cheek as she says goodbye, and I

catch Eloise watching. She bites her lip as though to hide her smile, then makes her way over.

"Quite a hit with the older generation, aren't you?"

"What can I say? I'm charming."

I'm not sure if it's my deadpan delivery or the idea of me being charming that causes a laugh to burst out of Eloise. Her sisters' heads jerk our way, and Eloise folds in on herself a little. The brief warmth in her expression cools. Right— because the Markhams seem to see me as the enemy somehow.

Eloise excuses herself. I shouldn't be disappointed watching her walk away or feel anything at all when she glances back over her shoulder at me, blue eyes sparkling.

Maybe I should go. Things are winding down, and it's not like I'm Gennie's family. Even Ken is glancing at his watch. No surprise there.

But when Eloise catches my gaze again, a certainty settles into my gut. I'll be here as long as she's here. And everywhere else she is, too.

Because it's my obligation, I tell myself. One last thing I can do for Gennie.

Benedict may own the island, but Gennie asked *me* to make sure her house is taken care of. I won't let her down.

Once, right after we finished Gennie's will, I indulged myself enough to think through the logistics of what it would take for me to buy the house from her family, assuming they decide to sell.

I practically grew up in that house. It feels more like a home than my actual childhood residence—an apartment above Ned's bar—ever did. But even my salary in Savannah, which was almost double what I make doing business on Oakley, wouldn't have been enough to cover the mortgage.

All I can hope for now is the chance to convince the sisters to choose their buyer carefully.

Oakley isn't completely untouched by commercialism. We get tourists, sure. But they're the sleepy kind. The kind looking to get away from the bustle, not the kind looking for sky-high condominiums and go-kart tracks. It just isn't that kind of beach. A bed and breakfast is one thing. But anything else? It isn't what Gennie would have wanted.

My gaze catches on the framed photo of Gennie propped on an easel to the right of where the sisters are standing. *I wish I knew what you were up to, Gennie.*

I can almost hear her answering laugh. *I bet you do, Jacob. I bet you do. Now, forget about me. Which one of my granddaughters catches your eye the most?*

The strangest feeling spreads from my gut outward. The terms of the will, the way Gennie required at least one of her granddaughters to be living onsite while I'm living next door, available to help and support ... It would be just like Gennie to figure out a way to play matchmaker even from the grave. And now to be haunting my thoughts.

I shake the idea away. I'll never know for certain, so it doesn't do any good to speculate. But that doesn't stop my brain from wondering if Genevieve knew exactly which Markham sister would catch my eye.

FIVE

Lo

"AS FAR AS FUNERALS GO, that wasn't so bad," Sadie says.

I stare open-mouthed until Merritt laughs, and then I turn wide eyes to my oldest and least-likely-to-laugh-at-anything sister. Her head is thrown back, and she's wiping tears from her eyes. I don't know the last time—has there BEEN a time?—when I've seen Mer laugh *or* cry. Both at once is stranger than when the sun shines through the middle of a rainstorm. Merritt flops back on my bed, and I'm officially in *The Twilight Zone.*

My room at the bed and breakfast became our command center after Jake dropped the bomb on us from Gran's will. We got ready for the funeral together, sharing a bathroom like we grew up doing. And just like when we were younger, Sadie takes ridiculously long showers and Merritt has zero problem walking around in front of us stark naked. Nor should she. Merritt has a body an Amazonian would envy.

Right now, as she laughs, she's at least clothed in a bra and panties. Her black dress is puddled next to the closet door. I could be wrong, but this might be the first item of clothing Merritt has ever left on the floor. I pick it up, shaking it out before hanging it in the small closet. I collect her shoes and line them up below the dress, thinking of how Jake did the same thing for me last night.

My neck gets hot just thinking about it. From *embarrassment*. Definitely not for any other reasons.

When I turn back, Merritt's eyes are closed, her dark hair splayed around her.

"Mer, are you drunk?"

She doesn't answer, but Sadie holds up her finger and thumb, just a sliver apart. "I might have provided her with a little *something something*."

I put my hands on my hips. "And not me?"

After this morning's headache and subsequent embarrassment in front of Jake, I swore I'd never drink again. Maybe I made that promise a little too quickly.

Sadie slides a small, silver flask from her purse. "I forgot you turned twenty-one this week."

"Yesterday," I say. Not that I expected either of my sisters to remember. Maybe it's weird, but birthdays were never a big thing in our family. We always celebrated the pants off Christmas, Easter, and Halloween, but birthdays were a low-key affair.

Or, in my case this year, an almost forgotten one.

"Happy late birthday!" Sadie says. "Have a drink."

I take the flask. *Sadie Bennett Markham* is engraved on the side. Based on the weight and feel, it's real silver.

"I got it as a bridesmaid gift. You can finish it off." Sadie perches on top of the dresser, still in her black dress, and nods toward the flask. "I have to drive us back to the airport soon."

"You're leaving today?" I don't know why I thought the two of them would stay a bit longer. At least for tonight. Then again, they used my room to get ready instead of getting their own. I just wasn't thinking about what that meant.

"Some of us have to work," Merritt mumbles from the bed.

On that note, I uncap the flask and take a tiny sip, trying not to cough. Whatever this is, it's not red wine. I'm grateful for that, though the alcohol burns all the way down. My eyes sting, and when I catch Sadie grinning, I hold her gaze as I drain the rest. Thankfully, not much was left. I guess Merritt hit it pretty hard already.

I'm not sure what I expected after Gran's funeral but drinking from Sadie's flask with Merritt in her underwear wasn't it. The whole day has felt surreal. I cried throughout the service, even while feeling oddly numb. Sadie sat like a statue through the service, and I saw Merritt white-knuckling her purse during the short service, which was attended by basically the whole island. And, I guess, was planned by Jake, according to Gran's wishes.

Jake—Gran's lawyer and my rescuer from last night. He was in this room not twenty-four hours ago, tucking me into bed and leaving me water and pills for the headache he anticipated I'd have. Listening to me babble about his expensive smell. Fending off my proposition for him to stay the night.

I wonder what my sisters would think if they knew. The embarrassment is almost worth the shock factor of announcing it. *Almost.* I'd rather not deal with all their commentary and judgment, so I'll keep my secrets to myself.

Merritt and Sadie seemed to take an immediate dislike to

Jake. I'm firmly in the undecided camp. Though getting me home safely was a kind gesture, it seems at odds with his bristly exterior. I haven't seen him smile once, like his control switch jammed, leaving him in some permanently serious mode. Serious is a generous word. Grumpy might work better. Irritable, even.

I hand the flask back to Sadie and wipe my mouth with the back of my hand. She cocks her head and grins. "Aw, Mary Sue really is growing up."

"Could you please stop calling me that?"

"Maybe if you stopped acting like it," Merritt says, and the statement is so harsh, both Sadie and I whip our heads her way. She's still lying on the bed, eyes closed.

"Mer," Sadie says, "be nice."

"Nice is overrated," she says.

"Wow." I drop into the chair by the window. "You guys can leave any time you want."

Sadie swings her disapproving gaze my way. "Lo, come on. Don't be like that."

"Like what? You two dumped this responsibility on me even though you continue to talk down to me. And now you're about to bolt just hours after Gran's funeral. What, pray tell, do you want from me?"

"You're the only one who could do this," Merritt says. "We both have—"

"Important jobs," I interject. "I know. While I'm just a jobless college grad with no life and no plans."

"I wouldn't quite put it that way," Sadie says, swinging her bare feet. "You could say that you have your whole life in front of you. The world is your fried oyster!"

"Ew," Mer says. "Oysters should only be consumed raw."

I roll my eyes and toy with my cell phone. "So, my life is a bivalve mollusk that involves renovating Gran's house on an island full of busybodies."

And a hot, nosy lawyer who's seen me at a very low point.

"Just think how much content you can create for the 'Gram," Sadie says.

I soften a little because I can tell Sadie is genuine. I might have expected her to be critical of my Instagram side hustle. I'm not a huge influencer, but I've slowly built a following and make a few hundred dollars a month with sponsorships and affiliate links.

I haven't had time to think about it, but Sadie's right. Moving here temporarily and doing whatever needs to be done on Gran's house will make for great content.

Merritt snorts. I'm glad she doesn't follow up with a smart-aleck comment because I'm about ready to tackle her. It's been years since the three of us have had actual fights. So long, in fact, that in the last one, I was still very much outweighed and outmatched. Now, however, things would be much more equal. But I don't have the energy for a fight of any kind. I sink down on the bed, jostling Merritt.

"I'm going to miss Gran's letters," I say, looking at my clasped hands.

"You two wrote letters?" Sadie asks, and I nod.

"For years." I loved seeing Gran's looping cursive on a brightly colored envelope. She must have a giant stash of stationery, as she never used the same style twice.

Without moving, Merritt says. "We kept the same email thread for three years running. Gran sure knew her way around a meme."

Sadie snorts. Pauses. Then leans over, laughing silently while her shoulders shake. Merritt cracks one eye open and smiles. I'm not sure the last time I saw her genuinely happy. I don't want it to end.

"Was Gran on Team Gif or Team Jif?" I ask.

Merritt props herself up on her elbows, the same almost unfamiliar grin softening her whole face. "Obviously, the superior Team Gif."

I expect Sadie to argue because she will die on the hill of Jif like the peanut butter. Instead, she sighs and says, "We texted every Thursday while watching a cooking show. You know—the one with the terrible chefs competing against each other."

I don't know, but I can imagine. It's so very GRAN that she found different ways to keep in touch with us over the years.

The three of us sit in silence, and this moment feels nostalgic and also somehow like the first of its kind. I miss Gran. I miss my sisters. I miss ... family. The dull ache in my chest becomes a strangely comforting warmth.

"Should we go over to the house? Maybe do a walk-through together?" I ask. I'm not sure I'm ready to face Gran's empty house, but the prospect doesn't sound so bad if we're together.

Merritt makes a rough sound that's a no if I've ever heard one. Sadie hops off the dresser and claps her hands.

"Actually, Mer and I need to get moving so we can catch our flights."

The special sisterly moment is over, like it never happened at all.

Sadie digs through our oldest sister's bag and comes up with what I guess is Merritt's travel outfit: black pants and a loose gray blouse that's miraculously wrinkle-free. Mer groans but takes the clothes Sadie tosses and starts putting them on even as she's walking to the bathroom.

When the door closes behind Merritt, Sadie pins me with an intense gaze. "Look, if Mer gets a little micromanagery with Gran's house stuff, go easy on her," she says in a low voice.

"Me? Go easy on *her*?"

This is the strangest piece of advice I've ever received from the wild child among the three of us. I cannot imagine a world in which I need to go easy on my bulletproof oldest sister. Especially if she's going to overstep when she isn't willing to step up and do the job herself.

Sadie glances toward the closed bathroom door. "Shh! Look, you don't know all the particulars. Coming here is hard for her."

Why *here*? What memories of Oakley is Merritt trying to avoid?

As always—I feel like the one getting the short end of the sister stick. The moment of bonding has been snuffed out faster than a flame doused in a cooler of ice water.

I shake my head. Sadie moves around the room, collecting their things and packing for both her and Merritt. Out of habit, I turn on my phone, opening up Instagram. I'm still on my self-imposed posting and engaging ban, which is starting to make me feel twitchy.

Does this mean I'm addicted to social media? Maybe. Do I care? No. Because, honestly, the eight thousand strangers who follow me are more supportive than either of my sisters. And that realization stings.

"Hey." Sadie's hand lands on my shoulder, and I click my phone off before meeting her gaze. "I'm sorry this is falling on you."

Falling on. Like she and Merritt didn't basically force me into it.

"But," she continues, "I do think you're the right woman for the job. You've got the most creative vision out of all of us. And, come on. Were you looking forward to moving in with Mom and Craig?"

None of us like Mom's new husband, who smiles too big and keeps trying to get us to call him Dad. *Gross*. We already have one failure of a father. We don't need a second one. At least Mom waited until we were grown, unlike Dad, who didn't even wait for the marriage to end to start seeing other women.

"Not particularly. I guess I can make the best of things here."

That's downplaying. As much as I don't like the way Merritt and Sadie just assigned this project to me, I AM secretly excited. Sad too, in a way I wasn't at the funeral. Maybe being here a little while will help me connect more with my grief and with my memories of Gran.

I swallow hard, still feeling the burn of whatever alcohol I just drank.

"Hey, another bonus. Our very hot lawyer is your new neighbor," Sadie says with a waggle of her eyebrows.

"He's not—"

"Hot? Uh, yeah he is. And he's most definitely your neighbor."

My heart is already pitter-pattering out of control at the thought of Jake. I shake my head vehemently. Too vehemently, based on the way Sadie's grin stretches even wider.

"I thought you and Merritt didn't like him."

"Meh. I wasn't sure, but I think he's doing what Gran asked. And you know what they say about men who seem like they're all business."

In all honesty, I have NO idea.

"There's a lot of passion hiding underneath, ready to be unleashed." Sadie makes a growling noise and swipes at me with fake claws.

"Um, no thanks." I can feel my blush heating me all the way down to my toes.

Sadie takes a strand of my hair and gives it a little tug. "First comes love, then comes—"

"Shut it, Sadie. I'm serious."

Her eyebrows shoot up. "Is there already something going on between you two? Wait, were you *actually* with him last night?"

"I was not," I whisper-yell. "And you aren't going to make Merritt think I was. Don't make me tell her about the yellow dress."

I've been saving this one. My sisters and I are masters at keeping and holding secrets—holding them over each other's heads, that is. Being the youngest, I've accrued a massive amount. I needed the currency more than they ever did, and I was always good at being sneaky. I made it my business to know their business. And to file it away for blackmail purposes.

The yellow dress in question was one Merritt bought with hard-earned babysitting money—only to have Sadie borrow it without asking. I caught Sadie sneaking back in her bedroom window, the dress in tatters. Sadie swore me to secrecy before shoving it in the bottom of the kitchen trash, hiding it under a pile of coffee grounds and eggshells.

"You wouldn't," Sadie says.

I give her a look that says, *Oh, wouldn't I?* The ruined yellow dress might hearken all the way back to my sisters' high school days. But Merritt's memory is long. And her need for payback is even longer.

As if sensing that secrets are being spilled, Merritt bursts out of the bathroom, looking totally sobered up. "Who wouldn't what?"

"Mary Sue wouldn't date our lawyer," Sadie says, only laughing when I shove her.

Merritt makes a face. "Ew. No. He's older than *me*. Don't even think about it, Lo."

Doesn't she know that telling me NOT to think about something only makes me want to think about it more?

"As I told Sadie, I'm *not* thinking about it."

Except I am. And I have been.

"Someone's protesting too much," Sadie says under her breath.

Yellow dress, I mouth.

"Is it time to head out?" Sadie asks Merritt.

My oldest sister looks conference-room-ready, no sign that she was at a funeral earlier or laugh-crying a few minutes ago. She slides into her heels, then surprises me with an unexpected, rib-crushing hug.

"Long past time," Merritt says. "Get me off this island, ASAP. You'll do good, kid."

"I could do without the condescension," I say, knocking her hand away as she pats my head before walking out of the room.

When Sadie hugs me, she whispers, "Have a good time with the hot lawyer overlord."

"I'm not sure he'd know a good time if it ran over him —twice."

The grin Sadie gives me is laced with pure, wicked glee. "Maybe the two of you will figure out how to have a good time together."

By the time I throw my shoes, the door is closing behind my most irritating sister.

SIX

Jake

MY DETERMINATION TO keep my eyes off of Eloise is challenged again when three hours after the funeral, she's already moving her stuff into the vacant half of the carriage house. I was hoping before I saw her again, I'd come up with a plan for how to ... *handle* her.

As in, handle the weird draw I feel in her presence.

I'm dressed and ready for a run. After the day I've had, I need to blow off some steam, but I'm hesitant to leave now. Instead, I watch from my living room window as Eloise struggles to maneuver an oversized suitcase across the path, which, like the driveway, is made of crushed oyster shells. The carriage house is a bit of a distance from the main house, built so it wouldn't obstruct the ocean view from Genevieve's house. Or, I guess, Eloise's house now.

With a sigh, I push aside the pang of sadness that thought brought to the surface and open my front door. I need to leave if I'm going to get in a few miles before I'm supposed to meet Benedict for drinks, but I know better than to stand by and watch Eloise without at least offering to help. Gennie would have my hide.

I make a conscious effort to ignore the tiny shred of resentment bubbling up in my chest and walk outside. I don't *want* to resent Eloise and her sisters for ghosting their grandmother, but a part of me is afraid that exact feeling has already colored our interactions. Maybe that's why they were hesitant to trust me this morning, why I felt a little like an enemy combatant. The sisters sensed my internal struggle.

Or maybe they just thought I was mean. Which wouldn't be all that surprising an accusation.

Eloise left her suitcase at the base of the porch steps and is trekking back to her car. I meet her when she's on the way back, struggling to carry a single box. It doesn't help that she's still wearing her funeral attire, including a pair of heels. The crushed oyster path adds charm, but it isn't easy to navigate in normal shoes.

"Need some help?"

She tilts her nose into the air. "Nope. I'm doing just fine," she says, gritting her teeth through the effort to hold the box.

"You can let me carry a box or two, Eloise."

"Or I can carry it myself," she says with a grunt. "I'm … managing." Even as she says this, the box in her arms starts to wobble.

I grab the other side, steadying it and her. This box is stupidly heavy. I'm not sure how she managed to carry it this far, save for the force of her sheer stubbornness.

"I don't mind," I say, holding her gaze over the top of the box.

She bites her lip, hesitating, but her grip relaxes slightly. "Are you sure? It's heavy."

"I managed to carry *you* just fine last night. A box shouldn't be a problem."

She gasps in outrage at my comment, and her cheeks flush pink. With a fierce yank, she tries to take the box back.

"I didn't ask you to carry me! In fact, I should file charges."

It's unlike me to goad people. In fact, I'm not sure why I'm pushing this. Somehow, her flustered reaction only motivates me to push more. "For?"

"Assault." Her eyes dart from side to side like she's trying to come up with charges on the fly. "Unsolicited touching. Kidnapping."

"Kidnapping," I drawl. "Really, Eloise? Another option would be to thank me for making sure you were *not* assaulted or kidnapped in your inebriated state."

We're still holding opposite sides of the box, and I give it a tug, but she doesn't yield, her jaw tensing as she pulls it back to herself. Beads of sweat dot her forehead.

I grunt and pull a little harder, and she finally relents. I stumble back a few steps when the full weight of the box hits me. What does she have in here—a library of hardbacks? A set of free weights? Sandbags?

"And stop calling me *Eloise*. No one but my grandmother ever calls me that." She winces. "Or *called* me that, I guess."

I don't like the way my gut wrenches when sadness eclipses Eloise's bluster and sass. I can't look directly at the shine of tears in her piercing blue eyes. So, I do the mature thing and ignore her words, ignore the downturn of her mouth, and ignore the ridiculous notion I have to wrap my arms around her.

I'm not the person Eloise would want offering her

comfort. Not when she's mock-threatening me with assault and kidnapping charges. I walk away and set the box next to her door.

When I make my way back, she's still standing there, hands on her hips. I can't tell if she's recovering from trying to carry the box or still dealing with her emotions. I take a risk as I pass by and nudge her a little with my shoulder.

"Giving up? That's okay. I can get the rest."

She takes the bait, and with an irritated huff, catches up with me. "I don't give up easily. But I don't expect you to know that, since you don't know me at all."

There is one more box, plus a few duffle bags and a lumpy trash bag in the back seat. I lift the last box with a grunt. If possible, it's heavier than the first. Cinder block heavy. Eloise probably doesn't weigh a hundred and thirty pounds soaking wet. There's no way she could have carried this thing on her own. It makes me wonder how she got it in the car to begin with.

I grunt as I hoist the box higher in my arms, not missing the way her eyes catch on my biceps. Pink tints her cheeks.

Again, I can't stop myself from pushing her buttons. "Do you usually invite men who don't know you to spend the night?"

Not that I need her answer. I already know that the other night was out of character for Eloise. Grief can make you do funny things. And it didn't come across as an invitation for a hookup. More like she didn't want to be alone.

The idea of staying was more tempting than I'll ever admit.

Eloise sputters, "That was ... I was ... we've already established I was tipsy."

"And is that normal for you?" I start to walk with the

56

boulder of a box, and Eloise scurries behind me with a few bags.

"For your information, that was the first time I've ever tried alcohol."

I almost drop the box. Because her statement reminds me how young she is. *Twenty-one, Jake. Practically a baby.* I walk a little faster.

This also tells me something else I file away about Eloise —she's a rule-follower. Sadie calling Eloise *Mary Sue* earlier makes more sense now. I won't lie. As a fellow rule-follower, I respect this.

"Before you say anything else insulting, I'm not a goody-two-shoes," she says.

Eloise seems to have missed the fact that I've been teasing her. I have a sudden flashback to being a kid and getting blank stares when I joined in conversations. Social cues aren't hard for me to read, but clearly communicating how I think and feel is a bigger challenge. I've never been particularly good at small talk or teasing.

Flirting, that Gennie voice in my head says. *Call a spade a spade—you're flirting with my granddaughter, Jacob. And I approve.*

Perhaps it's a good thing I'm terrible at this. Because I don't need to be teasing—or flirting with—my very young new neighbor. Even if Gennie would be delighted.

"I wasn't going to say anything like that. I respect your choice."

"Oh." Eloise seems surprised by my response. "Well, good."

We've reached the porch, and, for the moment, a kind of truce. She angles her body so we're face to face, then studies me. I swear, I'm about to keel over from the sheer weight of this box, but I keep my features even.

"Do you ever smile?" she asks, finally.

"When I have a reason to, yes."

Eloise rolls her eyes and gives a little laugh before pulling out the keys I gave her that morning. She unlocks the door, then drags the bags she has inside. I follow her inside.

Her half of the carriage house is the mirror image of mine in terms of layout, though my side could be described as masculine minimalist. This space bursts with bright, beachy colors, from the furniture to the curtains to the prints on the walls. There are throw pillows and a few fake potted plants to add a touch of green.

I hoist the heavy box onto the small, white dining table, afraid if I leave it on the floor, Eloise will throw her back out trying to lift it. I head back out to the porch, returning with the first box, heaving it onto the table as well.

"Did someone live here before?" Eloise asks, looking around the space. "It's so pretty."

"Gennie kept it up for you and your sisters. Just in case you came to visit."

Eloise looks like I slapped her. Tears pool in her eyes, and I immediately wish I'd softened my words, even if they're true.

"I didn't mean—"

"Don't," Eloise snaps. "I think your meaning is perfectly clear. I appreciate your help, Mr. Fieldstone. Have a good day."

The dismissal stings, and I swear, I can almost hear Gennie grumbling about how much of a bad impression I've made.

I clear my throat and take a step backward. "The power and water are already turned on. Utilities will be paid for out of the trust, so you don't need to worry about putting anything in your name. And there's wifi. I've got the password. I can text it over later. Gennie gave me your number."

Eloise looks surprised by this last bit and opens her mouth as though to ask a question. Instead, she clamps her mouth shut and turns her back on me, starting to rip open the packing tape on one of the boxes.

I head straight down the steps and to the street, not even going back to my place to get my phone or Air Pods. Today, I'll just run.

Until I can't feel anything.

Until I can't see Eloise's tropical-blue eyes narrowing on me like I'm public enemy number one.

SEVEN

Lo

THE BAR LOOKS NO LESS piratey when I walk inside the next morning. I'm not sure why I thought it might be different in the bright light of day, but it's almost MORE than I remember. I honestly wasn't even sure Ned's Place would be open so early. But the door swung open easily, even if I appear to be the only person here.

I woke up when the sun was still below the horizon to the sound of a door slamming on the other side of the duplex. Jake would be an early riser—of course he would. An early riser and a door slammer.

Not Jake—*Mr. Fieldstone!*

I've decided to use Jake's formal name rather than his first name. Jake is far too friendly of a name to be uttered bitterly under my breath. Or shouted at the wall after I heard him stomping down the porch steps. I made a mental note to play obnoxious music after nine p.m. and do a lot of door-slamming of my own.

Since I couldn't go back to sleep, I got up, showered, and dressed, and now I'm a woman on a mission. I think my mission should have included coffee first, but I don't have coffee. Or a coffee pot. The grocery store is next on my list. First up, I need to find Ned.

My walk up to the empty bar feels very walk of shame-y. Or maybe more like returning to the scene of a crime. A wine crime. A crime of wine proportions.

As I pass the wooden mermaid, I give her a quick smile. "I've gotta say, this look really works for you. I'm slightly jealous of your ability to fill out that tiny top."

She doesn't respond. Not that I expected her to. Though I'd never be TOTALLY shocked if an inanimate object moved, or a woodland creature offered to help me with my wardrobe. I may have focused my studies on poetry, but I've read enough fantasy to prepare me for just about anything.

"Are you talking to Gretchen?"

I'm so startled by Ned's voice, I walk into the corner of a table. "Oof!"

"Sorry," Ned says. "Are you okay there?"

I hold up a hand. "I'm all good!"

Just bruised. Both my ego and my hip.

I perch on a different stool than my first time here—a symbolic choice. Bard the bird appears to be sleeping. Otherwise, the room is empty. Ned makes his way down to me, wiping a glass dry with a white towel. His mustache twitches with a smile.

"What can I get for you today?"

Offering him an apologetic smile, I say, "My dignity?"

He laughs, the sound warming me through and through. I take a breath and settle onto my seat, letting go of the death grip I've had on the hem of my dress. Today, I chose a sunny yellow with tiny white polka dots.

"I don't think I can give you that," Ned says, and I'm about to agree when he winks and says, "You can't give back what someone never lost."

He is *way* too kind. "Oh, I'm pretty sure I lost it after the second glass of wine. Which, to be fair, was only my second glass of wine ever. Apparently, I have less than zero tolerance. Mine is more like a negative fifteen."

"You also mentioned you hadn't eaten," Ned says. "That can have an impact, even on someone used to drinking. In any case, I thought nothing of it, and neither should you. How about a glass of water? Or breakfast? I make a mean egg sandwich."

"Maybe just water? Thank you."

Ned returns with a glass of water with ice and lemon. I peel the wrapper from the straw, tying it in a knot. Back in junior high, this was one of those silly games. If you pulled until the straw paper ripped and the knot came undone, the boy you were thinking about was also thinking about you. If the knot held, they were not. When the flimsy paper pulls apart, I am in no way shocked to see the knot hold tight.

I don't even have a guy—who would be thinking of me?

Jake Fieldstone's face shouldn't suddenly appear in my mind, but it does. Ugh! I don't need straw paper to tell me he is NOT thinking about me. Unless he's thinking of ways to permanently remove me from the island.

"So, what brings you back in?" Ned asks. "Not that I mind your company."

I like how he said *your* company, not just *the* company. Maybe it's a bartender trick to make everyone feel at home, but I get the sense it's just who Ned is.

I toy with a flier resting on the bar, spinning it along the wood surface with the blank side facing up.

"I wanted to apologize," I say. When Ned looks surprised, I add, "For the other night. I feel really foolish."

Ned makes a dismissive sound, smiling again underneath his mustache. "Like I said, no worries. Totally understandable given the circumstances."

I wonder if he means the wine on an empty stomach or the fact that I just lost Gran. Either way, I appreciate his kindness and feel slightly less idiotic. Then I think about Jake picking me up and carrying me back to my room. Most of my memories from that night are messy and blurred, like an impressionist painting when you're standing too close, but Jake's role in my humiliation is painfully clear.

"Thank you. It's just … that isn't like me."

"Hey," Ned says, a fatherly gentleness in his tone. "You don't need to explain."

I straighten my spine and lift my chin. "I'd like to though. It's important to me."

Setting down the glass he's been drying, Ned gives me a firm nod. "Okay, then. Apology and explanation accepted."

"Thank you."

Bard the bird suddenly squawks to life. "'It was the best of times, it was the worst of times.'"

"Who's the literary lover?" I ask, leaning my elbows on the bar, still spinning the flier. "Is it you?"

Ned's eyes turn guarded, and his mustache twitches, almost hiding his frown. "No. That was my wife—ex-wife. And my son."

I fidget with the flier, unsure what to say next. If I were Ned, I'd probably have the perfect response, something that would hit the right notes of comfort and kindness for what's obviously a sore subject. But I'm at a complete loss.

I turn over the flier, and suddenly, I don't give a rip about the right words. I'm totally focused on the ones swimming in front of me, all caps Times New Roman on a plain white half-sheet of paper. I swallow hard as I try to process what I'm reading.

Because the flier is for a celebration of life for Genevieve Markham. The date is two nights ago, the night I came here. My birthday. I grab the bar with my free hand so I don't topple from the stool.

"What is this?" My voice breaks a little at the end of my question.

Ned glances down, and his brows draw together. "Did you not know about it?"

I shake my head and drop the flier. A haze of anger settles behind my eyes. How could I NOT know about this? Who would have left us out of something like this?

"He should have told you," Ned mutters.

"Who?"

Sighing, Ned gives his head a shake. "My son. Jake."

I GET no small amount of satisfaction pounding on Jake's door. I guess I could have just as easily banged on the wall we share, but that seems far too intimate. For my own peace of mind, I definitely need to pretend like Jake isn't just a wall away.

Doing ... whatever he's doing over there. It's been quiet, which makes my imagination come up with all kinds of scenarios involving my grumpy new neighbor. Jake eating. Jake lounging on his couch in his running clothes—which unfortunately look every bit as good on him as a suit does. Jake sleeping. Shaving. Taking a shower. Looking all handsome with his stupid, unsmiling face.

Jake doesn't answer right away, and I bang some more, switching hands. Because if I'm being honest, my fist is getting sore. I thought I heard the quiet close of a door earlier, in between the Olivia Rodrigo songs I've been blasting. Maybe I was wrong.

When the door flies open, I'm mid-bang, and the momentum carries me forward and right into Jake.

Correction: right into Jake's wet, bare chest.

His bare, wet TATTOOED chest.

Jake—Mr. Fieldstone—has a tattoo? My brain shorts out at the sight of the ink trailing over one shoulder and across his chest. I don't have time to examine it because I'm still basically sliding down his body.

He's wet, but why in the world is he so *slippery*?

I try to steady myself, but my hands slide along his pecs— which I would rate as a solid ten out of ten—and on down to his abs. (Also a ten out of ten, just to be clear.) Before my hands slip even lower toward the towel around his waist, Jake grabs my upper arms, saving me from further embarrassment and accidental exploration.

I make a very undignified squeak and then practically shout, "You have tattoos!"

At this point, I have zero dignity left in front of this man.

"Just one," he says, like that makes a difference.

Jake's movements are harsh and jerky, but there's a gentleness underneath. He doesn't send me flying off the porch, which I might have done if some almost-stranger mauled me when I was fresh out of the shower.

And here I accused him of assault and unsolicited touching. Oh, the irony!

Jake lets go quickly, and his hands go straight to the towel around his waist, which is on the verge of being indecently low. He hikes it up, holding the knot, and clears his throat.

He's obviously mid-shower, slippery because he's covered in body wash. A few suds trail down his chest. I get a little lost watching their slow progress over his tanned, muscled skin. What I can see of his tattoo is black inked feathers, trailing over his shoulder where it must continue onto his back. I would never have guessed that my grumpy lawyer neighbor has all this going on under his suit.

Sadie's words pop into my head, though I can't remember them exactly. She said something about what guys are hiding under their buttoned-up exterior.

"Eloise."

I blink, averting my eyes. Ugh, with the name again! Does every word out of his mouth have to be so ... dry? So curt and grouchy? And why am I starting to like hearing the sound of my full name on his lips?

"You banged?" he asks, looking one part annoyed, one part amused. Which makes me all parts furious.

Fury—that's why I'm here.

Focus, Lo. Forget the miles of gorgeous man-chest you'd like to map out with your fingers. Remember who he is and why you're mad at him.

"How could you not invite me to my own grandmother's celebration of life?"

I'm spitting mad. Literally, it seems, because I think I might have projected a little more than words just now. Serves him right!

"I could have been there," I continue. "I was here—on the island. Why didn't you think to let me or my sisters know?" Something about my merlot-addled birthday night hits me with startling clarity. I gasp. "That's where you were coming from! You and all the people dressed up who came to the bar!"

"I'm surprised you remember any of that," he says.

I'm not sure a face has ever been so perfectly punchable. But seeing as the hotshot lawyer would probably have a suit filed before my knuckles healed, I keep my violent urge in check.

I am not this woman. The fly-off-the-handle, want-to-punch-handsome-almost-strangers woman. I've been described as sweet. Quirky. Full of sunshine. But Jake's grumpiness is clearly contagious, and I've caught a wicked case. Hence the narrow-eyed glare I'm giving him.

He barely notices. At least, if his indifferent eyes and unchanging stance are to be believed. How can he care so little? He knew Gran. She wrote me and my sisters into her will—wouldn't he have realized we wanted to be there?

"It was more of an informal gathering," he says, looking away.

"Informal?"

I yank out the crumpled flier and smack it against Jake's chest. He's so wet, it sticks like a Post-It note.

If I weren't so mad, I'd laugh. Jake peels it off slowly, one hand still on his towel.

"I wouldn't call *that* informal," I tell him.

Though he has to know what it is already, he still looks at the flier. Honestly, I wouldn't be shocked if Jake wrote it. The wording definitely reads like a robot composed it. He carefully folds the paper, one-handed, which I'd be impressed with if I weren't so righteously angry. And righteous anger trumps dexterous fingers. Every time.

With no pockets, there's nowhere for him to put the note, so he curls it into his palm. I snatch it right back, smoothing it out, even though I was the one to crumple it in my angry fist.

"You've only been here a handful of times in the past ten years," Jake says. And though what he's saying is a hard truth, for once, his tone is gentle. "You rarely called. Why would I think you wanted to celebrate her life?"

"I wrote her," I say, but there isn't much fire in my voice. Our letters back and forth didn't replace the need for a real, in-person visit.

Still, I was young when my family basically imploded after Mom and Dad's divorce. Most of the drama I still don't fully understand. Dad and Gran had some sort of falling out around the same time as the divorce. Merritt thinks it had everything to do with him wanting Gran's money.

After we moved all the way to Arizona, Mom didn't do much to facilitate us maintaining our relationship with her ex-husband's mother. She and Gran hadn't been close before the divorce. There wasn't much reason to keep up after.

It was hard to manage much more than writing letters without adult help. I didn't have my own phone I could use to call or text. At least not at first.

But my sisters and I have been bona fide (if not fully legal, in my case) adults for a while now. Even while I was in school, I could have made more of an effort to come visit on my own. We all could have.

Not that it justifies Jake leaving us out. We are her family —her only family!

"I wrote letters," I repeat. "Every month. I was just a kid when my parents divorced, Jake."

He breathes out a sigh. "Eloise—"

"Stop," I say, somehow finding the fire I'd lost moments ago. "Stop calling me that. It's *Lo*. And—"

Sniff. Oh, no. It's happening. The burning eyes. The stinging nose. The tightness in my throat.

Not now, tears! You are banned!

"I would have been here!"

What I mean to be an angry shout comes out as more of a hiccupping sob. Because I cry at *everything*, and that's on a normal day. I cry at sad events, whether for me, a friend, or a total stranger ordering a cappuccino at the coffee shop where I worked during college. I cry at commercials. Before my period. During my period. After my period and until my next period.

My tears are like ready soldiers, prepared for battle and marching out at the first hint of trouble.

But I don't want to cry here. Not in front of *him.*

I already feel about twelve years old in front of Jake. Crying after practically groping his bare, inked chest? Ugh. I feel stupid. I feel small.

I'm about to run away—completing the picture of the little kid I feel like—when he speaks.

"You're right," Jake says, and I hate how his voice has gentled. "You were young. Family is complicated. And I didn't know about the letters. I shouldn't have assumed."

I appreciate his kindness, but I'm not sure I want it. A stack of letters doesn't fix the countless times Gran reminded me her door was always open.

I made plenty of plans. *I'll come during fall break,* I'd write. Or, *I'll fly down over Christmas!* But there was always a research paper to finish or an important exam for which I was woefully unprepared.

Gran was so healthy. So young and vibrant and accommodating. She never pressured. And I always thought I had more time.

69

"No," I say simply. "I should have done more. I should have *been here* more."

Jake steps forward and reaches toward my arm, but just before his knuckles brush my skin, he seems to think better of touching me and pulls back. I stare at his bare feet, fixating on a cluster of bubbles on his big toe. While I watch, they all pop.

"This is on me. I should have let you—all three of you— know about the celebration of life. I'm sorry." Jake's voice is so achingly sincere. He sounds somehow younger, though I know it takes maturity to apologize so well. "I should have given you the choice."

"Yes. You should have." I sniff, try to wipe my nose discreetly, then sniff again.

I don't know how to escape this conversation, only that I need to. Immediately. I head across the five feet of porch to my door, trying to keep my lip from wobbling until I'm safely inside my place. I'm unsuccessful, but as long as I don't start making ugly crying sounds, I can live with myself.

"Eloise—Lo," Jake calls.

I stop but don't turn around, scuffing my flip-flop along the wooden porch. "Yeah?"

"I've got the name of a contractor who is available to help with the renovations. Maybe I could bring it by later? When I'm a little less soapy and a little more dressed."

Did Jake Fieldstone just try to be funny? A very lame attempt.

But lame though it may be, I have to bite my lip to hold back a smile. I keep my back to him. Jake Fieldstone doesn't get to see my tears *or* my smiles.

"I would appreciate that. Maybe we could have dinner?"

No, no, no! Bad Lo! Why did you tack that on when you were THIS close to walking away from the conversation on a high note?

I don't even have wine to blame for my offer, which is only slightly less embarrassing than asking Jake to stay the night. Because it totally sounded like I was asking him on a date. Which I'm not! Totally not. I'm sure that would violate some kind of lawyer-client thing, and I get the sense Jake is every bit the rule follower I am.

Plus, why would he want to have dinner with the drunken deadbeat granddaughter who cries *before* the drop of a hat?

I squeeze my eyes closed, waiting for his answer, wishing I could take my invitation back.

"I've already got dinner plans," Jake says finally, his tone as blank as I imagine his face to be. It's impossible to read into his words, other than to take them at face value: a rejection.

This is the part where someone else might soften it and say, *Thank you,* or maybe even, *Rain check?* But not Jake. He says diddly squat, so I simply angle my chin like a woman who laughs in the face of rejection. I head inside where I can safely fall apart while NOT thinking about Jake finishing his shower on the other side of the wall.

EIGHT

Jake

I CHOSE The Big Tuna to meet Margo for dinner because it caters more to the local crowd than the tourists. After a week being around a lot of people, I was going for small and quiet. But as I cross the restaurant to the table where Margo is already seated, I realize my mistake. A local restaurant means nosy locals who will be trying to hear every bit of our conversation.

Already, I can feel the way they're all watching while pretending NOT to be watching.

Which means the gossip mill will be turning at warp speed tonight. I'll probably have half a dozen voice mails from people wondering, like Harriett did, if Margo and I are getting back together.

Which, to be very, very clear, we are not. Even if Margo's low-cut dress and her wide smile broadcast her intent loud and clear. Completely unbidden, I'm suddenly imagining Eloise in her ridiculously adorable pineapple dress.

Okay, that is definitely *not* where my brain needs to be right now. Or ever.

Margo stands to greet me when I reach her, stepping around the table so she can lean in and plant a kiss on my cheek. "Jake. Good to see you."

"Hello, Margo."

As she moves back to her seat, Margo eyes the casual jeans and polo I'm wearing. "Is casual Friday happening on a Thursday this week?" she asks. "Or is this the new, island-life Jake?"

Neither. Despite the more laid-back style of Oakley (not to mention the humidity), I still wear a suit to work every day. Honestly, my clothing choice tonight is an intentional statement. I need Margo to accept—FINALLY—that we don't fit in each other's lives. We are not a match.

There was a time when we seemed perfectly suited. I'd been working for her father for a few years when she came to work for the family firm. Margo went right to work in Atlanta after she finished law school, wanting to establish herself apart from her family—a sentiment I understood very well.

I respected her drive, her independence, and—keeping with total honesty here—her polished beauty. Together, we were her father's darlings and the firm power couple. Until … something I can't explain shifted.

I scoot my chair closer to the table and resist the urge to check if my collar is straight. "Sorry—didn't get the memo about the dress code."

Margo shifts, picking an invisible piece of lint off her dress as the waiter comes by for our drink orders. I choose a beer, which makes Margo wrinkle her nose.

"Sparkling water with fresh lemon, please," she says.

When we're alone again, a cloud of super-awkward hangs over the table between us. Margo lines up her knife and fork in a perfect row, edges aligned with her plate, then shifts her water goblet so it's just so. I'm half expecting her to pull out a tape measure and make sure the distance between the plate and her wine glass is acceptable when she finally looks up.

"Are you really going to stay on Oakley forever?"

I clench my jaw and hold her gaze for a long moment, long enough that when our waiter brings our drinks, he scurries back to the kitchen without asking if we're ready to order. "This is my home."

"Right. You grew up here. But with Gennie gone—"

"My father still lives here."

"You would never stay on the island for Ned," Margo says dismissively, and I hate that she knows me so well.

Ned and I get along fine. No, scratch that. Let's say we've figured out how to coexist by not discussing the many, many ways we irritate and don't understand each other. We definitely aren't close enough that I feel compelled to stay on the island just for him.

"I'm staying for *me*. I don't expect you to understand. I know it isn't the life you'd choose."

Honestly, I never thought it was the life I'd choose either. My life plan included college, law school, and then settling down to build a life anywhere but here. I can't quite pinpoint a moment when this changed. It was more like years of pretending I didn't feel the tug toward this island. A tug that —by the end—was more of a violent yank. Oakley is by no means perfect. But what I said was true—it IS home.

Call me small-minded or old-fashioned or whatever else you want, but I *like* being a small-town attorney. I like knowing my neighbors.

I like that Frank, the barber next door to my office on

Main Street, will call and check on me if I don't show up to work on time, and that Harriett, who owns the deli at the corner, will personally walk my lunch order down just so she can show me pictures of her granddaughter's dance recital.

When our mom left, the island raised me and Naomi as much as Ned did. Maybe that kind of closeness would scare some people away. But for me, it did the opposite. Oakley Island earned my loyalty, even when I was making plans to leave. That same sense of home and loyalty drew me back.

Margo's eyes dim the tiniest bit, but she sits up a little taller, like she's rallying for round two. "Daddy would make you a partner, Jake. We could—" She gives her head a tiny shake. "*You* could really make something of yourself."

We. I don't miss her use of the word. I also don't want it. Or the implication that I need to make more of myself.

"Margo, I'm not coming back to Savannah. I appreciate everything your father has done for me, but my life is here. Right where I want it to be."

"Even without me?"

Her voice is softer, and for a moment, I feel guilty. Then her eyes lift and fixate on something—maybe some*one?*—behind me. Her expression hardens, one side of her lip curling. The hairs on my arms stand up, and somehow, I know who it has to be.

"So, you'd rather stay around here and babysit?" she asks, all softness leached from her tone, which has all the subtlety of a Brillo pad.

I turn and look over my shoulder. Eloise is standing at the takeout counter wearing fuzzy pajama bottoms and a tank top. Her toned arms are almost enough to distract my gaze away from her outfit. *Almost.* The pink flamingos all over her pants make it tough to notice much else. Neon pink flamingos.

Does the woman not own any solid-colored clothing? Anything in a neutral color palette? Somehow, Eloise still manages to look cute. More than cute. She's endearingly pretty, even with no makeup and her hair in some kind of messy knot.

"Are those bunny slippers?" Margo asks, so loud I have to fight the urge to shush her.

The snide remark is another reminder of why Margo and I could never work. She has far too many sharp edges. And, apparently, where Eloise is concerned, claws and fangs as well.

My eyes drop to Eloise's feet, which are, in fact, ensconced in fuzzy slippers.

"They're teddy bears." A laugh catches in my throat. I glance at Margo. If looks could kill, I'd be dead right where I sit.

"And you trust *her* to renovate Gennie's house?"

"She's not going to be renovating by herself," I say. "She's got her sisters to weigh in on decisions."

Her sisters are probably five states away by now, but something in my gut has me needing to defend Eloise. Probably Gennie. It's what she would want, and I'm loyal to her.

You keep telling yourself it's about me, Gennie's voice says in my head. *I think you like her.*

I most certainly do not.

Though … she might be growing on me. I can admit that. There is something effervescent about Eloise. She seems unsinkable somehow, like no matter what life throws her way, she'll bob right back up to the surface with a smile.

And teddy bear slippers.

"And she'll have you to *oversee* things—isn't that right?"

"Yes." I want to argue because the way Margo says *oversee*

76

implies something else. But arguing would be like chumming the water, and Margo already seems to scent blood.

Margo rolls her eyes. "The fact that you're choosing *this* over being a partner at Daddy's law firm completely baffles me. What is it about this island? And that house? You've always been weird about it." Her eyes dart back to Eloise. "Or is it *her*?"

The waiter approaches for a second time, but I wave him away. I know Margo, and the crease between her brow and the way her fingers are nervously drumming against the table tell me we probably aren't going to make it through dinner. It'll make everything easier if we don't order anything. I take a few sips of my beer, needing a pause before I respond to Margo.

"Eloise arrived a few days ago," I say pointedly. "She doesn't have anything to do with me choosing life on the island. I'm here because I want to be here. I'm helping with the house because Gennie asked me to. That's it."

"Is it, though?" she asks.

Without meaning to, my gaze flicks back to the woman in the bear slippers waiting to pick up a takeout order. Margo's question should be easy to dismiss. And yet ... like the island, Eloise seems to have an inexplicable pull on me.

Unlike the island, I will NOT be giving into this pull.

Margo shakes her head tightly and stands up. "You're making a mistake. We were good together. If you would just come back to Savannah, we could be *great* together." When I don't answer, Margo huffs. "If you say no right now, there won't be another offer, Jake. From Daddy or from me. I'm serious."

I'm not even a little bit tempted. "Tell your dad I said hello, Margo."

She shoots me one final icy glare before turning and stalking away. Except, she isn't headed toward the door.

She's headed toward Eloise.

My skin prickles, and my heart rate climbs. What could Margo possibly have to say to Eloise?

As Margo reaches her, Eloise's gaze darts over to where I'm sitting before her focus turns back to the woman towering in front of her. Margo is tall without her heels on, but she's wearing what she always called her power heels now, making her a full foot taller than Eloise. Not that being taller than Eloise is much of an accomplishment.

I can only see the side of Margo's head, but I have a full view of Eloise's expression. My jaw tightens as I watch her face shift from surprise to something that looks more like disdain.

Another second passes before Margo flips her shiny blond hair over her shoulder and disappears out the side door next to the takeout counter. Eloise shoots me a look, one eyebrow raised, but then it's her turn at the register, and she shifts her attention away from me.

For the first time since I walked in, I remember all the eyes and ears. This time, no one is being subtle. Everyone is watching this little drama unfold. And if they aren't watching, they're tapping on phones. I give them all a look that I hope accurately conveys how ashamed of themselves they should be. When I look back, Eloise is gone.

I toss a twenty on the table and catch Eloise in the parking lot just as she's unlocking her car. I really hope Margo is already long gone.

"What did she say?" My question comes out more like a demand, and I'm already wishing for a reset button for this conversation.

Eloise stills and turns to face me. "Hello, *Mr. Fieldstone*. Nice to see you too."

"Sorry. I just know Margo was upset, and I worried she might have—"

"Said something negative about you?" She sets her food on the driver's seat, then leans back against the car, crossing her legs at the ankles. I do my best not to stare at her slippers. "Are you worried she'll taint my very lofty opinion of you?"

Whatever Eloise knows about me or thinks of me, I want it to be because I've told her or she's judged for herself, not because she's learned some skewed version from Margo, of all people.

Although, in all fairness, Eloise hasn't gotten the best impression of me so far.

"She *did* seem a little upset," Eloise continues, raising a brow. "What did *you* say to her?"

I sigh. "Nothing that I haven't said before."

"Poor Mr. Fieldstone, having to fight off the ladies. Must be so hard to be you."

"That's not—no. Eloise, please just tell me what she said."

"I won't tell you anything as long as you keep calling me Eloise."

I prop my hands on my hips. *"Lo,"* I say with extra emphasis. "Tell me."

She shifts and drops her gaze like she's suddenly uncomfortable. "It's nothing. It doesn't matter."

"Then why won't you tell me?"

"Gee, I don't know. Pick a reason. Maybe because I feel totally silly talking to you while wearing teddy bear slippers. Or because I really just want to go home and eat my coconut shrimp and fries while they're still hot."

My stomach rumbles. The Big Tuna's coconut shrimp are legendary. An image flits through my brain. Me and Eloise sitting on the front porch of the carriage house, sharing fries and the best coconut shrimp. Laughing. Talking about nothing. Arguing about everything. Making up afterward ... maybe twice.

Eloise huffs, a slight pink coloring her cheeks as she drops her folded arms, her hands curling into fists at her sides. "Fine. Margo told me not to get any ideas about you," she blurts out. "She said a relationship with Jake Fieldstone isn't a good idea."

I scoff. "Like there's any reason for her to issue *that* warning."

Eloise narrows her eyes, but I don't miss the hurt flashing there. Once again, I'm tasting leather as I shove my whole foot in my mouth.

"What's *that* supposed to mean?"

"I just mean you and I"—I gesture between us, suddenly realizing how close I'm standing to her—"isn't something for Margo to worry about. You're a client."

Eloise pushes off her car and closes the scant distance between us until we are toe to toe—or, loafer to fuzzy slipper.

"And you have the emotional availability of a dinner plate."

So *that's* what Margo said to Eloise. I shouldn't be surprised. I think Margo threw that exact insult at me during an argument before our final breakup. I want to defend myself, to explain that I have plenty of emotions. I'm just not good at expressing them easily in ways that other people understand.

Case in point: I keep goading Eloise when I never should have come out here. She's close enough that I can smell that

80

same floral scent wafting off her skin. It's messing with my head, making my thoughts feel hazy and slow.

"Is that why you asked me to have dinner? Or why you couldn't keep your hands off my chest when I answered the door earlier?"

Maybe it started as an accident, but the way her hands slid over my skin felt all kinds of intentional—something I still haven't forgotten. Accident or no, Eloise's fingertips lit a fire under every inch of me she touched. Which makes this whole conversation and especially our proximity particularly dangerous.

She grits her teeth as her cheeks go from a pink flush to ruby red. "I was being neighborly asking you to have dinner. And maybe you shouldn't answer the door in a towel."

"Maybe you shouldn't bang incessantly on people's doors. I thought it was an emergency."

"Either way, I wasn't touching you on purpose. It was just momentum when you threw open the door."

And once again, it feels like Eloise and I are fighting. But something about her fury is intoxicating. I feel more alive than I have in months.

"I'll be sure to open my door more slowly next time to avoid being groped."

She shakes her head. "Jake Fieldstone, if I didn't have to stay on this island, so help me, I'd get as far away from your smug face as I possibly could."

This is a good reminder that Eloise is leaving. More than anything else—beyond her being too young and my client (though technically, Gennie was my client)—Eloise never planned to move here. She isn't planning to stay. I need to remember this. Before I get used to this sparring, to her scent, to her ridiculous fashion sense.

She takes a slow, deep breath and a giant step back.

Something like disappointment falls heavy in my chest.

"I have a dinner to eat," she says.

"Don't let me stop you."

She stomps the few short steps to her car, an entirely ineffective gesture—can fuzzy slippers truly stomp?—and throws herself inside.

"Hey, Eloise," I call right before she slams the door shut.

She pauses, her arm poised on the door, and lifts her eyebrows. "Yes, Mr. Fieldstone?"

"I'm also allergic to flamingos."

Why I fired this as a parting shot, I'm not sure. Why I even felt the need to get in the last word is beyond me. It's a stupid comment, and I want to shrivel up where I'm standing as soon as I say it.

And yet, when I see the corner of her mouth twitch like she's fighting a smile, I feel like I've won.

NINE

Lo

THOUGH I'M USUALLY NOT one for putting things off, I wait a full two days after moving into the carriage house to enter the main house. I spend my time puttering around the carriage house, unpacking, and shopping for essentials like coffee, a coffee maker, and razors. I also do my very best not to think about the man on the other side of the wall. But today, we're having lunch, so at the very least, I need to have seen the inside of Gran's house.

Still, I find myself hesitating on the wraparound front porch, key in hand, giving myself a pep talk, which comes mostly in the form of singing halfway-correct song lyrics off-key. I'm terrible both at deciphering lyrics and singing, but somehow this is still my go-to for empowerment.

Who cares whether what I'm singing is technically correct?

"I'm the eye of the tiger, vanilla coffee with ice! Baby, be a firework—go on, let 'em do their worst! I won't stop believing—I'm higher than the ceiling!"

I put the key in the lock after butchering Journey, then mutter a little not-quite Sia lyrics for good measure: "I'll put some armor on, and then I'll eat some ham!"

The key turns, and I push open the right side of the double front doors. Taking a fortifying breath, I step inside and immediately stop short.

Grandma's house lives large in my memories, but the reality of it knocks up against my mental image, making it crumble to dust. The two-story foyer somehow seemed grander in my mind, spacious and open and full of natural light, but this space is smaller and dim, the chandelier hanging in the center gaudy and outdated. I must have merged my memories of this house with a scene ripped straight from a movie.

The wallpaper that lines the room and climbs up the stairway is peeling around the edges and at the seams, revealing a sliver of other wallpaper underneath. Joy! It will be like a wallpaper treasure hunt. I have a sudden urge to pick, to peel away long strips of the maroon and gold print to see what's underneath. Probably something even more outdated. Though, with the way trends circle back around, maybe I'll discover a layer of wallpaper from years ago that's all the rage now.

The wide, curving staircase could maybe be called grand —if it didn't look like someone yanked a carpet runner from its center, leaving a swath of darker wood beneath. The stairs —and all the hardwood floors, really—will have to be sanded down and refinished. Does Gran own an industrial sander? Probably not. Those things can't be cheap. Could we rent one, maybe? As my eyes drift around the room, I start to see things in dollar signs.

Before Merritt and Sadie left, they both impressed upon me the importance of staying on a budget. "I'll send you some projections later in the week," Merritt said.

I imagine a color-coded spreadsheet full of numbers that I won't look at. Excel is like my nemesis. Cut up, Merritt's spreadsheets would make fabulous confetti.

I should ask Jake about renting a sander or other supplies. That is, whenever I get over my embarrassment from running into him at the restaurant the other night. Which might be, oh, never.

I'm not sure what was worse—being accosted by gorgeous Margo or arguing with Jake in the parking lot right after. All in my pajamas and fuzzy slippers. You know, like the VERY mature adult I am.

No more thoughts of Jake! I scold myself.

Last night while eating coconut shrimp straight out of the to-go container, I promised myself that Jake would get no more space than absolutely necessary in my brain. And the only thing necessary is what we need to discuss in relation to the house. Which may be less than I thought. As promised, he texted me the name of a contractor named Hunter. I'll ask *Hunter* about the sander. Once I finally text him, that is.

I pull out my notebook and turn to a fresh page, writing the date at the top and then starting a list. Some people love making lists and some people hate them. For me, it's not about the list-making (though that is fun), but the resulting hit of dopamine when I mark through a completed item. I have a feeling this house is going to end up giving me the biggest rush of happy feelings ever. Because my to-do list is going to be LONG.

As I move through the rooms, I make not one list, but two.

The first is a list of obvious things that need to be done,

like refinishing floors and removing the wallpaper. The other is a list of questions I need answered. Things like: where can I get a sander, and how long can I keep it? How do you decorate the living areas in a bed and breakfast? Should each rentable room have its own style, or should it all be uniform?

I add a third list on a third page to capture my ideas. This one is my favorite and includes things like: pick a color palette and see about building a window seat in the bay window in the breakfast nook. Which then inspires a fourth list of videos and posts I can create on Instagram around the renovation. Because my focus has mostly been lifestyle oriented, I need to do some research on the kinds of posts, hashtags, and content that will hit the renovation and restoration niche. Maybe stuff specific to beach houses, too.

Before I have to make a list to keep track of my lists, I tuck my notebook back in my purse and open up Instagram. I've been ghosting my account for long enough. If Pinterest is good for inspiration boards, maybe Instagram can be something of a sounding board.

I head outside and take a photo of the house with the blue island sky and puffy clouds overhead. In the caption, I write a little bit about the project, sharing that it was my grandmother's house, but not mentioning the will or its stipulations. It's always a balance trying to decide how much to share. I've managed so far to make my Instagram *personable* without getting too *personal*. The distinction matters.

Life update! I've got a new project and I'll need YOUR help. I get to turn this big old beach house into a bed and breakfast. Amazing! But … I'm hoping you can help me pick colors and styles. Anyone up for the challenge??? Follow and share with friends! For starters, this is the outside of the house. Any ideas for updates? xoxo -LO

I do a quick search and add relevant hashtags, hit post,

and then am shocked when my phone starts buzzing with notifications almost immediately.

Well, okay then.

Sadie calls before I can get too deep in the weeds with comments, which are coming hard and fast. The sight of Sadie's name on my screen makes me happy—until I realize she's probably been ordered by Merritt to check in on me. Merritt has to know I probably wouldn't answer if she called.

"Hey," I say, trailing my finger along one of the shutters. What would it look like painted bright teal? Then I head back inside for the AC.

"How's it going? And before you ask—no, Merritt didn't ask me to call."

I laugh because it's scary how well she knows me. My sisters and I may not be super close, but there's this inescapable bond between us. A pang of longing shoots through me—a surprising desire to have Sadie, and maybe even Merritt, here with me.

"I just did my first walkthrough of the house."

"And?" she asks.

I glance around the kitchen—tidy but outdated with tile countertops and wallpaper with lemons on it. "I thought it would be weird, you know? Like, I'd have this emotional connection or all these memories flooding me."

"Not so much?"

"Barely. I mean, I have a few vague memories, but they might not be real. It's like I'm confusing memory with stories you and Mer told me. You both spent way more time here than I did. Or, at least, you were older when we stopped coming. I'm surprised you didn't want to see the place before you left."

I suddenly wonder if my sisters scattered simply because they *do* have more memories tied to this place, because they're running instead of processing, using their jobs as inarguable excuses.

"Can you video chat?" Sadie asks.

"I'll try, but I don't know the status of Gran's Wi-Fi." The carriage house is too far away for that signal to reach, but apparently, the cell reception is top-notch because Sadie's face appears before me. Her hair, a few shades darker than mine, is in a messy top knot, and her oversized shirt hangs off one bare shoulder.

"Must be nice to work from home, bra optional," I mutter.

Sadie smirks and takes a sip of coffee. "You can work without a bra on if you want." She waggles her eyebrows. "I'd love to see how that would go over with our hot lawyer slash overlord."

I know I'm blushing. Probably because I'm remembering Jake's bare chest and the tattoo I never got to fully see. I flip the camera away from my face. Hopefully *before* Sadie caught my blush.

"Not happening. He hates me." And has seen me in too many embarrassing moments to count now. "Look—what do you think about the kitchen?"

Sadie totally ignores my attempted diversion. "Your protesting only fuels my ideas. If you'd just admit he's objectively hot, I'd be more likely to let the issue drop." Her grin stretches wider.

She wants me to be objective? *Fine.* Jake is hot. He is also a gruff jerk and has the emotional bandwidth of a dinner plate. At least, according to Margo, who is just bitter enough not to be fully trusted. Though I can see where she got the idea. His face for sure has the emotional energy of a dinner plate.

He's also the kind of guy to see a tipsy girl home safely,

even when he doesn't particularly like her. I get the sense that he and Gran were close—closer than just attorney-client. If Gran loved him, he can't be all bad.

But I will admit none of these *fully objective* observations to my sister. *Commence a moratorium on the subject of Jake. Now, and forever after. Amen.*

"Ready for the grand tour?" I ask.

"Yes?" Sadie says, the question in her voice making me think I'm right about her hasty departure. "I think? No, just yes. I'm ready. Let's do it."

A surge of compassion flits through me. Eventually, I'll talk to my sisters about Gran. I want to add their memories to mine. Fill the gaps that my younger age caused in my own recollections. But not yet. Not until they're both ready.

Having Sadie on the line gives me a renewed sense of energy and purpose as I walk through the first floor. I keep hoping, keep preparing myself for an onslaught of memories, brought on by the sight or the smell of the house. But nothing I see sparks much emotional response or pulls me back to the past the way I thought it would. Even the smell isn't familiar at all. The let-down from the lack of connection makes me feel like I showed up wearing battle armor on the wrong day.

I flip the camera around so I'm facing Sadie again. "Do you have time for the upstairs?"

Upstairs to Gran's bedroom, the last place she slept. My stomach churns with nerves. Or maybe that's more a lack of breakfast.

Sadie sniffs and looks away from the camera. "Actually, I better go. Someone needs to keep those missiles from pointing our way."

"Missiles? Who's pointing missiles where?"

Laughing, Sadie straightens her shirt, her mask of cool and calm back in place. "No worries. Just a security joke."

I can't tell if she's joking now to make me feel better or if she was joking about the missiles. Either way, I'm unsettled when she says, "Byeeee" in a sing-song voice and hangs up before I can respond. She is the queen of abrupt endings.

Rather than heading upstairs, I decide to give the place a good airing-out courtesy of open windows and the ever-present ocean breeze. It's been a little over a week since Gran died, which means the rooms have been shut up tight since then. The house is clean and not at all musty, so it could just be mental, but fresh air feels like an obvious next step. I go room to room, opening windows, my soul lifting with every cross current that stirs the hair at the nape of my neck.

The breeze carries the distinctive, sharp smell of salt. I wonder if it's something you ever get used to. Since I arrived, every time I step outside, it's like my lungs feel starved for great, big lungfuls of ocean air.

I haven't seen much of the ocean yet. Obviously, I drove over it on the bridge connecting Oakley Island to the mainland. And the water is almost always in view, even if it's just a slice of blue-gray water between buildings or over the waving sea grass dunes.

What I haven't done is gone to the beach. I suddenly itch to stand before the ocean with my toes in the sand. I lean on the windowsill in the living room, drinking in the air and the view. The back lawn slopes down, ending in dunes that obscure the beach itself and only leave a ribbon of deep blue water edging toward the sky.

That will be my reward, I decide. I'll work all day, then tomorrow, I'll spend the afternoon at the beach. Maybe go swimming. I'm trying to visualize where my bathing suit is as I head toward the screened-in porch, the only room I haven't explored down here. The only bathing suit I own is a little old and stretched out. I wish now I'd bought the cute yellow two-piece that kept showing up in ads on Instagram. It was one of those fifties pin-up styles with a high waist with a lot of support in the bikini top.

Just to be clear. Me wishing I bought that bikini doesn't have anything to do with knowing my grouchy (and hot) lawyer lives right next door and might see me in it.

Jake?

Jake, who?

I'm not thinking about him. I'm not distracted by him, I tell myself as I throw open the creaky doors leading to the screened-in porch.

My totally non-distracted thoughts about Jake leave me completely unprepared for a bird the size of a pterodactyl to come flying at me. The bird slams into me with a surprising amount of force and a flurry of feathers.

I do the only natural thing when attacked by a winged, beaked murderer. I go limp, fall into a protective ball, and shriek like the kind of banshee who scares off other banshees.

When the bird doesn't resume its attack, I stop screaming long enough to crack one eye open. Then I scream again.

Because the pelican is standing a foot from my face, tilting its head to stare at me with a tiny, beady eye.

It's not easy to read a bird's expression, but I'm pretty sure this one wants to eat my face off. He's not even remotely bothered by my screaming. When I wave my hands in a shooing motion, he simply tilts his head, studying me.

Probably trying to decide the best way to eat me.

I've seen pelicans before—flying, diving for a fish, bobbing on the surface of the ocean. None of that gave me any sense of how large they are up close. They are MASSIVE. Or, at least, this one is.

Why is there an attack pelican on the screened-in porch? And why isn't he afraid of me?

"Go on," I tell him from my fetal crouch. "Bad bird! Return from whence you came!"

That last command is a quote from *Arrested Development*, a show my college roommates and I binged whenever we were procrastinating. The pelican, clearly not a fan, doesn't get the reference. Or maybe he's offended because one of the characters was tossing a dead dove into the ocean when he said it.

I slowly sit up, prepared to curl back in my protective ball or maybe run, if needed. I don't particularly want the bird to come any farther into the house though, and if I run, he might chase. And then I'll probably pee my pants.

"Are you going to eat me?" I ask.

He tilts his head the other way, shifting from one webbed foot to the other as I slowly scooch away until my back rests against the couch.

"Why are you in the house? Did you get stuck on the porch?"

Maybe he just needs me to prop open the porch door that will free him into the backyard. What if he's been trapped inside since Gran died? I have a sudden vision of the screened-in porch covered in piles of bird poo. Let's hope that's not the case. More likely, a screen is broken, and he wandered in.

"Let's get you back outside, yeah?"

As if he understood me, he turns and waddles back out to the screened-in porch. His head is brown, his feathers are a brownish gray, and he makes little chuffing squawks. He glances back once, making a noise that sounds like the pelican equivalent of exasperation.

"You want me to follow you?" Getting to my feet slowly, I follow him, wondering if this is going to end up being a Lassie situation. "Did Timmy fall down the well?"

I swear, the bird rolls his eyes at me, like he is totally above Lassie comparisons.

The screened-in porch is more like a lack-of-screen porch. Or flapping-screen porch, which is more accurate, as all the screens are present but ripped, flapping in the ocean breeze. The furniture out here is the first thing in the house that sparks real memory: white painted bamboo with worn teal and pink cushions. I suck in a breath at the force of the emotion hitting me.

It's a mundane moment—Merritt and me sitting on the love seat, eating those small round crackers meant for soup. Oyster crackers? I think that's what they're called. Our legs are bare, one of my knees scabbed over. Somewhere, Nat King Cole croons.

I blink and the memory is gone. The swell of emotion stays, making my breath feel shuddery and my knees a little weak. Or maybe that's just leftover adrenaline from the pelican attack.

The bird in question hops up onto the love seat and settles into what is now, apparently, a pelican nest. Or roost? The cushion erupts foam filler, tangled with sticks and brush and a fishing line, only a little thicker than a spiderweb, blowing in the breeze. My attack pelican looks perfectly content sitting on top, fluffing his brownish gray feathers and tucking his beak to his chest.

"Really? All that beach, all those dunes, and you build a nest *here*? Does that mean you have eggs, or are you just ... sleeping here?"

He makes a chirruping sound.

"Hm. We'll see about this," I tell him. But I have no idea

how to handle a pelican living on the screened-in porch. Are pelicans endangered? I make a mental note to google pelican stuff.

There's a loud knock, and then I hear Jake's voice calling out. "Eloise? Lo?"

Of all the bad timing! I'm supposed to have lunch with Jake, but he's fifteen minutes early. Jake CANNOT find out about this. He'll label me a total failure from the start. I walk into Gran's house and BOOM! There's an attack pelican inside.

"I'll be right there! You're early."

I quickly close the doors to the screened-in porch—now, the Pelican Porch—and scurry toward the front of the house, hoping Jake stays in the foyer. Instead, we nearly run into each other in the kitchen doorway.

Jake looks alarmed, but I remind myself that Jake's face and whatever expression it's wearing is none of my concern.

No matter how handsome it is. Or how much I like the worry creasing his eyes. Is that worry for me?

He also looks totally edible in his light gray dress pants, his button-down rolled up to his elbows, even if he looks like he ran the two blocks here. His forehead shines with a light sheen of sweat, and his shirt is partially untucked above his left hip. It's the perfect combination of put-together and pulled-apart. His tie is loose, and his collar is open, revealing a triangle of tanned skin that has me inexplicably itching to press my nose to the spot, to breathe him in while I'm exploring that tattoo I'd really love to see again—

Don't get any ideas, I scold myself. *This man is NOT for you.*

"Are you okay? Billie from across the street called me. Said she heard screaming?"

I cross my arms, a tiny act of defiance. "I'm fine. I was just … singing."

94

"Singing," he repeats, looking like he doesn't believe this for a second.

"Yeah. Singing. Maybe I was off-key. Singing is more Sadie's thing." Or, at least, it was. Until she decided to choose computers rather than performing. But whatever. "She's the singer and Merritt was the artist, but they both chose more stable career paths. Which—good for them, but if I had a gift like that, I'd use it. Meanwhile, I'm over here wanting to study American poets. Talk about impractical. Academia, folks. Am I right?"

I'm babbling, and Jake looks like he's searching for a response and coming up empty. I'm totally fine with that. I'll babble all day if it will keep Jake from finding out there's a pelican roosting on the outdoor love seat. Logically, I *know* the pelican was likely here before I was. His presence on Gran's clearly dilapidated porch is not my fault.

But it still feels like Jake would use the information against me, adding it to the growing list of evidence he's probably keeping that I am a total disaster. A total disaster, *and* a poetry nerd. Did I see his eyebrow go up at that admission?

Maybe nerds are Jake's type. Ned *did* say it was Jake and his mother who trained Bard the Bird to quote famous lines from literature.

Not that it matters! I don't care about Jake's type. I care about him not finding out about the pelican on the porch. Although … maybe he's allergic to pelicans like he is to pineapples and flamingos (I think he was joking about that last one) and I can use this to my advantage.

"What?" Jake asks.

"What?"

"You're smiling in a particularly villainous way."

I scoff. "I'm pretty sure I'm not the villain in this story."

"You think the villain is me?" His brows slowly climb his forehead until he's giving me the equivalent of side-eye but from the front.

Is *front* side-eye a thing? I think it is now. I'll have to add it to the urban dictionary site later.

Jake and I stand there, facing off. His gaze feels like one of those scanners at the grocery store, able to pull up information from a single bar code.

Only, he's getting nothing from me. Not. A. Thing.

"Do you need something else?" I finally ask.

I can't take the tension crackling between us. It started out like frustration or irritation, but it grows and changes every time we're together. Whatever it is has stretched tight, shifting into something else. It has me feeling all hot and bothered, and only ONE of those emotions is acceptable where Jake is concerned.

"No. That is, if everything is okay." He shoots me a questioning look, then peeks around me as though looking for a robber hiding behind the kitchen island. Hopefully the pelican isn't visible through the glass doors from this angle.

"I'm just fine. How lovely of you to be concerned."

He blows out a breath, dragging one hand through his dark hair. I try and fail not to track the movement, noting how soft his hair looks and how nice it is to see it slightly mussed. I'd like to get my hands in there and muss it myself.

Alert! Alert! Alert! Defenses have been breached! Abandon ship! We're going down. I curl my fingers to my palms just in case they get any ideas about touching Jake.

"You can go back to your fancy job now," I tell him, immediately regretting the bite in my voice. It's a total defense mechanism. Not the most mature thing, to lash out, but if it gets Jake out of the house, I don't care.

Jake opens his mouth, closes it, then frowns. "Eloise—"

"Lo."

"Lo, I feel like we should—"

Waving my hand in a shooing motion, I shake my head. "Nope. We shouldn't."

"You don't even know what I was going to say."

What I know is that any minute now, that pelican is going to bust through the doors. I start walking toward Jake, hoping he'll take the hint and back up. Or better yet—turn and walk right out the front door and we can go to lunch as planned. He doesn't budge, which just leaves us standing much too close.

"I can guess. Anyway, shouldn't we go?"

"Eloise, you don't need to—"

"It's Lo!" I yell, perhaps loudly enough that Billie, obviously the nosy sort, might be placing another phone call of complaint.

Jake's mouth tightens, and I wish that were a bad look on him. But he doesn't seem to have a bad look, and that's just not fair. Especially when we're practically chest to chest.

"Fine," he grumbles. "As long as you're sure you're okay."

"I'm fine."

"Fine."

"Fine," I repeat.

"Fine." Jake is clearly the kind of man who needs to have the last word. Color me unsurprised.

When he finally backs away, I feel like I can breathe again. Just before he reaches the front door, he turns back. "By the way, you've got a feather in your hair."

A feather? Oh, no. My stomach sinks as I dig through my hair, finally pulling out a giant feather. My brain blanks on ways to explain this. Which means Jake is going to find out about—

"Don't worry about Steve," Jake says. "His bark is worse than his bite."

"Steve?"

"The pelican living on the porch."

He gives me a look that clearly says, *Keep up, Markham.* I can almost hear the words.

And then ... he smiles.

Jake Fieldstone smiling—even if he's smirking, and it's totally at my expense—is devastating. It doesn't soften all his hard edges—nothing could make a dent in that jawline—but it's like a protective layer has been peeled back, revealing the man underneath.

I think the sight of his straight, white teeth and a slightly crooked tilt of his mouth stopped my heart. It absolutely stopped the flow of information from my brain.

I'm still frozen when Jake pushes open the front door. He pauses long enough to look back over his shoulder with a smile that's way too charming for Jake's good. Or MY good.

"Are you still coming?"

And then, while I'm standing there like an idiot holding a feather from a pelican named Steve, Jake and his unfairly hot smile walks out.

TEN

Jake

I'M BARELY DOWN the porch steps when Eloise comes barreling out the door behind me. Just like I thought she would.

"Wait a minute," she calls. *Yells* is more like it. "Are you telling me you *knew* about the pelican living on the screened-in porch?"

I hide my smile before I turn around. "Your grandmother liked him," I say, as if that's explanation enough.

"I don't care if Gran fed him right off the table."

She basically *did*. But I'm not sure Eloise needs me to point that out right now.

She puts her hands on her hips, drawing my eye to the pair of jeans that do very good things for her shape. I may be a man who voluntarily chooses to wear a suit every day, but there is something about a woman in well-fitting jeans.

"It might have prevented my—" She pauses, her gaze shifting toward Billie's house across the street. "My singing."

"Your *singing*, huh?" Billie absolutely said screaming. Not singing. But it's amusing to watch Eloise flounder as she tries to cover this up.

She scowls and folds her arms across her chest. "Jake, don't push me right now. I just had an encounter with a dangerous, venomous creature who could have done real harm."

I breathe out a dramatic sigh. "Steve won't hurt you. He might squawk and flap his wings a little bit, but that's it. If you ignore him, he'll ignore you. And birds are not venomous."

She frowns and presses a hand to her forehead. "But surely there are rules about giant pelicans hanging out on screened-in porches." The hand slips to her chest where she presses her palm against the stretch of smooth skin visible above the deep V of her t-shirt. "I mean, we need to get him out. He built a nest in the love seat."

I haven't given much thought to Steve's presence since Genevieve's passing. But she's right—he can't roost inside, even on a screened-in porch. "In that case, you might want to look up one of the wildlife rescue places."

Taking a slow, deep breath, she pinches the bridge of her nose, looking like she wants to throw a rock at my head and is only just keeping herself from doing it.

"Is there anything else you need to warn me about? Squirrels in the attic? A sea bass living in the master bathtub?"

There aren't any more animals lurking inside the old house, at least not that I know of. But I like the idea of Eloise creeping around every corner, afraid of whatever she'll find next.

"I really can't say." I start off down the sidewalk.

With a little huff, Eloise catches up to me. "Can't or won't?"

"I truly don't know all the things Gennie had hidden in the house. I only know about the bird. With your grandmother—"

"You never know," she finishes for me.

The conversation dies there, and we make our way down to Sweet Tea and Toast in a silence that—given our typical back and forth—is surprisingly comfortable. Other than the heat. Which makes me rethink my commitment to wearing suits. I hold the door open for Eloise, who gives me a small smile, like she didn't expect the gesture from me.

It makes me want to find ways to show her just how gentlemanly I can be. Except that's not the purpose of this lunch. Today is about setting the tone for our relationship going forward. And that tone is: distance. Space. Unscalable walls.

I have a list of resources to give her and financial statements detailing what's in the trust and how much is available to spend on renovations so she can get started. Technically, I could email these things to her. I probably will anyway, so I can copy her sisters on the message. But a business lunch in the middle of a crowded deli seemed like the perfect setting to establish a firm professional boundary between us. One that I started smudging the moment I carried her out of Ned's bar.

"How's my favorite attorney?" Harriett sidles up to us with a warm smile, the long white braid she's worn since I was a boy, and her customary twinkling eyes. She waves away the server who was ready to seat us.

"Hello, Harriett," I say, steeling myself as her gaze darts between me and Eloise.

"Eloise," Harriett says, beaming. "My, you do look just like your grandmama. Pretty as a picture. Isn't she pretty, Jake?"

I hold back a groan. This is not helping set the professional tone. At all. Perhaps I've made a grave miscalculation.

Eloise looks as uncomfortable as I feel. She opens her mouth to respond, but Harriett walks us over to a table in the corner. "For privacy," she says with a wink.

The table might be in the back, but it's also in full view of the whole deli and all the prying eyes. This is even worse than the other night at The Big Tuna with Margo.

"So lovely to see the two of you having lunch together." Harriett presses a hand to her heart, and I tense, already guessing what's coming next. "Oh, it would make Gennie so pleased." She leans toward Eloise. "She loved Jake, you know. Like he was her very own. I can't think of anything that would make her happier than the thought of her Jake and—"

"This is a business meeting, Harriett," I bark out loud enough that the matronly deli owner flinches the tiniest bit. "Sorry," I quickly add. "But Eloise and I are only talking business today. Or any day."

Harriett gives me what can only be described as the stink-eye. "I thought you had an office for talking business?"

"I do." But my office has a door that can be closed. And a desk that would look just perfect with Eloise sitting on top of it. Not that I've pictured exactly that. Not that I'm picturing it now. I move to loosen the tie at my neck. "Killing two birds with one stone. Everyone's got to eat."

Harriett frowns. "Hmph. Well that's a disappointment. You sure would make a lovely couple."

Eloise's palms are pressed flat against the table, her eyes fixed to a spot just between them, as if the spidery design on the formica will reveal the true meaning of life if she stares long enough.

I clear my throat. "We've got a lot to discuss today, Harriett. What do you say you bring us a couple of turkey melts with fries and something to drink?"

It's a bit of a risk to order for Eloise, but Harriett's turkey melt is the best sandwich on the island, and the fries are legendary. And I'm really ready to get this lunch started—and finished.

Eloise holds up a hand. "Actually, I'd prefer something cold. A ..." Her eyes scan over the menu, much too quickly to be reading. "A chicken salad croissant. No fries. A fruit salad."

It doesn't escape my notice that Eloise ordered something that's basically the other end of the spectrum from a turkey melt and fries. One part of me wants to roll my eyes at the way I suspect she's just trying to fight with me. Another part of me admires the way she's not going to let me come in here and roll over her. She might be younger, but she's smart and not afraid to speak her mind.

Harriett nods, not even attempting to hide her smirk. In fact, she winks at Eloise. *Winks.* Already, this lunch is off the rails.

"Coming right up. I'll leave you two to your *business.*" She chuckles as she saunters back toward the kitchen, pausing at the elevated lunch counter where Frank from the barber shop next door is enjoying his lunch. "Hey, Frank," Harriett says, too loud to be anything but intentional. "Did you say hello to Jake? He's here for a business meeting"—she emphasizes this part with air quotes—"with Genevieve Markham's youngest granddaughter."

Frank spins around, his deep russet skin gleaming and his smile wide. Maybe it's a stereotype that town gossip goes through the barbershop, but it is very true when it comes to Frank's Fades. The man is worse than the ten most gossipy women on the island combined. Gennie used to visit him weekly for a trim she didn't need just to catch up with the island news.

"Oh geez," I mutter, my eyes darting up to Eloise. "I should have guessed this would happen. This is only going to get worse."

"A business meeting?" Frank calls. "Is that what you kids are calling it these days? Don't think I don't know the song. 'Business Time'—am I right?"

Eloise has a blank look on her face. She's probably too young to know Flight of the Conchords and their most famous song.

I huff out a breath, tapping my folder. "No, Frank. Actual business."

"Well that's just plain stupid. Are you blind, young man? Can't you see a woman like that needs to be wined and dined and treated right? Business meeting? Bah," he says with an air of disgust that makes Eloise snort.

At least she's laughing. That's better than the scowling she was doing two minutes ago.

Not that I want her to laugh. Or think all this good-natured teasing is anything other than completely inappropriate. It's the exact reason we're here—to make it clear that Eloise and I have a professional relationship.

"Thanks, Frank. I'll keep that in mind." I turn my attention back to Eloise. "We should have done this in my office."

She raises an eyebrow. "Are they always this interested in your love life?"

"They're always this interested in *all* of my life. That's just the way Oakley is." I hold her gaze for a long moment. "It's a lot for most outsiders. Too much. But it's just the way

104

people are here. They treat everyone like family. Whether you want them to or not."

Eloise's expression turns wistful. "I think it sounds amazing. To have so many people who care about you."

"Hey Jake, have you kissed her yet?" Frank calls. A few other patrons sitting around the deli chuckle. "Might get you out of the 'business zone' if you kiss her."

"No kissing ... yet," a voice calls from another table. Sarah Beth Rowland and Lucie Cotton, both friends of Gennie's, have abandoned their food in favor of watching me and Eloise.

"We'll let you know," Lucie calls to Frank.

"Frank, you aren't taking a video are you?" I ask, giving him my fiercest stare. He doesn't so much as flinch. "That better not end up on Facebook."

"*Facebook?*" He laughs. "Naw. This is for TikTok."

Eloise presses her lips together, her eyes dancing as color rises in her cheeks. She looks caught somewhere on the spectrum between entertained and embarrassed. I've firmly pitched my tent in the embarrassment camp.

"Still sound amazing to have so many people care about you?" I ask, and Eloise only shakes her head.

Harriett returns with our food and drinks. And a rose in a vase and a candle, which she lights while I silently fume. Eloise bites her lip to hold back a smile. I'm not sure if she's more amused by Harriett's obvious matchmaking attempts or by my reaction to them.

"Just a little ambiance. For your *business*," she says.

I am never going to speak to anyone on this entire stupid island again.

"Thank you, Harriett," I grind out. She's lucky her turkey melts are so good. I glance at Eloise and tap the folder on the table next to me. "Food, then we'll discuss ..." I search for a word that is *not* business.

"Our very professional business," Eloise says with a smirk, taking a big bite of her sandwich.

I notice the way she only picks at her fruit, and when I push my plate of fries her way, she only hesitates a moment before digging in. By the time we've both inhaled a good portion of our food, I've almost forgotten our audience. Then I hear the distinct sound of someone taking our photo. I catch Frank sliding his phone into his pocket.

"All right, Mr. Fieldstone," Eloise says, pushing away her half-eaten sandwich. "Since we're clearly only here to discuss *business*"—I don't miss the way she emphasizes the word— "shall we get down to it?"

I force a polite smile and reach for my folder. She almost seems disappointed, and I suddenly wish I knew why. Disappointed to be talking business? Or disappointed to *only* be talking business?

I open the folder, turning it to face Eloise as I briefly explain the financial information, then flip through the various resources I've collected for her. I realize I missed one important document on the requirements from the historic preservation, but I can get that to her later.

She nods, looking overwhelmed but clearly trying to cover. "And the contractor you texted me about—would he just do the structural things? Rescreening the back porch? Fixing the broken banister on the stairs—stuff like that?"

"Hunter will do just about everything. And anything he can't, he'll know someone who can. He's had a lot of experience renovating old houses, so he knows how to handle the kinds of challenges Gennie's house might present. Original flooring you want to preserve. Layers of wallpaper. Ancient plumbing. All of it."

"I want to do some things myself, but a lot of it is above my pay grade," Eloise says. "He sounds perfect. Maybe he'll be willing to work with me. Teach me how to do some of this stuff so I can be more hands on."

Perfect.

Work with me.

Hands on.

An uncomfortable feeling swirls in my gut. Hunter will be spending a lot of time with Eloise, and because he's a man with a pulse, he's going to notice her. According to my sister, Hunter is *the goods,* though Naomi swears she'd never go for him herself.

After Liam's dad ditched her during pregnancy, Naomi wrote off the male population. Understandable. But Hunter is a solid guy. Steady. Reliable. Naomi could benefit from his influence. *And it would keep Hunter away from Eloise.*

But no. It doesn't matter. It *can't* matter. Hunter is exactly the buffer Eloise and I need, professionally speaking. He can communicate with Eloise. The two of them can make plans. Talk numbers. Make decisions.

And what if Hunter finds her as charming and irresistible as I do? What if she falls for him, too?

I push my plate away, even though I've only finished half my turkey melt. It just doesn't taste right.

"I'm shocked you didn't take a photo of your lunch. Aren't you an influencer?" I didn't mean for the ire to be so apparent in my voice.

Eloise doesn't even flinch, meeting and holding my gaze with the fire I find a little *too* attractive. "Not all influencers post every meal."

I wait for more, and when she doesn't offer it, I can't help but ask, "What do *you* post about?"

"I'd fall under the lifestyle category. That can be food or

107

fashion or everyday living." She pauses and plays with her straw. "But I may shift to focus on the house stuff. There is a lot of interest in renovation, DIY, and home decor. People love a good glow up."

I don't know the term glow up, though I can guess at the meaning. Another lovely little reminder of the age gap between us.

"But it's a hobby more than anything," she continues. "I make a little money here and there from brand partnerships and affiliate marketing."

That has me blinking in surprise because it sounds so ... formal. I may not exactly know what a glow up is, but I'm absolutely familiar with brand partnerships and affiliate marketing. One of my clients in Savannah was the pitcher for the Savannah Bananas—yes, that's the actual team name. While he didn't have the clout of a major league player, he had his fair share of smaller sponsorships whose contracts I read.

Maybe I need to revise my view of influencing.

"But my first love is literature, not Instagram," Eloise says. "Specifically poetry."

And that's how the conversation shifts from the bullet points I planned on discussing to a discussion about books. No one in my life enjoys discussing what they're reading—or maybe no one in my life reads?—so talks about books are relegated to Reddit threads. It's no surprise that Lo is as passionate about literature as she is about everything else.

I eventually finish the rest of my food, even snagging a few strawberries from Eloise's plate. Harriett brings by a couple slices of her famous peach pie, and we eat that too. We didn't order it, but nobody says no to Harriett's peach pie. I don't even pause the conversation long enough to roll my eyes when I notice the whipped cream on top of each slice has been shaped into a heart.

I love the way Eloise gestures wildly with her hands when I question what should determine whether a book is canonized as literature. And when I make a remark about poetry—admittedly, just to get a rise out of her—her cheeks flame an alluring red. She recites several lines to me as a rebuttal, reminding me of how I trained Bard the Bird to recite quotes when I was little. For once, thinking about Bard and Ned's bar and even my mom's love for literature, which in turn sparked mine, doesn't leave me sad.

When Harriett apologetically interrupts with the check, I feel like I've been slammed back down to earth after floating above it. For what's been almost an hour, I forgot the professional boundary I'm supposed to be putting up between me and Lo. Forgot the age gap. Forgot the lingering resentment I held for Gennie's granddaughters.

I also forgot where we are—a very public restaurant surrounded by far-too interested eavesdroppers.

We definitely should have met in my office. With the door open.

I pick up the check—loudly reminding Eloise and Harriett and anyone else in listening range (including myself) that it's a *business expense*—and we head for the door together. The distance between us returns, as though I'm not the only one who remembers the space we're supposed to keep between us. I'm far more disappointed than I have any right to be.

"Thanks for meeting with me," Eloise says with a smile that makes my chest tighten. "If I have questions, it's nice to know you're right next door. I'll just knock."

She must remember—as I do—the last time she came banging, because she quickly amends her statement as I open the deli door for her.

"Or maybe just knock on the wall. Oh! We could do Morse code! You do know we share a bedroom wall?"

Oh, I'm *aware*. TOO aware. Knowing our beds are separated by a few inches of drywall is the reason sleep has eluded me since the night she moved in. I'm torn between wanting to flirt back and wanting to bolt down the sidewalk, not stopping until I can throw myself into the ocean for nature's version of a cold shower.

"I'll probably just text you if I have questions. That's easier."

I follow her outside, where the sun turns her brown hair a burnished gold. "Probably the best way to reach me is to contact my secretary."

Eloise spins and turns to face me. I stop, leaving a good bit of distance between us. I swear, I feel every inch of it. She studies me, opening and closing her mouth twice before speaking.

"I get that you want to keep things professional between us."

I nod. "It's for the best. I'm supposed to be impartial, Eloise. You're a client."

"Right. I mean, sort of right. Gran was your client. My sisters and I aren't though. Are we?"

"Maybe technically speaking, yes. Gennie was my client. But as long as I'm still handling her estate, you and your sisters are de facto clients."

That isn't even the right terminology. I don't know where it came from. But if it keeps distance between Lo and me, I'll take it.

"Okay. But more than one person has mentioned that you and Gennie were close."

She's got me there. "We were," I say cautiously, unsure of what territory we're about to step into.

"So, sometimes you *can* mix business and personal?" The question feels beyond loaded. And the glint in Lo's blue eyes is even more concerning. Especially when she adds, "You just don't want to mix them with me?"

I'm surprised by the boldness of her question. Though I usually appreciate people getting straight to the point, at present, I'm left floundering.

"I'd prefer to avoid the appearance of impropriety," I finally say.

Eloise nods, her face expressionless. Is it wrong for me to feel disappointed by her lack of disappointment?

"I think it's a little late for that," she says, tilting her head toward the deli window.

The entire crowd inside Harriett's is practically pressed up against the glass, watching us with wide, knowing smiles. And ... Frank appears to be filming.

I drop my chin to my chest and breathe deeply. When I look up, Eloise is halfway down the block.

"Eloise!" I shout, but she doesn't turn.

Instead, she lifts one hand and waves without slowing her pace. I watch her walk away, not realizing I'm staring until I remember half the island is still watching from the window. I glare at Frank, who's blatant in his filming now. Probably another TikTok. I should slap him with a lawsuit for not asking permission. Instead, I start back to my office.

On my way, I mull over the truth settling in between my ribs: I meant for our lunch to put distance between Eloise and me, but I'm pretty sure it did the exact opposite.

ELEVEN

Lo

THERE ARE a few things that really scare me. Spiders. (Or things that look like spiders, which means most insects.) Heights. (Other than climbing trees, which somehow is an exception to the rule.) Having stomach issues and not being able to find a bathroom. (Very specific, but still a very real fear.)

But right now, as I stand on the front porch of Gran's house, I'm about to face another specific fear: Recording a live video.

I've managed to avoid going live in the year I've been growing my account. I know it's important—all the articles I've read and courses I've taken have reiterated this. But I've avoided all video until now, posting only images that fit into my brand aesthetic. With images, I can crop them just so, adjust the filters, and write the narrative.

Videos in general are more work. Getting just the right

shot, retaking over and over if you say something stupid or have a weird hair sticking up on the side of your head, having your cat randomly wander in front of the camera, blocking the view of *you* with a view of its butt.

Fine. I don't actually have a cat. But I'm positive if I did, things like that would happen. Then there's the hours of editing. Adjusting the sound. Trimming out the excess. Overall, it's way too much work and not my favorite medium.

Live video might require less in post-production, but it opens its own door to Pandora's little box of horrors. I mean —ANYTHING could happen. Especially considering the way my life has been such a hot mess lately.

Standing here with my finger hovering over *Start Live Video* feels like waiting in a chute on the back of a bull for my eight seconds of an unpredictable ride.

At least I *look* cute. It took some time and a hair tutorial, but I'm outwardly camera ready. If only inward preparation were as simple. I'm not even sure what I'm afraid of. There aren't specific scenarios of what could go wrong, just an intense nervousness that has me practically panting. I use my free hand and fan myself a few times, creating a minuscule breeze. My deodorant, which has held up well in the heat I'm finally getting used to, is completely ineffective when it comes to nerves. Better start now, or I'm going to *look* as nervous as I feel.

I need to do this. The still images and the stories I've started posting about Gran's house have garnered a surprising reaction. My follower count is up. My engagement has been ridiculous, to the point I have to schedule time throughout the day to respond to comments or they get out of hand.

But one thing people keep asking for over and over is

video. Specifically, ME on video, giving a full tour of Gran's house, not just the bits and pieces. Not just pictures.

The hand holding my phone is shaking. Probably because I've been standing on the porch for ten minutes like this, trying to work up the confidence while I sweat through my dress.

I whisper-sing jumbled words from one of my favorite Taylor Swift songs to bolster my confidence. "Feels like a perfect time to dress up like hamsters ..."

A throat clears, and I look up to see Hunter standing at the front door. "I think it's hipsters. Not hamsters."

"Are you a Swiftie?"

Hunter scratches his beard, which is almost the same light brown as my hair. In the same worn jeans, boots, and tool belt he's worn the last few days working here with me, he doesn't fit the typical image of a Taylor Swift superfan. I try to picture the incredibly reserved (read: basically silent) contractor in a concert crowd shoulder to shoulder with girls waving glittery posters. If mental images were printable, this one would totally go on my wall.

"I guess?"

I can't help but grin. "Favorite song?"

His answer is immediate. "'All Too Well.' Taylor's version."

"Obviously. Nice choice."

His chin dips in acknowledgment, and his eyes shift away, like he's used up his eye contact quota for the afternoon.

At first, Hunter's closed-off demeanor reminded me of Jake. But after a few days, I realized that where Jake is all scowls and seriousness, Hunter is simply more reserved. Introverted. Shy, even. And when it's a giant, muscly, bearded man who is quiet, it can come across as grouchy, at least on the surface. Underneath, there's a kindness and

114

steadiness to him. He doesn't get irritated when I have a million ideas and talk his ear off about all of them. Hunter simply listens—or pretends to—and either grunts or emits one- or two-word responses.

Unlike Jake, Hunter doesn't get under my skin. He also doesn't go out of his way to avoid me—which Jake absolutely has been doing. He doesn't take me out to lunch, talk literature, then tell me I can call his secretary if I have any questions.

Not that I'm taking it personally or anything. (Spoiler alert: I'm absolutely taking it personally.)

All Hunter's quiet serves him well when it comes to his work. He's done a huge amount in a very short time—stripping all the wallpaper from the downstairs rooms, ripping up carpet in any room that had it, and tearing the kitchen down to its studs. Other than the screened-in porch—still home to Steve, whom I've taken to feeding—and Gran's bedroom, every room has seen changes. The house is becoming more of a blank slate now, ready for me to start making some choices on paint colors, cabinet styles, and the really fun stuff.

Hunter clears his throat. "You're not taking a video, are you?"

"No." I'm still holding my phone up like an idiot, and it's not until I glance at it that I realize somewhere in the middle of imagining Hunter at a Taylor Swift concert, I must have hit the start button. "Wait—yes. Oh my gosh!"

I am recording a live video.

I am recording a live video, standing on the porch in the middle of a conversation with Hunter. There are already hearts and comments flying across the screen over my face, which looks totally panicked. (Even if my makeup is perfect.)

"Um, hello!" My voice takes on a desperately high pitch,

and I wave to the camera, feeling every bit the idiot I was afraid I'd be in a live video. "I'm Lo, and we're live."

Hunter ducks into the house without a word, leaving me with whatever followers are watching.

Taking a breath, I adjust the phone, which was cutting off the top of my head. "You'll have to forgive me. I've avoided live videos mostly because of this." I giggle, then gesture to myself with my free hand. "I'm awkward. And maybe a little prone to bad luck. So, this might end in some kind of viral fail video where I faceplant into the bushes. I hope you'll stick around anyway. This is just what you'll get with me. Who's ready for a house tour?"

Before I go inside, I try to read the comments zooming up the screen. There are a lot of them. Like, moving so fast I can hardly read one before it's replaced by the next. From what I can tell, they're all viewers saying things like, *Yes! Show us the house! Can't wait!*

"I'm going to turn the camera around so you can see. I'll do my best to answer comments, but I might have to come back later and reply. Do comments from live videos stick around after I stop recording?" I honestly have zero idea. Laughing, I say, "Guess we'll figure it out together!"

With that terrible but very authentically me introduction, I flip the camera and start the tour. I'm definitely going to need a shower after this. My deodorant may be extra-strength, but it's not live-video strength.

"Aren't these doors amazing? They need a fresh coat of paint though. I was thinking something bright and beachy. Maybe turquoise? Yellow? Coral? Let me know what you think! I'll set up a poll in my stories later. Let's head inside."

Sweating profusely, nervously babbling, and every so often tripping because I'm holding the camera and not fully able to watch where I'm going, I livestream a tour of the house, fielding as many questions and responding to comments as I go.

People want to know EVERYTHING. From countertops to color scheme to my memories of visiting Gran. I did end up sharing about losing Gran, not sure how personal I want to be.

Steve threatens to steal the show, which isn't surprising. The moment I enter the sun porch, he starts preening and strutting. Some viewers think it's hilarious that he's living on the porch, while others mention bird droppings and diseases.

"Steve is a very polite house guest—for the most part. He's also a very good listener but doesn't have much to say in terms of house design. Sadly, I'm going to need a rescue organization to relocate him soon. But I'll be sure to update you on all things Steve."

I start to relax after ten minutes—*how have I already been filming for ten minutes?!*—even if the adrenaline has me all jittery. Now, though, I feel more excitement than nerves.

Why was I scared of live video? It's honestly kind of a rush! And I've never experienced anything quite like interacting in real-time with my followers.

Though I don't mean to chase him, Hunter keeps trying to avoid the camera, somehow ending up in whatever room I'm headed for next. When I walk into one of the upstairs bedrooms where there's no other escape, he ducks into the closet.

Who's the lumberjack?

Is that your boyfriend?

Introduce us to the hottie!

The comments make me giggle. Especially because I know Hunter would HATE them. Maybe later I'll see if I can convince him to film a segment with me.

I give myself a mental pat on the back. Not even done

with my first video and I'm already planning more. This really isn't so bad. I should have done this ages ago.

"You might have glimpsed my contractor, Hunter. Not my boyfriend. He's also not a fan of the camera, so let's head to another room and let him work in peace. Sorry, Hunter!"

He grunts a response from the closet, and I close the bedroom door on my way out.

What's in that room?

Wait—you didn't show us the last bedroom!

I see several comments like that as I head back down the hall toward the stairs. Taking a breath, I say, "The room I didn't take you inside was my gran's room. I'm ... not ready for that yet."

There is a flurry of hearts then, and comments commiserating about my loss. I swallow, feeling grateful for the support offered up from virtual strangers.

"Thanks, y'all." I don't know when, but sometime since I arrived, I slipped back into y'all-ing, a word I haven't used since I spent summers here. It feels oddly natural.

Before I head back downstairs, I flip the camera around again so it's pointing at me. My cheeks are pink and there's a sheen of sweat making my forehead glisten. But overall, I look ... happy.

I grin. "This has been so fun! I need to actually get some work done—I'm stripping wallpaper from the upstairs bathroom today—so I'm going to sign off. Also, I'm not sure I can make it all the way down the stairs while filming without falling."

True story. I'm already halfway down, taking jerky steps while gripping the railing with one hand. It's a bad idea waiting to happen. I'm about to sign off when Jake walks through the front door, wearing a suit that looks tailor-made for him and a scowl to match.

Of course, that's exactly when I trip.

At least my instincts are good, even if I can't say the same about my coordination. I toss the phone and use both hands to try and stop my forward trajectory.

Here's the thing about gravity though—it's pretty impossible to stop an object (in this case, me) from falling once momentum has started. Something about mass versus velocity versus tripping while going down stairs.

I'm sure I read that in a textbook somewhere.

I desperately try to grip the railing, but the wood is too smooth. The next thing I know, I'm not just tripping down a few stairs. I am airborne—headed straight for the bottom and certain doom. I squeeze my eyes closed and hope I don't break my neck when I land in the foyer.

But instead of hitting the hardwoods, I slam into something—no, some*one*. Hunter?

No—JAKE. I recognize his scent—woodsy, smoky, sexy—before my brain processes the fact that he caught me. Correction—that he *tried* to catch me. The man may have more muscles than what seems possible, but he's no match for my weight combined with my momentum. (See: above physics equation.)

"Oof!" The sound leaves my chest as Jake and I tumble, and I hear a similar grunt escape him.

His arms come around me, pulling me into his body before his back hits the floor with a thud. He groans again, much louder this time.

I can't make any sounds. Because the wind has been completely knocked out of me. We lie there, him panting and me starting to panic. When my diaphragm finally loosens or whatever it does to allow me to breathe again, I take a gasping breath.

Only then do I take note of very important details. Like,

the way I am totally starfished over the front of Jake's body. His hands grip me—literally, one of them is holding onto the back of my cutoff overalls—and my cheek is pressed against his neck. Which, let the record show, smells delicious.

"Are you ... nuzzling me?"

I freeze, realizing that I absolutely am doing exactly that.

"No?"

Jake grunts and starts to sit up, moving me with him like I'm just some rag doll. I try not to get all swoony over the flex of his muscles. Admittedly, it's hard. Even under his many layers of suit, I can feel his pecs and the bunching of muscles in his shoulders and arms. The man is a specimen.

A very off-limits specimen, I remind myself, though I'm ready to call bull on Jake's whole attorney-client reasoning. He's Gran's attorney. Not *really* mine. There has to be something else going on in his handsome little head. I just wish I knew what it was.

But off-limits or not, I can still ogle.

The guys I dated in the past were exactly that—guys. Maybe even boys. At best, boy-*ish*. Jake is so completely out of that league—and let's be real, out of MY league—that it's mind-boggling.

I refuse to grope—because I do have SOME standards—but with one hand on his shoulder and the other gripping his biceps, I don't need to grope. They're just right there, being all muscly.

When he's finally sitting up all the way, and I realize I'm still draped over him like a beach towel, I jerk away. Because that's what I *should* do. It's most certainly not what I WANT to do. I'd prefer to stay right here, thank you very much, and enjoy his warmth and scent and—

I shift all the way off his lap, and my tailbone hits the hardwood. I wince, all at once feeling the soreness from the

120

whole incident. Before Jake caught me, I think I banged my shins and arms into the steps and railing and walls. But plopping unceremoniously off his lap right onto the floor did more damage, as pain radiates from my butt all the way up my spine.

"Are you okay?" he asks.

I wince, scooting a little farther away and trying to adjust so my weight isn't directly on my tailbone. "I think so. Are you? Thank you for catching me."

"No problem," he says, though the tightness around his eyes and the way he's gingerly shifting in place tells me that taking the brunt of my weight in a fall didn't leave him unscathed.

"I'm so sorry. Is your back okay? Did you hit your head?"

"I'll probably be a little sore tomorrow. But I'll be fine." As though suddenly remembering it's ME, Eloise, that he's talking to, Jake frowns. "What were you doing with your phone, anyway?"

MY PHONE!

"I was, um ..."

Words fail me as Jake gets to his feet with another soft groan and locates my phone where it landed halfway down the stairs. I can't tell if it's cracked or not, but what's immediately clear even before Jake makes his way back to me is that the screen is still lit up.

But that doesn't mean it's still recording. I'm sure hitting the floor was enough to end the live video.

My luck is bad, but surely it's not THAT bad.

Unfortunately, my luck proves to be the worst in the world. Because Jake frowns down at the screen, then turns it my way, his glower also turning my way.

"Is this ... recording?" he asks. It shouldn't be possible, but his frown actually *deepens*. "Is it live?"

I snatch the phone, seeing a flurry of hearts and comments shooting across the screen, which shows my panicked face, framed by my hair, which has come loose from its ponytail.

Oh, it absolutely is recording.

"Eloise?" Jake's voice is steel, matching the hard gray glint of his eyes.

I jab my finger at the screen to end the video. I also inadvertently hit the button to post it on my feed. Which I was planning to do anyway, but with the way it ended, I would have probably checked to see if I could edit it or something beforehand. Honestly, I'm so unfamiliar with going live, I'm not sure if that's even a thing.

This is why I avoid things I can't control.

"It's not recording." I clear my throat, withering a little under Jake's glare. "Now. It's not recording *now*. But it was a few minutes ago. When I, um, fell down the stairs. Apparently, I can't manage stairs and a live video. Who knew?"

Jake looks like he's about to tear my head off when Hunter strides in, glancing between the two of us.

"What happened?" Hunter demands in his gruff voice.

I could have used your help a few minutes ago. But I'll happily take the interruption now!

Hunter is exactly what I need to escape what feels like a brewing confrontation with Jake. One in which he tells me how foolish social media is and how I've invaded his privacy. Even if I had no intention of putting him on camera. I'm internally cringing, already thinking about the comment section. Hunter barely made it into a shot and my followers went bananas.

Jake in a suit? I can only imagine. And what did the video capture before I turned it off? Were we even in the frame? Hopefully not. I really hope, once I get home and can watch the video, I'll see the camera filming the ceiling or wall, barely picking up on our conversation.

Because if it WAS facing our way, and it WAS close enough to hear our words—like, for example, Jake asking if I was nuzzling him?

I squeeze my eyes closed. I don't know how I'm going to survive on this small island when I cannot seem to escape Jake. Or my undimmable attraction to a man who has made it clear he wants to keep a massive wall of professionalism between us.

This wall does not leave room for falling on him, nuzzling him, or smelling him. Discreet ogling is also probably frowned upon. I take a step closer to Hunter.

"We're fine," I say.

"How are things going with the renovation?" Jake asks, like he's just come by for a report.

Actually, I bet that's *exactly* why he came by. It definitely wasn't to catch up or to catch me falling down the stairs.

"Things are going so well. Hunter is the *best*." My praise makes the lumberjack of a contractor look like he wants to disappear in a puff of smoke. Which only inspires me to lay it on thicker. "He's been listening to my ideas and giving feedback. Plus, he's a beast. I swear, yesterday, he pulled a whole cabinet off the wall like it was a picture frame or something. I don't know what I'd do without him and his muscles."

Hunter dips his chin, and I swear a tiny blush hits his cheeks. It's hard to say for sure because his massive beard hides so much of his face. Meanwhile, when I glance at Jake, he does NOT look pleased by my good report. Or by the way I'm patting Hunter's giant bicep.

Is Jake ... *jealous?*

Mr. Let's Keep Things Professional, Mr. Call My Secretary Even Though I Live Next Door, Mr. Let's Have a Great Talk

123

about Books Over Lunch and Then Pretend It Never Happened—THAT guy is jealous?

Color me amused.

Before Jake realizes there's nothing to be jealous about AND before he remembers to ask about the video he unwittingly starred in, I say a quick goodbye and dart for the exit.

TWELVE

Lo

I MAY NOT HAVE KNOWN the first thing about renovating a house when I arrived on Oakley. (Truthfully, I still don't.) But it's happening! Mostly thanks to Hunter, but I have been here every day, hands-on. I even have a few blisters to show for it. Who knew swinging a sledgehammer through drywall would make me sore OR be incredibly cathartic—especially when thinking of my grumpy next-door neighbor's face?

I've had lots of dopamine hits marking off my to-do lists. And if the lists keep getting longer for everything I mark off, I'm here for it. So is my daily-growing following on Instagram.

Now that some of the demo is done, it's time to start considering the foundational design choices. Fun things like flooring, tiles, and paint colors. I know as much about design and decor as I do about renovating. And even LESS about turning an existing home into a bed and breakfast. But not knowing things has never been a barrier for an optimist like me. As it turns out, I don't need to know reno and design. Because Pinterest does.

Sitting on Gran's back porch with Steve (who greeted me a little less violently today), I create two different boards for inspiration. One specifically about bed and breakfasts and the other about style and decor.

"Should we give each room a theme?" I ask Steve, who fluffs his feathers in response. "Looks like a yes to me. Maybe bright and fun, but modern. Not shabby chic or just straight-up beach vibes."

Is the aesthetic I'm leaning toward similar to my own personal style? Yes. Yes, it is. But if Merritt and Sadie want something different, they can blame their inability to stick around. If you ask me, their absence vetoes their right to an opinion.

If it were up to Merritt, the house would probably end up minimalist and stark white. Sadie would go the opposite direction with random, kitschy stuff like fake turf instead of carpet and those leg lamps from *A Christmas Story*.

"I'm here," I tell Steve, a little defensively even though he's not arguing. "That means I get to make the choices."

Steve squawks and stamps his webbed feet before waddling over to one of the ripped screens. He glances at me with one beady eye before heading outside.

"We have to get you off this porch," I call after him. "Birds don't live inside. Except for Bard, but he's—"

With a big flap of wings, Steve takes off toward the ocean. Probably to scoop up a fish since I don't have anything to offer. Hunter gave me the number of a wildlife rescue place, and I have every intention of calling to have Steve extracted.

Soon. But maybe ... not yet. He may be just a bird, but he makes me feel less alone. More connected to Gran somehow.

I glance up at the sky, noting the clouds rolling across the horizon. They carry hints of gray, but there's still plenty of blue in the sky. I still haven't gotten to the beach. With Hunter fixing some drywall emergency at another site, I don't need to stay.

There are a few more hours of light left, and it's the good kind. Soft, gentle sun that won't make me instantly crisp up like a fried turkey leg. I used to tan when I spent the summers here, my legs and arms turning deep brown to match my sisters. But four years in Illinois have left me pale and pasty.

"Time to remedy that," I say, feeling sillier talking to myself than I did talking to a pelican.

BEFORE PUTTING on the very old bathing suit I find at the bottom of my suitcase, I grab a glass from the kitchen. Putting it against the shared wall between my place and Jake's, I press my ear to it and listen. Ridiculous? Maybe a little. But it's also very practical.

Jake is normally home from work by now. He goes on a run every afternoon, and I need to make sure he's well and truly gone before I walk outside in this suit. He's been playing—and winning—at the game of avoiding me since lunch. Other than the live video—which he must not have seen or he would be beating down my door. It went viral. Not like "Charlie bit me" viral, but two million views followed by tens of thousands of followers.

And let's just say the people from Oakley Island aren't the only ones trying to ship me and Jake.

All the more reason I want to avoid him as I head down to the beach in a bathing suit.

It's not that I'm super self-conscious about my body, at least no more than a typical woman. I've made peace with the size of my thighs—generous—and my breasts—*not* so generous. But the only bathing suit I have is threadbare. It has those little pills on the butt and the top gapes to the point where I have to hold it in place if I bend over. Otherwise, what little I have up top makes a great escape.

Ask me how I know.

The point is: Jake has already seen me in my pajamas and slippers. He's carried me home after I accidentally drank too much and endured an accidental groping when he was in a towel. Seeing me in a worn-out, saggy bathing suit does NOT need to be added to the list.

I'd much rather our first "in a swimsuit" run-in occur once the yellow bikini from Instagram has arrived (yes, I caved and finally ordered it) and I'm tucked and accentuated in all the right places.

Not that I need Jake to think I look cute in a swimsuit. (Fact: I REALLY want Jake to think I look cute in a swimsuit.)

Not hearing a single peep on the other side of the wall, I pull on a pair of cutoffs over my janky suit, slide into my flip-flops, and head straight down the crushed oyster path. Something in my chest unfurls as the roar of the waves grows louder. I pick up my pace until I'm like a little kid, darting across the splintery boardwalk and not stopping until my toes touch sand. A full-body sigh moves through me.

While walking into Gran's house didn't flood me with memories, the beach does. It's the grit of sand immediately invading my flip-flops, the way my hair whips wildly around my head, the powerful bass of the ocean waves hitting the sand. A huge smile is on my face, and inexplicably, I feel a tear slip down my cheek as I lose my shorts and kick off my flip-flops.

And then I sprint for the surf.

Normally, I'm not one to run in a bathing suit—especially given the lack of support up top—but the urge to do so is impossible to ignore. Hardly a *Baywatch* babe, I stumble as the cold waves slap against my shins and almost fall face first into the surf, laughing. When I'm waist deep, I dive through a wave, calling on very rusty swimming skills to get past the place where the waves curl and tumble over themselves. I keep my eyes pinched closed, hearing the muted roar of the water and feeling the tug of the current.

My lungs begin to burn, and I burst through the surface, still smiling wide. I stand, shrieking and lifting my feet when I step on something hard. Probably just a shell, but I vividly remember the feel of a crab's claw closing on the sensitive skin of my feet. I tread water a few feet to the right and gently lower my feet again, feeling around with my toes until I find just sand.

This is *marvelous*.

I didn't know the ocean was a thing I missed until this moment, when I feel somehow *complete*. The sting of salt in my eyes, the warm burn of the sun on my shoulders and cheeks, the wild pull of the current. The sound and the smell and the *everything* about this moment is magical. I'm immediately sucked into a memory.

I'm digging trenches to save my drip castle from being crushed by the rising tide.

Merritt and Sadie are having a cartwheel competition where the sand is packed flat, arguing when Merritt insists she won.

Gran is fighting with an umbrella, jamming the pole into the sand as the wind tries to yank it from her grasp.

I'm stepping in the wet sand, then watching my footprint disappear before my eyes as a tiny crab scuttles past.

Sadie is tossing cheese puffs to the gulls, then running away screaming as they dive bomb her.

It's like a whole reel of memories plays in my mind, all the summers spent here blurring together into one visceral rush of emotion. I close my eyes and lean back, floating. Letting the ocean do its thing, which right now is cleansing. Healing. Washing away my tears.

Oh, yes—I could get used to this.

The thought barely passes through my mind when a rogue wave slaps into the side of my face, sending water straight up my nose. Half coughing and half laughing, I stand again. My nose stings, and I remember Gran's trick of looking toward the sun.

You'll sneeze that water right out, she used to say.

It works, and I sneeze twice, telling myself the tears I feel in my eyes are from that, not anything else.

"You don't have floaties."

Startled, I turn to see a frowning little boy on a boogie board a few yards away. His blond hair is missing a chunk right in front in an uneven line, like he took scissors or maybe garden shears to it. He can't be older than eight or nine.

"I'm a little old for floaties," I say.

He nods. "Me too."

I glance toward the shore, looking for a corresponding adult for this small person. There are several that look like they could be here with a kid, but none look particularly interested or alarmed. We're not terribly far out, but it seems a little odd to me that he's unsupervised. Though I'm no expert on kids.

As though reading my concern, he says, "My mom is

reading one of her kissing books. She said I should go ride waves because she's at one of the spicy parts." His frown deepens. "I tried to tell her books aren't spicy, but she doesn't listen."

I manage to swallow my laughter. I search the shore and see a pretty brunette in a beach chair, fanning herself with a paperback. Bingo! Spicy reading, indeed.

"Do you know how to ride waves?" the boy asks.

I tilt my head, shaking it a little in an attempt to get the water out of my ears. "I used to. I'm not sure if I still do. It's been a long time. I'm probably not very good."

He assesses me, nodding as he seems to come to that same conclusion. "Yeah, my mom isn't good either. Stuff that's easy for kids is sometimes hard for old people."

Am I now in the category of old people?

"Do you always say everything you think?" I ask, genuinely curious.

"I don't like lies. Not even the white ones, though Mom says they're okay." His frown deepens. "I think they should be called yellow lies instead of white."

"Why yellow?"

"Because they're cowardly."

"I think white lies tend to be more about kindness than cowardice," I say, a little shocked that I'm having this conversation at all with some child I don't even know. "What color goes with kindness?"

He thinks for a moment. "Light blue. But a lie is always a lie."

Fair point, little kid. Fair point.

"Come on," he says. "Let's ride a wave."

Though I'm not really in the mood for body surfing, his tone is so demanding that I find myself paddling over, lining up next to him as we watch for incoming waves. This is a kid

131

who seems like he'll run something important one day with exactly the same serious expression.

"This one?" I ask as a wave approaches.

"That one isn't good. The next one. Start paddling!"

I don't know what it is with this kid, but I find myself doing exactly what he says, paddling along as I feel the pull of the wave on me. Adrenaline surges through me, bright and happy. It's been years, but muscle memory kicks in, and I manage to put myself in the perfect position, kicking madly until the wave picks me up.

The swell in my chest matches the one propelling me toward the shore. It's a rush as the wave drops me in the shallows, foam rising up around me with a hiss. I laugh and turn, my bottom hitting the sand as another wave gently buffets me toward the shore.

"You did pretty good." The little boy stands in ankle-deep water, holding his board.

A high compliment from a kid who doesn't like white—or yellow or blue—lies. "Thank you."

"Okay, bye."

He runs off, dragging the board by its strap. I guess our brief time of bonding is over. Even though I should feel zero responsibility toward whatever his name is, I watch until he reunites with his mother. She has on a huge hat and sunglasses and beams at her son. He doesn't smile back, not even as she gives him a kiss on the top of his head. Undeterred, she shakes her head, still smiling, and begins to pack up. She's all smiles and spicy books—the boy must take after his dad.

The ocean calls me, and I make my way back out into the deeper water. The waves have picked up speed, angling sharply toward the shore, one after the other as the gray clouds I noticed earlier gather and thicken on the horizon.

Maybe I won't have as much time as I thought for swimming. I'm going to enjoy it while I can.

I dive through a wave about to break, just like I did earlier.

Only this time, when I start to swim, I feel a sensation I don't immediately recognize. At least, not until I feel the water, cold on my skin in a way it wasn't just moments ago.

Because my threadbare bathing suit caught a wave back to shore. Leaving me in the ocean, completely naked.

I stand, keeping my knees bent so my top half stays submerged, and scan the water for my suit. Why couldn't it be a bright pink or teal rather than navy? I see no sign of it. Which is ... ridiculous. It wasn't THAT old. Or THAT falling apart. I mean, I've heard of women losing their tops in strong surf, but I was just swimming a basic stroke. How in the world did my WHOLE SUIT just vanish?

As puzzling as this question is, the one that demands more of my attention is this: How am I going to get back to shore? More importantly, how will I get from the shore to the carriage house?

I didn't even pack a towel. My cutoffs will cover some of my bits, but they're at least forty feet away from the edge of the water. No way am I making a run for it. Public naked running is not in my wheelhouse. The beach is starting to empty out, but there are at least half a dozen people still around, including a grizzled-looking man fishing right near the shore. I'd probably send him into cardiac arrest if I emerged from the water stark naked. I could maybe get the attention of my little boogie-boarding friend—maybe his spicy-book reading mom would bring me a towel. But they're already making their way over the dunes.

Which means ... my only option is to wait until dark. I glance again at the sky. Two hours, maybe? Less if the clouds stay low? I can already feel my fingers turning prune-y. And the usually covered bits of me not used to direct water contact feel so exposed. Hours more in the water is not going to work.

"Okay, universe! I get it. Funny joke. Now, please—send me back my suit."

I'd even take a big bunch of seaweed I could drape over my body. Maybe a piece of driftwood? If I had shells and string, I could recreate Ariel's bikini ... but that would still leave the rest of me bare.

My stomach growls, followed by a low rumble of thunder.

Oh, great. Because what I want right now is to be stuck in the ocean naked and hungry with lightning flashing around me. Behind me, the clouds are moving in, fast and dark. At least this means most people are leaving the beach. Maybe the thunderstorm is kismet, the universe's answer to my plea. Once everyone is gone, I can stay low in the water as long as possible and then make a run for it.

If the beach is entirely empty, maybe I could at least put my shorts on, then make it back to the house using my arms to cover my front. Someone in one of the houses along the shore might get an eyeful if they look out their window at the wrong time. But that's a chance I'll have to take.

"Come on people! Go home," I mutter.

Thunder rumbles again, this time loud enough to make me jump. The first fat raindrops splat along the surface of the water. As the sun disappears behind the clouds, the water feels like it drops a few degrees. I shiver, then bite my lip to stop it from shivering. But the very last family is walking away with their backs toward me.

Yes! I can make a break for it!

I'm moving toward the shore, careful to keep everything

covered as long as possible, when a man decides to ruin my plan, coming over the boardwalk. I groan.

Who comes to the beach right as a storm rolls in? The rain is still gentle, but there's that sense that any second now, the whole sky is going to open up.

"Beach is closed, buddy. Head on back home. There is nothing to see here—please disperse!"

I close my eyes and take a calming breath, hoping that when I open them again, the man will be heading for cover like everyone else.

But I should be so lucky. The guy is still on the beach, and what's more—he's spotted me and is walking in my direction with purposeful steps.

Familiar steps.

I squint and rub my eyes. That can't be …

No.

No, no, and more no. Absolutely not.

I groan. It can't be, but it is.

Of *course* it is.

Because why would anyone else but Jake Fieldstone show up at this exact moment?

THIRTEEN

Jake

ONE LONE SWIMMER bobbing neck deep in the water when a storm is brewing would be enough to catch anyone's eye and cause concern. As soon as I realize it's Eloise, my concern shifts to full-on worry.

What is she doing in the water with a storm rolling in?

Not only that, but she's moving in the wrong direction, going further out to sea instead of coming in to shore like any sane person would. I could have sworn she saw me, but she's turned away now.

Is she in distress? Too tired to fight the swells tugging her into deeper water? Does she even know how to swim?

Or is she just being Eloise—wearer of quirky prints and doer of ridiculous things?

"Eloise!" I shout again, but over the surf and wind, there's no way she hears me.

I watch her another moment, looking for signs of distress,

my hand shielding my eyes from the increasing rain. Her head is staying above water, but I can't see her arms. I've been to the beach with my nephew enough times to know that drowning doesn't always include flailing and splashing about. My sister, Naomi, is very loose and free, which only makes me feel like I need to be more responsible. I can't count the number of videos I've watched on preventing drowning.

What I've learned is that drowning doesn't always look like a lot of shouting and splashing. It can be silent.

I don't see signs of drowning, but something is wrong. And Gennie would find a way to haunt me if I stood here and let her granddaughter die.

It's for Gennie. Not because of the worry gripping my spine. *Nope.*

I kick off my shoes, then strip down to my running shorts, leaving my socks and t-shirt in a pile on the sand. I wade into the water, jumping over waves until I'm close enough that she'll hear my voice. Even if she isn't in distress, she's crazy for staying in the water. The storm clouds are getting darker by the minute, and the rain is falling harder.

"Eloise!"

She hears me this time, because she glances over her shoulder, her eyes widening before she drops fully under the water. Is she ... hiding?

My worry and frustration and some other emotions I can't or don't want to name mingle until I'm practically bubbling over.

She pops up out of the water a few yards farther away, her hair plastered to her forehead and water streaming off the end of her nose.

As though we aren't on the cusp of danger, Eloise takes her time responding. She wipes the water from her face and lifts a hand out of the water to wave with forced casualness. But only a hand. None of her arm. Not even her wrist. Just five fingers and half of her palm.

"Hi, Jake. Out for a swim?"

The bubbling feelings inside me are now more like lava spewing from the mouth of a volcano. "Look around you! Of course I'm not out for a swim. I thought you were drowning."

She laughs a light, breezy laugh, but there's a forced quality to it that keeps me on edge. "Who, me? No drowning here. Just swimming."

"Swim time is over. Let's go. We should stay together. Conditions are getting dangerous."

"You go ahead! I'll get out before it gets too bad."

"It's already bad!"

She makes what I think is supposed to be a shooing motion. With so much of her hand under water, it's hard to tell. "Go on. I'll be fine."

"I'm not leaving you!" I yell.

"And I'm not leaving until you do!" she yells back.

I don't like that even like this, she still looks beautiful. Soaked messy hair, angry blue eyes, a scowling mouth. I don't like my desire to move closer for reasons that have nothing to do with dragging her to safety. I want to taste the salt on her lips, to feel her skin, slick and smooth under my palms.

It's not the first time since I've met her that I've felt this urge. More like every night as I try to fall asleep while pretending she's not on the other side of the wall. It's why I've worked so hard to avoid her. Because right now, standing a few feet away, her pull on me is stronger than the tide.

Thunder booms, shaking me out of my Eloise-induced reverie. The waves are choppy, rain is impacting visibility, and the rumble of thunder means lightning. My protective instincts surge.

"We have to go in!" I move steadily closer.

As if to prove my point, a rogue wave comes out of nowhere. Without thinking, I lunge, grabbing for Eloise's shoulders. I barely get out a warning for her to take a breath before I pull us both under. The wave moves by overhead with a pretty substantial tug. They're getting stronger, and we need to go. Now.

When we both break the surface, Eloise jerks away from me. It's only then that I realize when I held her shoulders, they were both completely bare. No bathing suit straps. No fabric of any kind.

Is that why she—oh. *Oh.*

I take a deep breath and force myself to swallow while banishing all invading thoughts of Eloise topless. Not appropriate. Not okay. Not going to help my preoccupation with her.

"Do you—are you ... um." I have to clear my throat. "Did you lose your top?"

She deflates, dropping a little lower in the water. "More like my whole suit."

I swallow. Hard.

Focus on her safety. It's storming, and you need to get her out of here.

But thinking about getting her out of here only makes my mind circle back to why she hasn't gotten out already. Because the beautiful woman I cannot be attracted to—the one just a few feet away from me—is completely bare beneath the dark surface of the water.

This is Eloise. My client. My very *young* client. Gennie's granddaughter.

Oh, don't let that stop you. You have my blessing. Go for it!

Gennie's voice is about as unwelcome as the thoughts pinging around in my head. I'm almost grateful for the crack of thunder and bright flash of lightning immediately after. Naked or not, we have to get out of this water.

"Promise you'll follow behind me, and I'll swim ahead and grab my shirt from the shore. It should cover most of you."

Eloise glares at me for a long second, then, as if accepting it's truly her only option, gives her head a quick nod.

We're side by side until we reach waist-deep water. Eloise stops here, her body crouched low so she's covered up to her shoulders. It only takes me another second to sprint to shore and retrieve my rain-soaked shirt. At least the rain is hiding the sweat, though I doubt Lo would care either way right now.

On my way back to her, I watch as she drops under the surface of the water like a pro to miss the wave crashing over her head. I'm not deep enough to do the same thing, so I jump over the crashing surf, holding the shirt above my head. When Lo finally resurfaces, I'm close enough to hand her my shirt, doing my best to keep my eyes averted from the stretch of her pale skin visible under the water.

I turn my back while Eloise puts on my shirt, but I don't go anywhere. She's crazy if she thinks I'm leaving her out here alone.

"This would be so much easier if I wasn't wet," she says grouchily.

I resist the urge to smile. I cannot think about Eloise wearing my shirt and *only my shirt*. I press my palms to my face and think about the stack of contracts on my desk. Maybe I can scrub the image away. Grind the salt water into my brain and wipe all visions of Eloise and her curves right out of existence.

"Okay," she says from behind me. "I'm decent."

I turn around. Swallow.

Decent? Hardly. This ... might actually be worse. She takes a few steps toward me, out of the deeper water, using one hand to pull the hem of the t-shirt over her hips.

I am frozen. Drinking her in. The way the shirt clings to her skin, hugging every curve. She makes my clothes look way too good.

"Jake," she says, snapping my attention back to her face. She's holding out her hand, and I slip my fingers into hers. How is her hand so warm? We're in the ocean, in the middle of a freaking thunderstorm. And still, her touch is lighting me on fire.

Wordlessly, we make our way to shore, stopping to grab my shoes, then heading over to where her shorts and flip-flops are piled on the sand. Now that we're out of the water, my shirt hits her midthigh, almost long enough to be a dress. I do my best to avert my eyes. She's more covered than she would be in a bathing suit, but it's not the same.

The rain lightens the slightest bit as we make our way across the sand and to the wooden boardwalk that will take us back to the carriage house, but I can tell by the look of the clouds we still haven't seen the worst of this storm.

"Were you really planning to just stay out there?" I ask after another low rumble of thunder.

"At least until it was dark. What choice did I have? I had no towel. No shirt."

"Even in the storm?"

"The storm ... did not make things ideal. But can you imagine me just strolling up to the house nude like it's no big deal?"

My step slows involuntarily. I *can* imagine it, but that doesn't mean I should. I shoot Eloise a look, eyebrows raised, and her cheeks flame red. "Please pretend I didn't just say that."

I'm so distracted by Eloise's comment, I don't even notice Naomi and Liam on the porch, standing outside my door. Of all the times for them to show up …

Eloise stops so fast beside me, I almost hear the cartoon sound of tires screeching to a halt.

"Surprise!" Naomi says. "I brought Liam over for some guy time tonight."

I want to groan. This has not been my day. Translated out of Naomi-speak, what she means is she has a date with some awful guy and even though it won't go anywhere, I get to babysit my nephew.

I love Naomi, and I love Liam, but babysitting is not what I envisioned for my evening plans. Not that I ever have the benefit of a plan when it comes to Naomi.

My sister can't make a plan farther in advance than she can throw a tractor tire, which means at least a couple times a month she shows up for what I like to call sneak-attack babysitting. If I weren't so crazy about my nephew, I would put a stop to this immediately.

"Were you swimming? I didn't see you, but we left as the storm rolled in." Naomi now notices Eloise behind me, and more importantly, what Eloise is and is *not* wearing. "Oh, hello," Naomi says, her grin taking on a dangerous glint. "Did you two get caught in the storm?"

"Something like that," I mutter.

Her eyes go back to Lo. "I'm Naomi and this is Liam. We're Jake's family."

Did my sister MEAN to make it sound like she's my girl-friend or wife, and not my sister? Because that's absolutely how it sounded. Based on the sharp intake of breath beside me, that's what it sounded like to Lo, too.

Great. First, Margo messes with Eloise. Now, Naomi. My sister's eyes are dancing, and I can read that expression like the kind of Level Four reader Liam likes. She definitely tried to make it sound like we're an item—GROSS—as a jealousy test for Eloise.

Not even a full two minutes have gone by, and my sister is already meddling. I'm about to clarify when Liam steps forward.

"We rode a wave together. She's not as good as me, but she's all right. Why are you wearing his shirt?" He looks from Eloise to me. "And why are you wearing *no* shirt?"

Eloise shifts so she's more hidden behind me, close enough that she brushes against my back as she cranes her head around to answer Liam. I do my best to ignore the way the light touch ignites a spark that travels up my spine like it's on its way to a stick of dynamite.

"I, um, had a wardrobe malfunction," Eloise says.

Liam's frown deepens. By the time he's twenty-five, the kid is going to have a permanent crease between his brows. He'll also probably be CEO of some company. Maybe president of the United States.

"A wardrobe like Narnia?" he asks. "That makes no sense."

Naomi snorts, then holds up both hands when I shoot her a look promising certain slow, painful death later. "Sorry."

I need to get this whole conversation back on the rails. "Liam, a wardrobe can be a piece of furniture, like in Narnia, or the clothing that goes inside the piece of furniture. To use it in a sentence—"

Liam interrupts. "I keep my *wardrobe* in my *wardrobe*. Got it."

Naomi is about two seconds from totally losing it with her trademark cackling laughter, while Liam looks completely serious, and Eloise is shifting nervously behind me. Every brush of her against me makes it harder to hide my reactions to her touch.

She pokes me in the back. "As fun as it is meeting your, um, *girlfriend*?" She whispers the word girlfriend. "And your ... *kid*? I need to get inside and change."

With a clap of thunder, the skies open up fully, sheets of rain falling all around the porch and the wind whipping leaves and branches across the lawn. The sound of rain pelting the roof is deafening. I'm distracted long enough that Eloise darts for her door and has it unlocked before I can even move.

"Nice to meet you," she calls, her voice trailing off as she slams the door behind her.

Disappointment leaves a sour taste in my mouth. I don't like how we left things, and I definitely don't like the idea that Lo thinks my sister is my girlfriend and my nephew is my son. But if I go after her, it will only prove the point I think Naomi is trying to make. I can try later, but if Naomi is leaving Liam with me, it may be a while.

"Uncle Jake, what's a wardrobe malfunction? Did the ocean eat her swimsuit?"

"Yeah, Jake. Was it the ocean? Or something else?" Naomi teases.

I narrow my eyes. "It's a long story."

"You can tell me while you make dinner," Liam says. "Unless it's a boring story. Then you can tell my mom after I'm in bed."

"Oh, it's very boring," I tell him.

"Do you have mac and cheese?"

"I'm sure he does," Naomi says. "He always keeps your favorites stocked. And if not, he can always ask his new neighbor. The one he hasn't ever mentioned before. Not even to *me*."

"It's because there's nothing to mention," I say through gritted teeth as I unlock the door. Even as I say it, I wonder if I can really still claim that it's true.

I felt real panic when Lo was out in the water, refusing to come in. And just now, when Naomi intentionally misrepresented our relationship, the fear that pulsed through me at the thought of Lo getting the wrong idea nearly made me irrational enough to chase her into her own apartment and force her to hear the truth.

Stalwart as I have been in my resistance to Lo's charms, that resistance is flagging.

"She didn't tell us her name," Liam says. "Isn't that bad manners? You always tell me that's bad manners."

"I think she was just in a hurry to fix her *wardrobe*." Naomi winks at me, then puts a hand on Liam's shoulder and steers him toward my door. Or maybe she's using him as a human shield, which is smart because I'm ready to kill my sister. "I have a feeling we'll meet her later, Liam. I think we'll be seeing her a *lot*."

"If she lives next door to Uncle Jake, of course we'll see her a lot. Also, she has to give back his shirt. Otherwise, it's stealing. We'll at least see her then. Why are you winking, Mom?"

"Because your mother doesn't value her life," I mutter, glaring.

Naomi grins widely and steps behind Liam, putting both hands on his shoulders as she pulls him closer.

Oh, yeah. Definitely a human shield.

While I wouldn't hesitate to fight my sister—who is scrappy and has no qualms about getting physical with me, a leftover vestige from childhood—she knows I am nothing but gentle with Liam. We both are.

As soon as we're inside, Liam is talking about food, so I pull out a box of the gluten-free, dye-free mac and cheese he likes. When Liam was really young, he was diagnosed with celiac disease, which means he needs a gluten-free diet. Together, he and I have been eating our way through some of the most popular gluten-free versions of things kids love. The mac and cheese is one thing we both love, though I'll only eat it with him. Otherwise, I feel like a kid or at least a frat boy.

I'm filling up the pot with water when Naomi emerges from the bathroom wearing date clothes, which for her is a flowy sundress and Birkenstocks. Her hair is in a messy bun, and she's even managed to put on eyeliner. Impressive, given the fact we've been inside less than five minutes. She gives me a hug and darts away before I can really squeeze her hard the way I want to. Liam is next, and she presses a kiss to the top of his head.

"Be good for Uncle Jake," she says. "He might need you to be his wingman."

I drop the saucepan in the sink, and half the water spills out. "I don't need a—"

"Go take a shower," Naomi says. "You stink."

"Yeah—you smell like pepperoni," Liam adds.

"Gee, thanks." I glare at my sister, before heading for the shower. Later. I'll get revenge later—both for the wingman comment and telling me I stink.

And now I'm worrying about whether or not Eloise also thought I smelled like pepperoni. Just before I close the bathroom door, I hear Liam say, "Mom? What's a wingman?"

Yep. I am going to get revenge. And it is going to be *good.*

FOURTEEN

Lo

I TAKE AN ANGRY SHOWER, which looks like me turning the water up to the point of scalding and scrubbing my skin so hard I accidentally send the bar of lavender soap flying across the bathroom. Twice. The second time, I slip in the water puddling on the floor and end up coming THIS close to face-planting into the toilet.

The very LAST thing I need is to knock myself out wet and naked in the bathroom. Because you know who would be the one to find me? The man who already rescued me once today while I was wet and naked. The man who apparently has a wife—ex-wife?—or girlfriend and a CHILD.

I shouldn't be so angry. Not when nothing has happened between Jake and me. It's just ... maybe I hoped something would. Admitting this makes me feel stupid and young again, like a child thinking the guy on the movie poster might actually show up in real life and ask her out. Jake isn't interested in me.

Even if he does keep showing up to rescue me. This time *shirtless*. With that gorgeous tattoo on full display. I think it's a griffin? If I hadn't been worried about flashing him my goods, I'd have paid more attention.

The point is: I should never have allowed these crushy thoughts to take root. Not when he has been SO clear from our lunch to his avoidance that I'm nothing to him.

I have enough wherewithal not to try shaving in my angry shower. I'd probably end up slicing an artery and needing an ambulance. When I'm starting to prune and the water is lukewarm, I finally get out. Clearing a circle on the foggy mirror with my palm, I examine myself. My skin is lobster-red from the hot water. My eyes look puffy and bloodshot—maybe from the salt water? I look every bit as drained as I feel.

"Pull yourself together, Lo," I tell myself, feeling like a living, breathing cliche as I give my reflection a pep talk.

The problem is—I don't know what to pull together. Since I arrived on Oakley Island, my life has been a bunch of unhappy accidents. Most involving me making a fool of myself in front of my lawyer slash neighbor slash lying jerk.

The wet shirt belonging to the lying jerk in question is puddled on the bathroom floor. I leave it there, hoping it'll mildew. Jake and I share the washer and dryer in a laundry room that both our houses connect to at the back, but I haven't been desperate enough to use it yet. The last thing I want is to run into Jake while washing my underwear. And knowing my luck, that's exactly when he would need to do laundry.

Seeing my dresses hanging in the closet, I get an idea that will help me take back some semblance of control. It's been more than twenty-four hours since I posted on my Instagram account, and four times that long since I've posted about anything besides the house. The renovation posts are already getting a lot of traction, but I don't want to abandon the rest of my content altogether.

I flip through my dresses and pull out one of my favorites —a bright turquoise with big green jungle leaves and pink flowers. A perfect dress for my first island-themed fashion post.

The interior of the guest house doesn't have as much natural light as I need, at least not at this time of the evening, but the storm has passed, and outside, the setting sun is blanketing everything in soft, golden light. I slip on pink, peep-toe wedges and peek my head out the door to make sure Jake and his *family* are gone. I don't think I could look him in the eye right now.

Jealousy isn't a good look on anyone, and it's an even worse feeling—a churning, burning, gross gut thing. Like indigestion times twenty. And there is zero reason for me to be jealous. Jake and I are not anything. And if he wants a Margo when he also has a Naomi and a Liam—well, you do you, Jake the Overlord. Not my circus, not my monkeys.

Thankfully, the porch is empty. It's almost like we didn't have a storm at all, other than the sun shimmering on the water droplets still lingering on the grass and leaves. It's honestly beautiful out, the golden hour everyone talks about. I get a few photos of the landscaping, leafy greens as bright as the ones on my dress, and water shining gold where the sun hits it. I can use those later. I've learned from experience to get extra shots when the light is good and save them for later posts. I'll have to start doing the same thing over at the house.

But now, it's time for me. Since I hate selfie sticks and

don't feel like setting up my tripod, I use one of my simple, go-to shots.

I stand on one of the porch steps, next to a pot where bougainvillea spills deep fuchsia blooms over the side. Making sure the flowers are in the frame, I take a few pictures capturing my dress and shoes. The steps are a little wet still, but I sluice the water away with my hand and sit, taking another few shots from above. Then it's just a matter of cropping, a smidge of editing, and then typing up a caption and finding relevant hashtags.

That's where I get stuck. The blinking cursor is mocking me. Or maybe it's the blank space where my words are supposed to go. Usually, writing is the easiest part. Now that I've gotten accustomed to posting house stuff, I'm not sure how to go back to my original brand, which is ... me.

"Don't be ridiculous," I tell myself. "Or—*be* ridiculous. It's your brand, and it's nothing to be ashamed of."

Drawing in a calming breath, I start to type.

Heyyyyy, Insta friends! You guys have been AMAZING with all the thoughts and suggestions for the house renovation. There are more of those posts coming your way soon, but for now, I'm settling into island life and loving the chance to match my wardrobe to my surroundings! Did I mention the house I'm renovating is on a tiny Southern island off the coast of Georgia? After enduring four years of Chicago winters, let me tell you, I am READY to enjoy a little bit of paradise! I can't wait to take you all on this journey with me! Don't forget to follow along for all the fun renovation updates, and of course, I'll still be posting my favorite fashion finds every Friday! xoxo - Lo

After tagging the sources for my shoes and dress, I do another quick typo check, add in some of my go-to hashtags, plus a few related to renovation, DIY, decor, and beaches.

Before I can rethink or overthink or any other kind of think, I hit publish and turn off my phone.

A throat clears behind me, and I spin around on the step to see Jake standing in his doorway with Liam. It takes about one point five seconds to remember I'm upset with him, then another point five seconds to remember I have no reason to be.

"Hello," I say, my attempt at being cool sounding more rude.

"Sorry to interrupt you," Jake says, rubbing the back of his neck.

"She's just sitting there," Liam says. "There's nothing to interrupt."

I may be unreasonably upset with Jake, but there's something about the no-nonsense, literal Liam that makes me smile.

"I was just finishing up a ..." I pause, not wanting to draw Jake's attention to Instagram. Where he plays a starring role. "Just taking some photos while the light is nice."

Instead, Liam only nods. "Cool. Want to have dinner with us?"

I stiffen. Dinner with ... Jake and the kid he didn't tell me about with the woman I also didn't know about? Yeah. Hard pass on that.

But my stomach grumbles at the thought of food. The last thing I ate was a handful of crackers. I'm a terrible cook and have basically existed on fruit and things that come in single-serve packages. If someone tested my blood, I'd probably be ninety-five percent preservatives.

"Um ..."

"It's gluten-free mac and cheese," Liam says. "I have celiac disease. Gluten damages my intestines and makes my butt explode."

151

Jake coughs to hide a laugh, covering his mouth with his hand. I can only stare because ... Jake is capable of laughter? Liam shoots him a glare, and I wish I could say my heart didn't go *awwwwwww* at the way Jake straightens up, looking apologetic.

"Not literally," Liam adds with an eye roll. "My mom says that's a nicer way of saying diarrhea. She doesn't like poop talk."

"Your mom and I have that in common," I say, trying not to laugh. I can see Liam doesn't appreciate being laughed at when he's being serious. Even if he's unintentionally hilarious. "But I'm not sure—"

Liam frowns, stepping closer. "The mac and cheese still tastes good. Uncle Jake buys the best kind—the one my mom says is too fancy."

"*Uncle* Jake?" I say, way too much emphasis on the *uncle*.

I glance from Liam to Jake, who is leaning against the doorway, his eyebrows raised in question and his mouth quirked into an *almost* smile. He could be laughing at me. But he looks more like he's enjoying this. Like he's *happy* I asked the question.

"You ran off before we could do full *family* introductions," Jake finally says. "Liam is my *nephew*. Naomi is my *sister*."

I nod my head like this is *no. big. deal.* "Cool," I manage to say, my voice way too wispy and light.

It is taking every ounce of my willpower to keep my expression neutral and my cheeks from flushing. While it was infuriating to think that Jake hid having a family (even if it was none of my business), it is dead sexy that he is a doting uncle—the kind who buys the fancy gluten-free mac and cheese.

"Are you coming to dinner or not?" Liam asks. "It's ready,

and I'm hungry. Uncle Jake made me wait to ask until you were done with your photos."

I swear, I feel each little hair rising on the back of my neck at the words. Was Jake watching me take photos? When the man has seen me wearing far less just hours ago, the idea shouldn't make me blush. And yet, it does. He glances away.

Guilty. He was totally watching me take photos. I resist the urge to do a little victory dance.

"Well?" Liam demands, clearly demonstrating the child's version of hangry.

I push off the stairs and take a step toward them. I might regret this later, but the half-smile playing on Jake's lips is just enough to push me into saying yes. I lift my shoulders in an easy shrug. "Why not?"

Potentially awkward conversation and gluten-free mac and cheese with a straight-shooting kid and a sexy uncle, here I come.

THE MAC and cheese really *is* good. And, since I'm still living like a broke college student, I'm quite the connoisseur of boxed meals.

"I told you it was good," Liam says.

I pause, caught with my tongue halfway out, ready to lick the last bits of cheesy sauce off my fork. Setting the utensil back down, I avoid looking at Jake. I can still see what looks like another tiny smile from the corner of my eye.

Who is this man and what did he do with my grumpy, all-business neighbor?

"It was delicious," I say. "Thank you for inviting me, Liam."

He nods. "It was Uncle Jake's idea. He said you probably

have no food because you just moved in, but you'd be too proud to say yes if he invited you. That's why I did. I didn't care if you came or not. Can I watch a movie?"

I'm not used to kids, or maybe just this particular kid, who speaks every thought in his head and changes subjects without warning. But, boy, do I love what he just said. I cannot stop myself from throwing a smirk Jake's way.

"Why don't you clear the table first?" Jake says, more of a command than a question. "Eloise and I will do the dishes."

I raise an eyebrow and meet Jake's gray gaze. *Oh, will we, now?* my look says. At least, I hope that's what it's conveying, rather than what I'm actually feeling. Because internally, I'm squealing and jumping up and down with excitement at the idea of washing dishes with Jake. Which is dumb. It's DISHES. But I am ridiculous levels of excited.

Jake helps Liam stack our plates, silverware on top. With exaggerated care, Liam sets them in the sink and turns back to the table.

"Thank you for making dinner, Uncle Jake."

"Did I do good tonight?"

"Five stars," Liam says, then turns to me. "And for what it's worth, you're much nicer than Margo."

"Liam," Jake says, a warning in his tone.

But this opportunity paired with my curiosity is too much to ignore. "Did you eat mac and cheese with Margo a lot?"

Jake looks ready to protest, but Liam jumps in first. "No. She doesn't eat things that come out of a box. Mom says Margo is a food snob. And also that she's the absolute worst."

Another point on which Naomi and I happen to agree. I'm beginning to think Jake's sister might be a good candidate for my new BFF.

"Liam," Jake says in a tone that's a warning but still somehow gentle. "That isn't very kind."

"But it's honest," Liam protests. "And *I* didn't say Margo is the worst. Or that she's a food snob. Mom said it. She also said you need to find a woman who doesn't have her head stuck up her—"

"Movie time!" Jake claps his hands and almost knocks over a chair in his rush to grab the remote.

"I'll just get started on the dishes," I say, turning so neither of them can see my smile.

Jake joins me at the sink a minute later, and I've already finished the plates and am just getting ready to start on the saucepans and colander. There's no dishwasher in this kitchen, same as in my half. It's really an odd sensation to be inside a mirror image of my new digs. Especially with how differently the two apartments are decorated.

Everything here screams Jake. Dark wood, clean lines—very masculine and un-fussy. But I did notice his bookshelf doesn't have the same clean lines. His books have broken spines and all look well-read, arranged in a way that seems haphazard at a glance. I'm sure I'd see an order if I looked through the shelves.

I'm surprised—and far too pleased—when Jake invades my space, nudging me over with his hip with a familiarity he hasn't quite earned. Not that I mind.

"Excuse you," I say, nudging him back.

"I'll finish this. You dry."

"So, you're bossy about everything. Even dishes."

He meets my gaze, and I swear, the look he gives me is scorching. "Yes. I am bossy about everything. I happen to like control."

Before I can burst into flames where I'm standing, Jake turns his attention to the pot and begins scrubbing, appar-

155

ently unaware that I'm suffering from some kind of cardiac event. I'm not sure if it's Liam's presence or the ocean rescue, but tonight, Jake is different. Less guarded. Almost playful.

I wish he showed this side of himself more. Especially—and maybe only?—to me.

"So," Jake says like he didn't just toss an innuendo grenade my way, "I'm sorry if Liam made you uncomfortable."

I laugh. "I'm not the one he was making uncomfortable. And I appreciate his honesty. He's almost like a mini-you."

"Really?"

"Seriously? You don't see it?"

"I'd like to see how *you* see it."

Jake hands me the clean pot. Our fingers brush as I take it, sending nerves skittering straight up my arm. I'm suddenly aware of nerve endings in places I have never noticed before. My scalp. The backs of my hands. Even that part of my elbow where people supposedly have *no* nerve endings.

I focus on the pot in my hands, rubbing the plain white dish towel over it. "He's serious. Intense."

"Are those good or bad qualities?" Jake asks.

I set the pan down and lean back against the countertop, crossing my arms. It's weird to be talking like this. So easy and casual-like. I want to enjoy it, because any minute now, I feel like Jake will revert back to his original operating instructions, which don't include what feels like friendship and maybe even mild flirting with me.

"They can be both good and bad, I think."

Turning off the water, Jake steps back, mirroring my stance with his back against the other counter. His kitchen, just like mine, has butcher block countertops in a little U-

156

shape with open shelving above. All of his dishes, like the dish towels and cloth napkins we had at dinner, are stark white.

"Are they good or bad qualities as related to *me?*" he asks.

I don't mean to make him sweat as I consider my answer. Okay, maybe I do a little. But I honestly don't know how to respond, not without tipping my hand to the very unwelcome crush I'm developing on Jake. The lawyer. The much-too-old-for-me neighbor. The sexy uncle. The playful dishwasher.

"I don't know you very well," I say, mentally tacking on the word *yet*. "But I get the sense that your best qualities might also be the things that trip you up and become struggles for you."

For a moment, he doesn't answer, and I wonder if I've offended him. Unlike my lit-marquee of a face showing every emotion I have as I have them, Jake is a blank wall. If I'd studied micro expressions instead of dead poets, maybe I'd get a read on him. But I didn't, so all I can do is wait.

"Very astute observation, Miss Markham," he says finally, one corner of his mouth lifting in a half smile.

"Thank you, Mr. Fieldstone."

Silence descends between us, and there's a little too much tension building in the small kitchen. Desperate to cut it but not yet ready to go, I tilt my head toward the living area, where Liam is watching a movie I don't recognize. Something with robots and cats. I think he's enjoying it because he's totally intent on the screen, but he's still frowning. Resting frown face is apparently his thing.

"Do you take care of him a lot?"

Jake's gaze cuts to his nephew, then shifts back to me. "My sister's situation is complicated. She's raising Liam on her own, so I try to support her as much as I can. Naomi has been through a lot, but she's a fighter."

This sweet protectiveness is like an arrow right through my Jake-proof armor. Though, to be honest, that armor is more like a soft burlap sack full of holes. The man is still a grump, but he's a grump who cares. I've seen it in the way he rescued me, that first night at the bar and then again in the ocean earlier this afternoon, and now I can see it with Naomi and Liam. I want to ask for more details, but I don't want to be too nosy.

Correction: I AM nosy, and I *want* to be nosy. I just have enough good sense not to be blatant about it.

"Does she live here? On Oakley?"

He shakes his head. "She's in Savannah. Just close enough to randomly drop by when she needs free babysitting. Which is usually fine by me," he adds quickly. "I enjoy spending time with him. But I appreciate having set arrangements, and Naomi does not function that way. Plus, it's hard to watch her wasting time with—" He sighs, his focus fully on Liam now. "Whatever. It's fine. I just wish my sister would finally pick a decent guy."

He would want that. Of course he would. Because Jake Fieldstone, grumpiness aside, is clearly a very decent guy himself. Realizing as much is not going to help my growing (exploding?) crush.

"Are you done talking yet? It's hard to hear the movie," Liam says.

Jake's gray eyes meet mine. "Do you want us to come watch with you?"

Once again, there's that hint of bossy control. Because he didn't ask me if I wanted to watch before volunteering us both. Is it possible Jake wants to spend more time with me and is using Liam to do it?

Be still my fluttering heart.

"That's okay. You could go outside and talk on the porch swing."

Jake raises his brows and gestures toward the door. "You heard the man. I think we've been relegated to the porch. Unless you have big plans?"

"I have zero plans, big or small."

Still, I search for an excuse. This is too dangerous. Too risky. Too tempting.

And yet I follow Jake out to the porch. Almost immediately, we're assaulted by a cloud of mosquitoes. And something bigger that looks a lot like a flying beetle. When it lands on my shoulder, I scream, flail until it flies off, and run right back inside.

Liam glances up as I bolt across the living room, tripping in my wedge sandals. "What?"

I'm busy sweeping my hands over my arms and hair, hoping none of the bugs hitched a ride inside.

"Mosquitoes and a flying cockroach," Jake explains.

My eyes bug out. "That flying thing was a cockroach?"

"Surely you remember them from when you spent summers here," Jake says.

"I think I'd remember flying cockroaches. They'd haunt my dreams."

"Your grandmother probably called them palmetto bugs. But that's just a fancy name to make people feel better about finding them in their house."

With a heavy sigh, Liam pauses his movie, then looks between me and Jake. "Are you going to watch the movie quietly or what?"

Jake shrugs, tilting his head toward the couch, and I sit down, disappointed that Liam is already in the middle. But as

Jake goes to sit, Liam scoots all the way over to the opposite end, forcing Jake to sit right next to me.

I notice Jake shooting his nephew a look. Liam only shrugs. "What? Mom said to be a good wingman."

"I thought you didn't know what that word meant," Jake says.

"She explained it while you were taking a shower. It's what you do when someone needs help getting a girlfriend. Can I put the movie back on now?"

I'm not sure who I love more right now—Liam or his mother.

With a deep sigh of his own—almost an exact echo of the one Liam let out earlier—Jake stretches his arms over the back of the couch, one behind me and one behind Liam. "Knock yourself out, buddy."

Liam looks like he's about to say something else, but then he huffs back into his seat and presses play. Meanwhile, I'm sitting forward stiffly, careful not to brush my back up against Jake. Though I am VERY AWARE of his arm.

"Relax," he mutters to me.

"I am relaxed."

He leans even closer, and I shiver when his breath brushes over my neck. "You wouldn't want Liam to feel like he's failing at his very important wingman job."

"Oh, this is for Liam?"

"Shhh!" Liam says, then adds in a more polite tone, "Please."

Pulling his other arm out from behind Liam, Jake grasps my shoulder gently and pushes me back until I'm leaning on his arm. When I glance at him, his gray eyes are dancing with laughter.

"I don't have cooties," he says. "Relax."

Liam presses pause again. "Cooties are a made-up thing.

Not a real disease like celiac. Jake doesn't have any diseases. At least, none that we know of yet. Now, can you please be quiet and watch the movie?"

"Yes," Jake and I say at the same time, and I force myself to lean back against his arm. Cooties may not be a real affliction, but my crush very much is, and nothing about our current scenario is going to help cure it.

FIFTEEN

Jake

YES. Yes, I am aware of the massive contradiction that is my current life. That it makes no sense how one minute I'm talking about keeping my meetings with Eloise public and telling her to call my secretary, and the next, I'm urging her to snuggle in beside me on the couch just so I can feel the warmth of her next to me.

I shouldn't like having her so close. But it's still not close *enough*. She's leaning into me, and her legs, which are tucked underneath her, are touching the outside of my thigh. I could drop my arm over her shoulders rather than just bracing it behind her on the couch, but that feels like an actual *move*, which, no matter how much I'm enjoying myself, I can't really make.

She's a client.

She's too young for me.

She's not planning to stay on Oakley.

She's ... sighing and leaning her head against my shoulder.

Oh man. I have never been so happy to watch one of Liam's kid movies. I hope this one is on the longer side. Maybe a double feature? Pretty sure that's not a thing on streaming services, but that doesn't stop me from wishing it were.

I silently drum my fingers on the back of the couch. Six inches to the right and I'll be touching her arm.

I *really* want to touch her arm.

My pointer finger jerks, and I ball my hand into a tight fist. The action does nothing to quell my driving need to trace it over her skin. I might as well be in the seventh grade working up the courage to hold a girl's hand for the first time. Except, I'm a grown man with a respectable amount of dating experience, so this shouldn't be so hard.

As the movie plays on, the tension builds and builds. A slow and steady heat crawls its way up my chest to my neck. Every place we're touching, even separated by clothes, feels scorching.

"Pee break!" Liam yells as he pauses the movie, startling Eloise and me both.

Eloise giggles, shaking her head, her body shifting so she's a tiny bit closer.

Liam's absence is the last push of motivation I need.

I drop my hand to her arm, tracing a line down the exposed skin below the sleeve of her dress. It's only a fingertip. But this touch is more electric, more *alive* than anything that has passed between us before. Because this is intentional. There's a message behind this gesture. It's a bright neon flash across the sky that says *I'm interested.*

Completely negating the message I've been sending her, which is more like *stay far, far away!*

Her breath catches, and she closes her eyes, and for a single moment, time stops. There's nothing else. No grieving. No attorney-client relationship. No renovation. No Liam or Naomi or Margo or Merritt hovering in the periphery. There's only us.

Liam barrels back into the room with enough *oomph* to startle Eloise, which is fine by me because she startles *into* me. She's practically in my lap, and when she tries to pull away, I hold her in place, my arm now around her waist. She faces the television, but I see the pink rising in her cheeks.

As the movie starts up again, I lean forward, whispering close to Lo's ear. "Is this okay?"

She nestles in a little closer. "It's okay."

"Just *okay*?"

Even in the dim light, her eyes sparkle. "Are you fishing for compliments? If you really must know, this is more than okay. Good. Maybe even great."

"Shh!"

Liam sounds totally exasperated with us both. He shakes his head when Lo giggles. *Lo*. I'm not sure when my brain made that switch, but I like it. I find a grin stretching across my face. We settle in, back to watching the movie, though my attention is much more on the woman pressed close to me.

Had Margo been the one sitting beside me while one of Liam's movies played in front of us, it wouldn't take her five minutes to reach for her phone to pull up her never-ending feed of business news and world events. She had a hard time staying engaged if we picked out a movie for *us*. But something like this one? With cats and robots and ... is that a dancing chicken? Yeah. Margo would never have gone for this. Honestly, she probably wouldn't have even stayed.

But Lo *is* watching the movie. Or she's at least pretending to. Liam glances back every once in a while, watching us watch, and smiles like he's glad we're there. Like he appreciates that we're interested in what he's interested in.

Or maybe he's just thinking about telling his mom later what a good wingman he was. I can't wait for the conversation Naomi and I will have after tonight.

"I don't trust that guy," Lo says, pointing to the screen.

"It's the eyebrows," Liam agrees. "He has very untrustworthy eyebrows."

"You're right! It is the eyebrows."

I had no idea eyebrows could be untrustworthy. "Eyebrows can be untrustworthy?"

"Yes," both Liam and Lo say emphatically. "What kind of eyebrows do I have?"

With another sigh, Liam pauses the movie. Then he and Lo are both examining my eyebrows, and I'm trying not to squirm, suddenly sorry I asked.

"Thick," Liam says, just as Lo says, "Intriguing. But definitely trustworthy."

Liam starts the movie again, and I spend the next half-hour wondering if intriguing is a good eyebrow quality or if I need to do some manscaping. Is that even the right term?

By the end of the movie, Liam and Lo have both fallen asleep. Liam's on the floor, stretched out with his head propped on a throw pillow from the couch, and Lo has her head on my lap, my arm resting on the small of her back. I'd sit here all night if I thought she'd be comfortable, but she's bent at the waist, her feet resting on the floor. She'll wake with a crick if she stays that way long.

I shift at the thought. I'm still in shape, and I feel pretty good most days. But the stretching I do at the end of my runs to keep my back from seizing up reminds me of my age every single day. A body that is thirty-two is not the same thing as a body that is twenty-two.

My eyes drop back to Eloise. *Or a body that's twenty-one.*

I do some quick math in my head. When I was a senior in high school, Eloise was seven. Oh man. That feels gross. She's just so *young.*

She isn't that young now, Jacob, Gennie's voice says in my head. *And you're not getting any younger.*

Maybe that's true, but it's hard to shake the reality of an eleven-year age gap. Are she and I even in the same generation? The thought makes me shudder. And yet ... millions of couples all over the world have crazy age gaps, and they're still happy. Genevieve's husband was eleven years older than she was.

Genevieve was also a relatively young widow. The age gap didn't help in that regard.

I'm getting ahead of myself. I don't actually *like* like Eloise, do I? There is attraction, sure. I wouldn't be sitting with her like this if there wasn't.

But is it more? Is this something beyond a physical pull? Do I like her enough to be debating the impracticalities of dating someone so much younger than I am?

A massive part of me—the smartest part—keeps trying to remind me of the boundaries I felt so sure I needed to keep in place. Another part, playing a very lawyer-y devil's advocate, wants to know if I REALLY need those boundaries and what's the worst that could happen.

The worst is also the best, Jacob. You could fall in love.

More than my own arguments, Gennie's voice in my head right now makes me feel like I cannot sit here another moment with my arm around Lo.

I give Lo a little shake, and she shifts and pushes herself up, looking around as if she can't quite place where she is. A strand of her hair is stuck to her cheek.

I reach over and smooth it away, pushing it behind her ear. Her sleepy eyes finally lock on me.

"Enjoy your nap?" I ask.

Her hand flies to her mouth. "Did I drool on you? Please tell me I didn't drool on you."

There is, in fact, a tiny damp spot on my jeans, but she isn't going to notice it unless I point it out. "No drool," I say. "But you did snore."

She gasps. "I did not."

"Like a chainsaw," I say. "It's a good thing the movie was already over, or Liam would have been so mad at you."

She shakes her head, the silver hoops dangling from her ears bobbing back and forth. "Jake Fieldstone, you better tell me you're kidding, because otherwise, I'm leaving forever, and you'll never see me again."

I try not to panic because she's joking. Except ... she will be leaving, won't she?

Swallowing, I try to infuse my voice with a teasing tone. "What about the renovation?"

"Gran would understand the magnitude of this embarrassment. I'll send for one of my sisters. You can be their overlord instead of mine."

Again, I know she's joking, but the idea makes my stomach drop.

"I do *not* snore, and I need you to admit it," she says.

"*Fine*. You didn't snore. Don't send for your sisters."

A blush creeps up her cheeks. "Why not?"

Yeah, Jake. Why not?

I can't really tell her why. The answers scare me, which means they'd definitely scare her. *Because I like you the most. Because you're the most beautiful. Because I like being around you. Because you're the one I can't stop thinking about.*

167

I've been fighting these realizations so hard, it feels invigorating to finally let them loose. At least a little bit.

Still, for Lo's sake, I settle for a safer answer. "You're the most like Genevieve, for one. If any of you is going to truly capture the vision of this place, it's you."

Her eyes glisten, and for a second, I worry I've upset her. "Am I really like her?" she whispers.

I want to swim back to the shallows, go back to the teasing conversation—maybe the first one ever I haven't screwed up. But it doesn't do either of us any good to pretend like we didn't just lose someone we care about.

"You have the same stubbornness," I say, and Lo swats at my arm. "And also the same smile. Same passion. The same joy for life."

She holds my gaze a long moment. "Jake, how did you get so close to Gran?"

I lean back and lift my hands, resting them behind my head. It isn't that I don't want to tell her, I just don't know where to begin. Genevieve Markham is woven into my earliest memories, as much a part of my life as Oakley Island itself.

"My mom left when I was a kid," I say simply. "Got a job up north but didn't want to take Naomi and me with her. Said she thought the island would do a better job of raising us than she could."

"Wow," she breathes out. "That's so ... cold."

I shrug. *Was* my mother cold? Her leaving seems to say that she is. But she's done a decent job of keeping up with us over the years. She calls regularly and shows up for the big events in our lives as long as they don't conflict with her own illustrious career in academia. I know she cares; she just seems to care best from a distance.

"Maybe. But she was right. Oakley was an amazing place

to grow up. The people here banded together to help Ned with me and Naomi, taking an interest in where we were and what we were up to. I spent afternoons after school at Sweet Tea and Toast. I'd do my homework, Harriett would feed me something better than the bar food I'd get if I'd gone straight home to Ned's—"

"Wait, you lived at the bar?"

"In the apartment above it. Ned still lives there."

She nods. "I was surprised when he told me he was your dad."

This surprises me. "*He* told you? You've been back to Ned's after your night of debauchery?"

"It was two glasses!" she protests.

"I know, I know. Your night of *accidental* debauchery?"

She huffs a sigh. "I went back to apologize. I felt ... silly, I guess. I know he wasn't trying to over-serve. I just wanted him to know I didn't hold him responsible for me being a lightweight who skipped dinner and also had never had a drink before. He told me not to even worry about it."

The thoughtfulness in this gesture makes something tighten in my chest. Ned and I haven't been all that close. Especially not after I left and went to work in Savannah. But the idea of Lo caring enough to go talk to him, to explain, makes me want to try and repair things. It also makes my respect for her climb a few degrees higher. She may be younger, but I could learn a thing or two from her.

"Why do you call him Ned instead of Dad?" she asks.

"I don't know, really. We were in the bar all the time as kids. Getting him to take a day off is next to impossible, so we just heard it all the time. Everyone else calling him Ned. And he didn't really talk to us like we were his kids. More like we were just ... tiny customers. The only parenting advice he ever gave me, he gave across the bar counter. I always felt like it was the same advice he'd give a random guy off the street."

"Like what?"

I lean forward, propping an elbow on my knee as I channel my best Ned impression. "Listen, Jake. You want people to like you? You listen to their problems, you buy them a beer, and even if you're lying, you tell them everything is going to be okay. One way or another, your lie will become truth eventually."

She smiles. "You do a good Ned voice."

"The world will knock you down, Lo, but as long as you've got your integrity, you've got something to hold onto."

"So you're saying Ned parented in memes."

I nod, smiling, because as simple as it is, that's a pretty solid way to describe it. Naomi and I are both grown now, but not much has changed. Now he just serves us a drink along with his helpful advice. "Gennie didn't like that we spent so much time at the bar, so she started bringing us here every weekend. Some school nights too."

"You stayed at her house?"

I arch a brow. "Is that so hard to believe? Your grandmother always had people staying at her house. She collected strays like some people collect antiques."

A flash of uncertainty moves across her expression. "I mean, I …" She sighs. "I guess I didn't spend enough time here to know her that well."

"You were young, Eloise."

"That's not really an excuse though, is it?"

"Could you have made the trip on your own? When you were in high school? Middle school? You said you wrote letters. You did what you could."

"Maybe. But once I was in college …" Her words trail off,

and she sniffs. "I don't know. I guess I just thought I had more time."

Deep in my chest, a coil of resentment I didn't know I was harboring unspools and drifts away. Logically, I knew better than to blame Lo and her sisters for the way their lives shifted away from Oakley Island after their parents divorced. They *were* children. They probably did the best they could.

But it still soothes me to hear Lo's regrets. To sense her awareness of what she's lost. I loved Gennie too much to want anyone to take advantage of her love and generosity.

"I find it hard to believe we never crossed paths," Lo continues. "We were playing with other kids around the island all the time, but I don't remember you. How did I not see you around?"

I pause. She does not realize how old I actually am, and maybe she needs to. If I'm lucky, she'll figure it out, be entirely repulsed, and run out of my apartment screaming. I'll finally be able to stop thinking about her, stop wondering what she's doing on the other side of my bedroom wall.

"Do you remember the summer you set up a lemonade stand out on the sidewalk in front of Gennie's house?"

A smile stretches across her face. "Gran made the best lemonade. But I only convinced her to let me have a lemonade stand once. She didn't think I was old enough to sit on the street alone, and my sisters were too old to be bothered."

Lemonade stand *singular* makes this an easier game.

"It was a Saturday afternoon," I say slowly. "And a guy driving a beat-up Corolla packed full of everything he owned stopped and paid you twenty bucks for a glass of lemonade."

Her expression brightens as she finds the memory. "That's right! Were you there? You saw—" Her words cut off, and I know the moment she realizes because her eyes become cartoon-character wide. "That was you?"

"On my way to college in Savannah. I dropped by to say goodbye to Gennie."

"That was the summer I turned seven," she says, her voice a little smaller than it was a moment ago. "And you—"

"Had just graduated from high school."

She shifts on the couch, tucking her legs up under her again, which has the added effect of putting a little more distance between us.

"Oh wow. I knew you were older than me. So that means now you're—"

"Practically geriatric," I say. "Approaching my thirty-third birthday."

"Thirty-three is not geriatric."

"No? Then why is your face turning red?"

"It isn't." She presses her palms to her cheeks. "Or if it is, it's only because I'm embarrassed. I knew you were older, but it doesn't seem so bad until you put it in that context."

I could tell her I don't see her that way now. I could tell her the age difference doesn't bother me so much, not after I've started getting to know her. But I'm still torn. I don't have good and bad angels on my shoulders. I've got a rule-following prosecutor pointing out all the reasons I wanted to keep my distance and an overconfident defense attorney casting shadows of doubt.

But then Lo straightens, like she's digging for some deeper resolve and determination. "But age doesn't really matter. Does it?" A sliver of trepidation sneaks into her voice as she reaches over to where my hand rests on my thigh. She slips her hand into mine, curling her fingers into my palm. "I don't want it to matter," she says slowly.

I might have been relieved had the age difference

mattered to Eloise. Relieved to be rid of the temptation. The uncertainty of possibility.

But the feeling growing in my chest is more intoxicating than relief. I am ... elated. Mystified. Sparked to life in ways that make it easy to ignore every sound and logical reason I ever had for keeping things professional between us.

I tug Eloise closer and lift a hand to the curve of her jaw. It feels like a bold move for me, but then, we've been inching forward all night. She leans into the caress, her blue eyes locked on mine.

"I sat next to you at the bar that first night, not knowing who you were at first. Then you turned and spoke to me. It was your eyes that told me who you were," I say. "I could never forget these eyes."

I lean forward until we're only inches apart and pause. Waiting, *asking*.

She closes the distance, nudging the tip of her nose against mine, then pressing her lips, feather soft, to the corner of my mouth. My eyes fall closed, but then pop open again when Eloise jerks away from me, scrambling off the couch like a teenager caught by a scolding parent.

Except, in this case, the parent is my sister. And she isn't scolding. She's laughing in the doorway.

"Sorry to interrupt," Naomi says as she sashays into the room. "Have we had a nice evening? Please tell me you didn't drug my child so you could make out uninterrupted."

Eloise shakes her head way too fast to look innocent. "We're not—I mean, we weren't—"

"Naomi," I growl at the same moment Liam sits up. Eloise is practically plastered to the wall, her hands bunching up the fabric of her bright print dress.

Liam speaks through a big yawn. "Mom?"

Naomi drops onto the chair by the door and ruffles Liam's

hair. "Hey, kiddo. Did you have as much fun as your Uncle Jake? Looks like you were an excellent wingman."

Liam swings around to face me. "Did you kiss her? I woke up, but you looked like you were about to kiss, so I pretended to still be asleep."

Could this night be filled with any more embarrassment? I think I've filled my lifetime quota.

At least Lo looks less panicked now. Actually, she looks like she's about to laugh, which is better, right? Even if it is at my expense.

"Excellent moves, kid," Naomi says, offering him a fist bump.

"I should go," Lo says, moving to the door. "But thank you. For everything. For the mac and cheese. And ..." She looks at Liam. "For the movie. We were right about the untrustworthy eyebrows."

He nods. "Yes, we were."

"Lo, wait." I stand to move after her, but she waves me back down and darts past Naomi.

"It was nice to meet you," she says hastily, and then she's gone.

I turn to glare at my sister, who shrugs sheepishly.

"I really am sorry about my timing. I'm all for any woman other than Margo. I promise I didn't mean to scare her away."

"Yes, you did."

"All I did was walk into the room. Maybe you're the one who scared her away. How long has it been since you've kissed someone? Wait. Let me rephrase. How long has it been since you kissed anyone besides a cold-hearted, fish-lipped, money-grubbing—"

I hold a hand up to stop her. "I get the point."

"Words should be used to lift people up, Mom. Not tear

them down," Liam says. I almost forgot he was a part of this conversation. My confidence that he will repeat every single thing he hears in front of someone else—possibly even Lo—has me wishing he'd stayed asleep.

Naomi rolls her eyes. "Are you using my own parenting against me now?" She motions toward the hallway. "Go pee before we leave. I don't want you complaining on the drive home."

Liam grumbles his frustration, but he gets up anyway.

"So who is she?" Naomi asks as soon as Liam is out of the room.

I don't really want to tell her, but she'll figure it out soon enough. I'm honestly surprised she hasn't already. She knows me too well to assume I'm spending time with a tourist, and Oakley is small enough that new women only ever move in once or twice a decade. Who else could Eloise be but one of Gennie's granddaughters?

"You couldn't tell by her eyes?"

"Wait. That was ... you were ... with one of Gennie's granddaughters? Which one?"

"Eloise," I say. "She goes by Lo."

"*Jake.* You're kidding me. The *baby?* She was, like, *eleven* the last time I saw her, and I was on my way to college. Is she even fully legal yet?"

"She's twenty-one," I say, not bothering to mention just how recent her twenty-first birthday was. Hopefully, it will be a while before Ned lets it slip.

Naomi shakes her head, her laughter growing. "You dirty dog. I'm actually kind of proud of you. This feels like something I would do, but you? Careful, responsible, respectable Jake Fieldstone? Never." She rubs her hands together like she can barely contain her glee. "I feel like I need to tell someone. My older brother is dating not just a woman who is eleven

175

years younger than he is, he's dating a *client's granddaughter* who is eleven years younger than he is. Ned would love this. Does Ned know? Please tell me I can tell Ned."

"Naomi, stop. Lo is—we aren't dating. We aren't anything."

"You were kissing," Liam says unhelpfully. "That's something."

Except we *weren't* kissing, thanks to Naomi. And the longer this conversation persists, the more grateful I am, my disappointment quickly melting into uncomfortable relief that we didn't fully cross that line.

What am I doing?

Eloise isn't a client, but she's client *adjacent*, which to me is too close. Gennie asked me to look out for her house. To look after her girls, as she called them. I was given this responsibility because Gennie believed I could be fair and impartial. Reasonable and forthright.

Or ... because she was trying to play matchmaker. The thought has struck me before, and now, I have to wonder even more.

"So, twenty-one," Naomi says. "Is she still in college? This story will be so much better if she's still a co-ed."

My jaw tightens. "She's not a co-ed. She just graduated with a degree in English."

"Aww, Mom would be so proud."

Naomi's comment hits me like a punch to the gut. Mom *would* be proud. And the parallel doesn't sit well. Because Mom's love for academia is what eventually convinced her to leave Oakley. To leave *us*.

During our not-all-business lunch, Eloise mentioned wanting to get her master's or doctorate down the road, just like Mom did. Her stay on Oakley is temporary. Out of all the reasons I should put back the distance I closed tonight, this reason is the most compelling.

"What do you think, Liam," Naomi asks as she shoulders Liam's backpack. "Do you like Eloise and Uncle Jake together?"

"Naomi," I groan, not wanting her to plant ideas in my nephew's head I'll just have to uproot later. The same way I need to pull them out of my own.

Liam shrugs. "She likes my mac and cheese. And my movies."

I only wish it were that simple.

SIXTEEN

Lo

"AND THERE'S the woman who made my brother go viral."

I yelp and trip over a pair of Gran's heels. People really need to stop startling me in this house. From my new vantage point on the floor of Gran's closet, I look up at someone I wasn't expecting.

"Naomi?"

She grins, tossing her dark brown hair over her shoulder, and slides down the wall in Gran's enormous closet to sit across from me. I haven't seen her again since I had dinner with Liam and Jake.

Also known as—the night I all but kissed Jake.

Or, maybe even better—the last time I've seen Jake, who has become a ghost. Even worse than after our business lunch. I'm honestly not even sure if he's sleeping next door. If avoidance were an Olympic sport, he would be standing at the top of the podium, waving as they play the national anthem.

But I won't take out my frustrations about him on his sister.

"Nice dress," Naomi says, looking me up and down.

I smooth my hands down the knee-length skirt. Compared to a lot of my dresses, this one seems a bit more understated in navy and white. But this one is special: the white details are really looping cursive lines from a Shakespearean sonnet. "Thanks. A little fancy for cleaning out a closet."

"I think it's perfect. Mind if I join you? The front door was open, and Hunter said it was okay to come up." She tilts her head. "At least, I *think* that's what his grunt meant."

I can't help but laugh. "I've thought about making a cheat sheet to decode Hunter's different grunts."

"You could probably sell that to any number of eligible island bachelorettes," she says. "They've all been trying to lock that down. To no avail, obviously. The man seems determined to live and die a hermit."

I wonder if Naomi is one of the women who'd like to lock that down. From her tone, it's impossible to tell.

"Are there a lot of island bachelorettes?" I ask.

Most of the people I've interacted with on the island—Jake and Naomi aside—are solidly in the over-forty crowd. Many in the over-sixty crowd. Naomi is the closest person to my age I've met, and she lives in Savannah.

"Unfortunately," Naomi says with a roll of her eyes, but then doesn't seem inclined to expound, switching quickly to another subject. "You're immune to Hunter's charms, right? Because I kind of have my hopes pinned on you and my brother."

So did I.

"Um, that ship has sailed. Or maybe it sank?"

I lift a shoulder, trying to locate an expression that says I'm totally A-okay with this. I don't think I succeed based on the way Naomi's gaze slices into me. Her grin definitely has a wicked tilt to it.

"Already? From what I've heard, your ship hasn't even had its maiden voyage yet. Since I interrupted and all."

I'm dying to ask what exactly she's heard and also dying at the idea that she's heard anything at all. I try to imagine what Jake might possibly have said about me. Probably something along the lines of: I'm too young, too silly, and keep getting myself into jams which require his rescue.

And that he's insistent on NOT dating me. Even if we did almost kiss—something I wish I could scrub from my memory. That would be better than playing the moment on repeat like I am now.

"I foresee zero voyages in my future," I tell her. "I am very firmly landlocked. Trust me."

"I'll take that bet," she says.

"Take it up with your brother," I mutter, adding a shoe box to the growing tower beside me.

"Is he being an idiot?"

I bark out a laugh. "Can we still be friends if I say yes?"

"You want to be friends?" Her eyes light up. "Yay! I wasn't sure if I scared you off."

I shake my head. "Nope. As long as you don't make me talk about Jake."

She sticks out her lip in a pout. "I can't promise I won't *ever* make you talk about him. But how about a temporary moratorium? And you're welcome to call him an idiot as much as you want. I'm happy to be a semi-impartial listening ear." Before I can answer, she plows on. "So, what are we working on? Need help? I'm Liam-free for the next few hours. He's at a robotics day camp this week."

I can completely picture Liam at a robotics camp. He'll probably come home with a perfectly functional model that performs a practical application like washing dishes or predicting fluctuations in the stock market.

"You really want to help?" I ask.

"Consider me your new, free work-woman."

I glance around at the closet, which looks worse than when I came in. I think that's how it usually goes when you're trying to pack up and clear out.

Today, after a few weeks on the island, I finally felt brave enough to crack open Gran's bedroom door. Also, Hunter basically said I was going to hold up the whole timeline if I didn't.

Not unlike when I walked into the house for the first time, I was disappointed by the lack of emotional connection. Nothing about the sight of Gran's perfectly made bed or the scent of her perfume—some old department store brand I found on the bathroom counter—stirred memories or deep feelings.

Same as it's been most of the time, I just feel ... numb. At some point, all the feelings are going to crash into me like a barge.

"I'm going through Gran's impressive shoe collection, all of which I plan to donate."

She might have been a minimalist elsewhere, but Gran was a maximalist when it came to footwear. None of the dozens of shoes, most of which look totally new and in the original boxes, are in any of my or my sisters' sizes. Despite our differences, we all wear an eight and a half narrow. Gran's shoes look like they'd fit a woodland fairy. Who in the world wears a size five?

"Oh! That's my size!"

I guess Naomi does. She picks up the box I just tripped over and examines the ruby-red heels.

"Did your grandmother ever wear these?" Slipping off her flip flop, she slides on the heel and turns her foot from side to side before wrinkling her nose and putting the heel back in the box. "The soles look perfectly pristine."

"I'm honestly not sure. I hadn't seen my grandmother in years."

Admitting that makes something pinch tight in my chest, but Naomi doesn't seem to judge me for it like her brother does. Or did? I'm honestly not sure where Jake landed on that. She slips on the heels, clicking them together three times like Dorothy, grinning.

"Feel free to keep anything you like."

"Really?"

"Yep."

"Sweet. Thanks. I'm impressed you can do this. Me? I am a total sentimental sap. I've still got everything my mom didn't take when she left. I've even kept things from my ex." She shakes her head. "And if anyone deserves to have his things burned, it's him."

I want to ask more about her ex and her mom, and while I'm debating which one I'm more curious about, she says, "So, did you and your grandma have a falling out or what? How come you hadn't seen her in so long?"

I wonder if Naomi is the only one on the island who doesn't know the story, or if she just wants to hear my side. Either way, I'm in a talkative mood. Probably because other than Hunter and Steve, I have no one to talk to with Jake playing his ghost game.

While we open shoe boxes, I explain about my parents' messy divorce, Dad being basically a deadbeat, and the way

182

we fell into a life where Gran was only in the periphery, aside from our letters back and forth. Naomi listens, nodding in understanding as she helps stack shoe boxes into two piles—one to donate and a smaller one she's going to keep.

"Family is hard," she says.

I don't feel like I can ask about hers without being overtly nosy about Jake. Specifically, why the strain between Jake and Ned? Is he really as low-key about his mom leaving, or did that have a huge impact he's hiding?

Thankfully, Naomi is in as talkative a mood as I am. Or maybe this is just her default setting.

"My mom took off when we were little to pursue a career," Naomi says.

I almost drop the box of strappy sandals I'm holding when she scoffs, "Like academics is really a career."

I try to make some kind of casual noise of agreement while staring a hole through the shoe box in my hands. But, as I'm all-too-aware, I have zero poker face.

"Oh no," Naomi says. "You're not in academics, are you?"

I smile weakly. "American literature. Specifically poets. I was hoping to be studying at Greenwood University out in Washington state this fall. But things didn't work out with the grad program."

Naomi groans. "I'm sorry. I'm known for putting my foot in my mouth." She holds up a black patent leather heel and pretends to take a big bite. It makes me feel marginally better. "What happened with the program?"

The box in my hands suddenly feels heavy. I take off the lid, then put it back on again. "The short version is that my advisor screwed me over. He messed up his recommendation letter."

"Well, that just sucks."

It does. But that's not the whole story.

The longer version is that Dr. Harding totally blew me off when I asked, not even looking up from his desk as he agreed to write the letter. And when I tried to explain in more detail what I needed, he glanced up, pushing his reading glasses down his nose, to glare with his beady little eyes.

"I understand how recommendation letters work," he said in an icy tone.

And, like the scaredy cat I can sometimes be, I bolted from his office and didn't even follow up—though I knew I should. Come to find out he wrote a letter—but it didn't follow the required format and arrived late.

Maybe I wouldn't have gotten into the program anyway.

Maybe if I pushed him, he wouldn't have written a letter at all.

Or, maybe if I stood up for myself, if I fought for what I really wanted, I'd be preparing to leave for grad school in a little over a month.

"Anyway, academics is a fine career," Naomi says. "I didn't mean to diminish it. Heck, right now, I'm paying the rent by calling to harass people about late medical bill payments. Who am I to talk? I'm just a little bitter because my mom chose it over us. I mean, mostly, it's fine. I was young enough when she left that the only relationship we've ever really had has been long-distance. It was much harder on Jake."

Her shrug is an attempt to cover a hurt I can tell runs deep. I wonder what Jake would think of my career path. I know I mentioned my desire to pursue a higher degree, but I can't remember now if he reacted to it.

If nothing else, it's probably one more thing to add to his long list of reasons why we shouldn't be together—I remind him of his mom.

Ew. That's almost as bad as being reminded he bought

lemonade from my stand when he was going to college. Triple ew.

I only wish either of those things meant I didn't still harbor feelings.

"Hey, you could probably sell these. I mean, most of them are designer and in perfect condition."

I glance at the names on the boxes. She's right. I do recognize most of the brands. "Maybe. It sounds like a lot of work."

"There are so many sites for resale. It's easy now." Naomi pulls out her phone and opens up an app, turning her screen toward me. "See? I use this one all the time."

"If you want to list them, you can keep the money." My sisters would not approve, but who's the one packing up Gran's house? Not Sadie or Merritt.

Naomi's eyes brighten. "Really? I'll totally do that if you really don't mind. I just need to take photos and I can upload them ..." She's already gathering boxes, dragging a stack out of the closet and looking around the room. "Is it okay if I move this table?"

I nod, and Naomi removes the book and lamp from one of the bedside tables and drags the small piece of furniture in front of the window for better light. Which reminds me of Instagram and what Naomi said when she walked in and scared me.

"Wait—does Jake know about the viral video?"

Naomi laughs. "He mentioned it. Which is a miracle, because I didn't think he knew what Instagram was."

"Is he mad?"

Naomi picks up another box, a smile on her face. "I think *mad* is his baseline emotion. Or, at least, serious. He came out of the womb like a grumpy old man. Just like my Liam.

Genes are weird. But I'd rather my kid take after Jake than the deadbeat dad who shall not be named."

I have so many questions I want to ask, but I'm not sure I want to press on what's clearly a painful subject.

She smiles, her expression clearing. "Don't worry about Jake. Seriously, it's fine."

I'm not so sure about that, but I figure if he was really mad, he knows where I live. "How did you find me on Instagram?"

Her look is shrewd. "Let's just say I'm too nosy for my own good, and I needed to know more about the woman my brother is *absolutely not* interested in." She puts the *absolutely not* in air quotes and adds an exaggerated eye roll.

I wish her comment didn't make hope flutter in my belly. I have declared it a butterfly-free zone, especially where Jake is concerned. Flutters are not allowed. Flapping and flying? Banned. Indefinitely.

"Now," Naomi says, grabbing a box from a high shelf. "What are we going to do about these hats?"

AN HOUR LATER, Naomi and I are lying in the closet, laughing hysterically, each of us wearing a ridiculous hat, when Hunter is suddenly standing in the doorway, blinking at us.

"Hey, Hunter!" I toss him a silver rhinestone-covered cowboy hat. "To enter, you must have a hat."

He catches it, turning it over in his hands while I hold my breath. I glance over to see Naomi biting her lip. Hunter sighs, then puts the hat on. It's too tiny—Gran was petite, and Hunter is built like a linebacker—so it rests on the very top of his head, giving him a cartoonish look.

When Naomi and I burst out laughing, he doesn't turn and run like I might have thought. Instead, he folds his long legs and sits down between us.

"That one," he says, lifting a hand to touch the oversized white sun hat I'm wearing. "She always wore it to the beach."

I swallow thickly. "She did?"

Hunter nods. For the first time in a long time, I really FEEL the loss. It hurts, but at the same time, it's good to feel. Without thinking, I reach out and squeeze Hunter's hand.

And because I win the award for the world's worst timing, that's when Jake walks in.

His gaze goes straight to where I'm holding Hunter's hand. I can practically feel the heat searing through me.

I jerk away from Hunter while Naomi just eyes her brother with a shark-like grin. Hunter grunts and lumbers to his feet. He hands me the silver cowboy hat before nodding at Jake and walking right out.

"Hello, brother," Naomi says. "Fancy meeting you here."

I haven't seen so much as a glimpse of Jake in days. I wish my thoughts and memories were too generous with the man, but Jake in the flesh is better by far.

Though I might prefer the Jake in my memories who doesn't totally ditch me only to show up randomly and tilt my world off its axis. This Jake looks more rigid than ever and absolutely green with jealousy.

Hunter-green with jealousy, one might say.

Which is ridiculous, seeing as there is zero anything between Hunter and me. I can see how it might not look that way. But if Jake makes the wrong assumptions, oh well! Call me cruel, but I don't mind the man suffering. He has no right to care whose hands I touch.

"Come on in," Naomi says. "The water's fine!"

"That's okay," he says. "I, uh, just wanted to check in."

I lift my shoulders in a casual shrug. "Everything's great. Hunter is *unbelievable*," I say, possibly with a little too much suggestion in my voice. "I'm so glad you hooked me up with him."

Jake's eyebrows go up, then slam right back down as his eyes narrow. Naomi swaps her fascinator for what I can only describe as a Sherlock Holmes-style hat, hiding her smile as she does so.

"He's also unbelievably hot," she adds. "Did you see the t-shirt he's wearing today? It looks like it was painted on."

Naomi tilts her head and winks. She's making her brother jealous, and I really want her to be my new best friend.

"Hot doesn't exactly qualify him to renovate a house," Jake grumbles.

"Are you worried about his qualifications?" I ask. "Because you were the one who recommended him."

He props his hands on his hips. Naomi opens another hat box and pulls out a purple beret. "Come on, No Fun. You need a hat. Lo, did I tell you Jake's nickname growing up was No Fun?"

"You did not tell me. That seems like a perfect name for him."

I've lost the edge to my voice now. My sisters have accused me of being too forgiving—*which, how is that a bad thing?*—and I can't maintain my irritation with Jake. Especially not when I find his irrational jealousy so amusing.

"I am *not* no fun." Jake glares at his sister.

I'm not sure what makes me grab the hat with the bears hanging from the brim, but I hold it out to Jake, a challenge in my eyes. "Prove it." I pause while we stare each other down, then add, "No Fun."

The moment he hesitates feels way too long. Just when I'm about to drop my hand, he reaches for the hat, our fingers brushing for longer than they need to while his eyes burn into mine.

Still keeping his gaze on me, Jake slips the hat on his head. Tiny bears dance around his still-frowning face.

"You look ridiculous," Naomi says, giggling.

Jake scoffs. "Lo, what do you think?"

He called me Lo.

I tilt my head to the side, pretending to study him. Actually, I'm not pretending. I *am* studying him, grateful for an excuse to do so without hiding it. His gray eyes look darker in the dim closet light, and his jaw looks freshly shaved this morning. I bet if I ran my hand over his cheek, it would make a delicious raspy sound.

"Well?" he asks.

My brain almost explodes as he strikes a dramatic pose, cocking one hip and raising one hand over his head to grasp the doorframe.

It is so NOT Jake. And despite the fact that he's channeling the playful side I saw the night with Liam, he still looks seriously hot.

Naomi erupts into laughter. "From No Fun to SO Fun!"

Jake is still looking at me, waiting for an answer. His gray eyes are like steel, slicing through me.

"It's a good look on you," I say finally. "The bears really bring out your eyes."

"I like yours too," he says, the tiniest of tiny smiles tilting his mouth up on one side, barely visible to the naked eye.

I'd keep any hat on for that smile.

"So, you're going through hats?" he asks.

"And stationery." I toe a box toward him, one I found on a shelf behind some shoes. "This box is full of it."

Jake crouches down, opening the box and thumbing through the various cards, papers, and envelopes. The bears on his hat dance as he moves, and I try not to laugh.

"I remember you saying you and Gennie wrote letters," he says, and I can only nod, thinking of how I won't see her familiar handwriting on the outside of any more envelopes.

"Like actual letters?" Naomi asks. "I didn't think anyone wrote letters anymore."

"It's a dying art, for sure," I say. "But Gran wrote me every other week, and I loved it. There's something lasting about a letter. Something tangible. And romantic, too—though obviously, my letters with Gran were *not*. But some of the most powerful declarations of love in history, we only have because someone wrote them in a letter."

Love letters—specifically love letters—have always held appeal. It's what drew me to Greenwood's Master's program. Dr. Banerjee, a resident scholar at Greenwood, is a leading expert on Willa Fremont, a 20th-century American poet who fell in love with her editor through letters.

Jake studies me closely, and I try not to squirm. "A romantic and a poet. That's quite a combination."

"You're only half-right," I quickly correct. "I'm not a poet. Just someone who loves to study them. I'm definitely a romantic though. Always have been."

Owning this aspect of my personality in front of Jake makes every part of my body feel warm. It shouldn't mean much, but it feels significant somehow.

He offers me another almost-smile in response, the corners of his lips barely lifting, but it still sets my heart to pounding. A small smile from Jake carries the weight of a thousand grins.

Naomi clears her throat. "Oh, shoot. I've got to go pick up Liam from summer camp." She hops up, bumping her hip into Jake's as she passes. "Don't do anything I wouldn't do in here!" she calls in a lilting voice that makes my cheeks flame.

I don't know Naomi well enough to know what she would or wouldn't do, but I've got a list suddenly forming of things I'd like to do with Jake. In here. Out there. Anywhere, really. Based on the way he's still scorching me with his gaze, I'm not the only one.

Whiplash much, Mr. Fieldstone?

Before we can do or not do any of the things we might be envisioning, a scream from downstairs breaks through the tension.

"Why is there a pelican in the house?"

SEVENTEEN

Jake

I LEAN against the back wall of The Round Up, beer in hand, while Benedict reracks on the only public pool table on Oakley Island.

We could play at Benedict's place. He's got his own table. And everything else he could possibly need. Not to mention all the stuff he doesn't need but owns anyway. But his house still feels a little too much like a museum for casual hangouts. He keeps saying he's going to do something about it. That he'll make the place he inherited from his mother his own. But that would require him to move off his boat, and I'd put money on that never happening.

The Round Up is the only other bar on the island besides Ned's place, and it's half as classy. Which is saying something, considering Ned's pirate decor and questionable taste in music. But the beer is cheap, and the company is mostly tourists. Important to Benedict because locals will always find reasons to talk to the man who owns the entire island, and, well, it isn't Ned's place. It shouldn't matter to me as much as it does, but there it is.

"Your break." Benedict straightens and steps away from the table. He reaches for his beer while I position the cue ball. "I could invite Jessa. You remember her?" he asks, diving back into a conversation I hoped was over. "The swimsuit model? For a week on the boat, I bet she'd come. She wasn't *not* into you."

"Way to convince me, man. That's one of my top priorities. I'm looking for a woman who isn't *not* into me."

"Look, I'm not the one being difficult. I'm asking you to spend a week on a boat with your very best friend and any number of beautiful women, and you've given me a dozen different reasons why you can't."

There's really only one reason. And the last time I saw that reason, she was wearing a dress covered in lines from Shakespeare's eighteenth sonnet. I read *Shall I compare thee to a summer's day* right off her shoulder.

And it took all my willpower not to keep her in that closet until I read every line off every inch of that fabric.

I miss my shot. "I don't know."

Benedict shakes his head and sinks his next ball. He hinted earlier that he knows what's really going on, that my mind is occupied elsewhere, but he won't come right out and say it. At least not yet. He'll give me the chance to tell him on my terms, which I appreciate. I just don't know what to tell him.

That I can't stop thinking about Lo? That last night, while I was trying to fall asleep, my heart rate spiked simply because I could hear her *walking* around in her bedroom?

That I pressed my palm against the wall, wishing for some point of connection to her?

What even *is* that?

Then I went a step (or ten) below that desperation.

I found Lo's Instagram feed. And I went through all of it. Looking at all the photos. Reading all the captions AND comments. Watching the videos.

Did I feel a strange dip in my stomach watching the sideways video filming Lo falling down the stairs onto me? Yes, I did. I did NOT read the comments there. But I may have watched the ending more than a dozen times.

In case there was any question—she *definitely* nuzzled me.

Her profile practically bursts with the vivacious energy and light I've come to associate with Eloise. She's funny and winsome and smart and responds to almost all the comments personally. It was strange to see Gennie's house progress on the screen when the actual house sits a hundred yards away from my front door. Seeing Lo's college days was even stranger.

But even being faced with how recently those college days were didn't make me glad for the distance. It didn't make me feel any better about the way I ghosted her after the almost kiss.

Seeing her wide smile and bright blue eyes only made me feel like an idiot for letting her go. And when I couldn't stand the distance anymore and stopped by to see her only to find her holding Hunter's hand today ...

Yeah. There's a reason I can't sink any balls.

"Dude," Benedict says when I scratch, sending the cue ball into a corner pocket. "Where are you?"

"Not here," I mutter.

"Clearly. Want to talk about it?"

The thing is, Benedict would understand. Not that people would know it from his outward impression, which I know is a mask. He comes across as the quintessential rich playboy—beach edition. His light brown hair is a little too long in the back. He wears designer board shorts like actual shorts and his loafers are worn almost to the point of falling apart—but retail for a few hundred dollars.

He hosts weeklong parties on his yacht and has several supermodels' numbers saved in his phone.

But at his core, Benedict is a genuinely empathetic guy. Better at talking about his emotions than most. Better than I am, for sure. If I admitted any of this out loud to him, Benedict would listen well and have great advice, thanks to the decades of family therapy his mother forced him to endure when he was a kid, therapy he willingly continued once she died.

It hasn't helped him figure his life out, but when you're a billionaire island owner, I'm not sure what there is to figure out. Maybe he doesn't ever want to settle down or buff out the tarnishes in his image. But I suspect underneath the devil-may-care attitude, there's something he's running from too.

Maybe I'll bring that up if he doesn't let this go, like a game of conversational chicken. We'll see who cracks first.

Benedict breaks this time, sinking two solids before he misses. I take my shot, and the ball rebounds off the far wall and rolls aimlessly into the middle of the table. I never play this badly, but considering how distracted I've been, I'm happy the cue ball is even making contact.

"What if we take the trip with just the two of us?" I suggest.

Well, the two of us and the ten-person crew it takes to

run the monstrosity that is Benedict's boat. He grumbles when I call it a yacht. Says it sounds pretentious. But is a boat that has a complete kitchen staff, housekeeping, and its own captain *anything* but pretentious?

"That sounds fun. Your company has been so fantastic lately, I'm sure we'd have a great time. A real-life bromance," he says dryly. "Come on, man. If you don't tell me what's going on, all I've got to go on are Frank's updates on TikTok, which have been admittedly colorful, but I'm positive they don't contain the whole truth."

I may have cracked in stalking Lo's Instagram, but I've vowed never to get on TikTok. According to a text from Naomi, Frank posted a TikTok of my conversation with Lo outside of Sweet Tea and Toast. According to him, it was a full-on proposal and we'll be getting married any day now. My love life has turned into the digital equivalent of Frank's legendary fishing story. The one where every time he tells it, the bluefin tuna he wrangled onto his own boat with a broken line during a raging thunderstorm gains twenty pounds and a foot in length.

Benedict sinks another ball into the corner pocket and levels me with a stare before rounding the table and positioning himself for a second shot. This one he misses, so he steps out of the way. "Talk to me."

I try to line up a shot, knowing before I even move that it won't go in. As predicted, it doesn't. "I don't know what you want me to say. There really isn't much to tell."

"See if this tracks. You met a hot girl"—he holds up a hand as I glare—"sorry, a hot *woman*. You fell for her, but because you're the star of your own tragedy, you blew your chance through severe self-sabotagery."

He's remarkably accurate. "Sabotagery isn't a word."

"It is now. I just trademarked it while you were busy with your self-sabotagery."

"She's a client."

"She's not a client. Her grandmother was. It's her estate that's paying you for your time, not any of the sisters. Try again."

"She's only twenty-one," I say.

"And you're only thirty-two. She's an adult. You're an adult. Who cares?"

I don't, really. I've dismissed most of the reasons to stay away from Eloise too many times in my own head to even *need* this conversation with Benedict. It feels like I'm guessing all the wrong answers on a multiple-choice test. But there's still one more reason I haven't mentioned. The biggest one. The one where everything starts out great, and she leaves me in the end.

Because I live on a small island with its own peculiar way of life. It isn't for most people. It wasn't for Margo, though I'm very clear that location wasn't our only issue. Would Lo want to stay on Oakley? Is the island enough for her?

Am *I* enough?

"It's okay to admit you're scared," he says, his tone serious.

If those words had come from anyone in the world but him, I would protest. Instead, I sink my first shot in a while.

"But answer this for me," Benedict says. "If she walked away tomorrow, if you never saw her again, how would that make you feel? Because if you keep resisting, keep giving into fear, eventually she *will* walk away. Women don't like to play games."

I lift an eyebrow. He's one to talk about playing games. His life is basically a Monopoly board where he's got hotels on all the properties. Hotels filled with available women, all hoping for a chance with him. Island life hasn't cramped his style. But I don't have a billion dollars. Or an island. Or a boat.

"You're the expert on women," I say with a shrug.

He smirks at my expression. "The women I spend time with know what they're getting right from the start. And it's not *that* many women. Despite the rumors and Frank's two cents on Tiktok. If I'm playing a game, it's only with people who volunteer willingly."

I sink two more shots before finally answering his question. "Eloise leaving is already a foregone conclusion. She isn't from Oakley. Why would she stay here?"

This conversation is pointless. I've never even kissed the woman, but it feels like I'm already justifying our breakup.

"I don't know," Benedict says, lining up a shot after I miss mine. "Because she just inherited a great house on the beach? Because she's falling in love?"

I roll my eyes. "She's not falling in love. And they're selling the house."

"So, change her mind. You've always wanted that house anyway. If you marry—"

"Stop. No." I run a hand through my hair. "I don't have any claim to that house. I wouldn't do that. I'm not thinking of it like that."

"I wasn't saying you'd marry her just to get the house. Might be a nice perk though."

"There are three sisters. They all have an equal interest in the house, and I can't factor myself into the equation at all."

"Honestly, Jake, don't you think Genevieve *expected* you to factor yourself into the equation? She wanted her grand-daughters here on the island. Long enough to renovate the house, all while you're right next door. She was explicit about that part, right? Haven't you ever asked yourself why?"

I have. And I don't have answers, only suspicions that Benedict may be right. "I was her attorney. We were friends, yes. But it still seems pretty far-fetched she would have banked on anything else happening."

"But maybe she *hoped* for it?"

"Hoped for what?"

I glance up to see Naomi leaning against the pool table like she's been there all night. Or at least the past few minutes.

Has she been listening to Benedict grill me about Eloise?

The gleam in her eye gives me the answer.

"Nothing," I answer, shooting Benedict a look that says he better keep his mouth closed. "What are you doing here?"

She shrugs. "Just meeting a friend."

"Where's Liam?"

She narrows her eyes. "Don't ask that question like you think I forgot him at a gas station somewhere. He's with Harriett. She's teaching him how to make gluten-free cookies with almond flour." She leans to the left, her eyes focusing on Benedict, who is about to beat me. Again. "Hi, Ben," she sing-songs. "How's the conversation? Has Jake admitted he's falling in love?"

"I'm not—" My eyes dart from Benedict to Naomi. "Wait, have the two of you talked about me?"

I'm not surprised they've talked. Benedict is almost as much a big brother to Naomi as I am. But I don't love that they talked about *me*. It's even worse than knowing Harriett and Frank and, let's be real, everyone else on Oakley is talking about me. This feels personal.

"If you weren't more stubborn than a pack of old mules,

we wouldn't need to," Naomi says, her arms folded across her chest.

"I don't even need to dignify that comment with a response."

"Then just admit you like her," Naomi says.

I distract myself by chalking up my pool cue, which is stupid because Benedict just won, and there are other people waiting to play.

"It doesn't matter even if I do," I finally say. "As soon as the house is done, she'll leave. She's got a life. Plans. A million reasons not to stay on Oakley."

"I got the impression her plans were pretty fluid," Naomi says. "I think you're just being cagey because you're scared."

"That's exactly what I said." Benedict gives my sister a high five. "He likes her, and he's freaking out."

"Totally."

I drop onto a barstool. "*He* is right here, and *he* is not amused."

"And *he* needs to stop being an idiot."

"You might as well admit it, man," Benedict says. "I saw the Instagram video. I've never seen you look at a woman like you looked at Lo."

"She should never have posted that video," I mutter. *Says the guy who watched it a dozen times.*

I finish the last of my beer. I don't need my best friend telling me this is something different, something real. I can feel the difference. Before Margo, I had a few other relationships I'd call serious, ones I thought had potential to last.

What I feel for Lo right now—without a relationship, without even a real kiss—makes all of those past relationships feel like child's play.

I think about the words Naomi and Ben are throwing around. Is it possible to fall in love with someone when you aren't even in a relationship? When you haven't known each other very long?

No. That answer feels clear.

But ... with Lo, my feelings are like standing on the cusp of something. I see what could be. And it very much involves love.

If she weren't leaving. I can forget my other reasons for wanting to distance myself from Lo. It's *this* one that made me run after the night we babysat Liam. It's this one making me want to argue with my sister and best friend about my feelings. This one I can't get past.

Maybe you should give her a reason to stay, Jacob.

I have to wonder—if Gennie were really here, is this what she would say? More importantly, if she really told me this, would I listen?

Because there's a nagging secondary reason I'm holding back that has nothing to do with Lo and everything to do with my inability to know how to manage this emotion. I've never been good at this. What Margo warned Lo about me wasn't so wrong. And if I couldn't handle a relationship where I felt so much less than I already feel for Lo ...

"Maybe it doesn't matter either way," Naomi says. "She and Hunter seem to get along swimmingly."

"Is that so?" Benedict asks.

"He's single. Hot. Probably emotionally available."

Even though I know she's just saying this to get a rise out of me, it does exactly that. I immediately feel my shoulders tense, and my grip on the bottle of beer feels like enough to shatter glass.

"She's a free woman," I say, though it comes out more like a growl.

Benedict shakes his head. "So, if they walked in here together, you'd be totally fine with that?"

"Sure."

"Let's put this to the test," Naomi says, giving me a look I do not like at all. It's the expression she wore every time she suggested something that got us both in trouble growing up.

"Fine. But how does that work exactly? Am I supposed to set them up?" Saying the words makes my whole mouth taste sour.

Naomi tilts her head toward the door. "You don't need to. They just arrived. Together."

My head snaps up. And just as my sister said, there's Lo, walking into the bar with *Hunter*. Smiling. Laughing. And is she … *touching him?*

"It's fine." I say the words I'm thinking out loud.

They convince no one. Not even me.

Benedict leans back against the wall and takes a long draw from his beer. Naomi hops up on the stool beside me, leaning in.

"I was supposed to meet Lo, but I think I'll give them a minute." She tilts her head. "They're really cute together."

"Just *adorable*," Benedict says, and I punch him in the shoulder.

It is fine. It will be fine. Hunter and Lo—as I watch, I try to wrap my brain around the idea. But my brain is firing back with *does not compute* signals, combined with jealousy rising like a tsunami in my chest. I feel a single bead of sweat track a slow and steady path down my spine.

Lo laughs again, though I swear Hunter hasn't said a word. And then she spins, pointing to something on her back. It takes me a minute, but when Hunter tilts his head, I realize he's reading the Shakespeare lines on her dress. Lo moves her hair out of the way, exposing her slender neck.

And that IS IT.

The fuse I didn't realize was lit reaches the end. I see not

202

red but black as I stalk across the room. I'm only vaguely aware of Naomi and Benedict laughing behind me.

I don't care about them.

Or how this looks.

Or my objections.

Nothing matters except Eloise.

EIGHTEEN

Lo

I LURED Hunter to the bar with promises of discussing bathrooms. I'm like someone in a windowless van proffering candy and puppies. But in this case, the van is a bar I've never been to, and the candy is a discussion about toilets. He's been pushing me to make a decision for a week, and I've been putting it off because who wants to talk about toilets? Not this girl.

But Hunter DOES.

"This isn't for fun?" he clarified before we left Gran's house.

"Not even an ounce. Just beer and talking about low-flow toilets."

THIS is the kind of promise it takes to get my contractor out to a bar.

Lies. All lies. But it worked! Naomi is meeting us here, and I'm hoping to do a little Oakley Island matchmaking of my own. I didn't see her when I came in, so Hunter and I headed to the bar where I put my Shirley Temple and his beer on my tab. I noticed him eyeing my dress, clearly trying to read the words.

"It's Shakespeare," I tell him, turning so he can read the clearest lines on my back. Also—it's a lot less awkward than Hunter trying to read my *front*.

I've just pulled my hair to the side when I glance up and see Jake storming across the bar. And I do mean STORMING. If little lightning bolts and a funnel cloud formed above his head, it would only be natural. I'm honestly surprised there are none.

Why is this sexy? And why does the fire in his eyes—which looks like it was lit by a blowtorch of jealousy—make a thrill move through me in a full-body shudder?

It shouldn't. Because talking to me for a few minutes at Gran's before running off (again) doesn't make up for days of ghosting me. Not after the night with Liam where we almost kissed.

Correction: where I almost kissed him. He started it. But I was the one putting myself out there. Even if it was just the teensiest peck not full on the lips but on the corner of his mouth. It counts for something! It was brave!

So, no. NO. Jake doesn't get to decide when and where he gets to stake some claim. He can't decide to be jealous when it suits him. I straighten my spine to counteract all the melting happening inside me and cross my arms, ready for this battle.

Do I want to win or lose?

I'm not sure. I only know I'm ready to fight. And if this fight ends with me in Jake's arms? Then I've won.

"Incoming," Hunter mutters into his beer.

For a moment, I don't think Jake is going to stop. I prepare for him to crowd me right into the bar, but he stops short before plowing into me. Just the toes of our shoes touching, his preppy leather boat shoes challenging down my yellow sandals.

Jake's eyes are wild. His cheeks and neck are flushed, and it's like all his muscles are flexed, veins popping out on his forearms and one pulsing right by his temple. Veins are highly underrated. Jake's could totally sport their own twelve-month calendar, and I would line right up to buy.

AFTER I tell him where he can stick his back-and-forth, wishy-washy attitude toward me.

I hold his gaze and keep my voice steady and devoid of emotion. "Mr. Fieldstone."

"*Ms. Markham.*"

He says my name like it's a curse. But the kind of curse you WANT. The deep timbre of his voice has goose bumps standing up and doing the wave all across my skin.

"What brings you to this fine establishment on such a lovely evening?" I ask.

He doesn't answer. But his eyes narrow and flick toward Hunter. *I knew it! He's jealous. If only he knew I brought Hunter to set up with Naomi.* But I'm not about to show my hand.

I'd rather test this theory. You know—because I'm all about scientific experiments. Almost failing bio taught me to be meticulous when it comes to testing theories.

Angling my body toward Hunter, I touch his shoulder. Briefly, because I'd like to still have a living, breathing contractor at the end of the night.

"Do you think you could find us a table? Somewhere"—I glance around the bar—"tucked away?"

A sound rumbles from Jake's chest. *Did he just GROWL?* I wish the sound didn't send euphoria zinging through my body from head to feet.

206

Hunter's beard twitches, and I could swear he's trying not to grin. With a nod, he walks off, leaving me to face the wrath of Jake.

I shouldn't be so excited by the prospect. Why am I?

I've never once gotten hot and bothered thinking about making a man jealous, and I've never been the type to poke an angry bear.

Except, apparently, when it comes to Jake Fieldstone. He is a grizzly, and I've got a poking stick in each hand, sharpened to a point.

I chew the tiny straw in my drink, and when Jake's eyes burn into me, unblinking, I gulp down the rest of my Shirley Temple until it's only ice. I lean back, slamming the glass onto the bar without even looking.

"I'll take another. Make it a double," I say, channeling my inner vixen. If such a thing even exists.

It takes half a second for Jake's intensity to crack. Now he looks like he's about to laugh. "Did you just order a double Shirley Temple?"

"What of it?" I've always wanted to say *Make it a double* in a bar. Even if it's about a sprite with simple syrup and a generous dose of cherries.

"The bartender isn't even here."

Jake tips his chin, and I glance over to see the bartender flirting with a small group of women. Guess I won't be getting that drink.

"What do you want, Jake?" I ask.

Come on. Tell me seeing me with Hunter made you raging jealous, and now you've realized you want me—despite the age gap and the excuse about being a client and whatever other excuses you can tack on.

SAY. IT.

"Did you know it's illegal to post public videos of other people without first receiving written permission?"

"What?" My head is spinning like a top shot out of a cannon. He wants to talk about the Instagram video?

And then it hits me: Mr. Avoidance is just being himself. He came over here to confront me, but not about Instagram. He's constructing a shield for himself, deflecting. Which is par for the course with him. But I'm not going to do this.

I take a slow, steadying breath and speak in careful, measured words. "If you want, I can take the video down now."

He opens his mouth. Closes it again. I gaze into those gray eyes of his. Not blinking. Not showing any sign of the weakness I feel in his presence. I channel my inner Sadie—the fiercest of my sisters. I channel Gran, who could hold her own while saying *bless your heart*.

"When you're ready to talk about why you're really upset, come find me."

And then I walk away.

I hope I look brave. Because inside, I'm terrified. Instinct tells me this is the right move. But maybe Jake really is just upset about being on Instagram. Maybe he doesn't think I was with Hunter, or if he did, he doesn't care. Maybe—

A hand slides around my waist.

Not any hand. I know this hand. Even after only a few weeks, it's like my body has programmed Jake's touch into the system.

It's why I don't resist as he tugs me through a side door and onto a dark area of the outside deck where the sound and scent of the ocean permeates the air.

I don't fight.

I should.

Maybe?

But I'm just so tired of the back and forth. We need to stop this push-and-pull. *It's one or the other*, I think as Jake lets go of me to pace on the small deck, his hands digging into his hair.

Push away, once and for all.

Or ... pull closer.

I know what I want. And for once in my life, I take it.

Stepping in his path, I slide my arms around his neck and drag his mouth to mine.

Only—it isn't so much dragging. Because the moment I touch him, Jake is right there. With me. Giving me exactly what I want.

For once, we're in sync, our mouths wild and desperate, all the pent-up tension releasing in a flood. I'm practically trying to climb Jake, needing him closer. I gasp against his lips as his hands find my waist, lifting me to perch on the railing so our heads are level and he's standing between my knees.

"You're so short I'm straining my neck," he whispers between kisses.

"And you're so tall you ... you ... mmm."

I have no teasing insults to throw back. Words have dried up like a desert. I'm living inside the mirage. Everything is hazy and bright and perfect as Jake draws me closer.

It's like we're trying to memorize each other, trying to consume one another. His stubble grazes my cheek, and I can't wait to see the beard burn he'll leave behind. I want him to mark my skin with it, not just on my cheeks. I want to see evidence of him on my neck and shoulders, my collarbone.

More places that are already eager for his touch, places that definitely are not going to be touched tonight.

Jake doesn't push for more than this, and this is enough.

It makes my heart want to burst at the way he's content to kiss me thoroughly without going for more. His hands aren't wandering far, remaining on my waist, my back, the curve of my hip.

Even this is almost too much. His mouth is hot and hungry, confident and sure. He touches me like he owns me —no awkward fumbling or sneaking toward what's next.

He's telling me this kiss is enough for now. I am enough. His willingness to stay right here, reveling in these kisses, tells me so much about the kind of lover Jake would be.

Not just in the physical sense. Jake is a man who, once he makes the choice, he will give himself wholly. Fully. All-consumingly.

He will love with all he has, treasuring each moment in itself, no rushing, no losing himself in desire. His passion is a roaring flash flood—but his masterful control banks it and holds it back.

I could kiss this man every day for the rest of my life.

The thought should scare me, but it only makes me fist his shirt in my hands, pulling him closer.

His lips slow, focusing all that wild heat into teasing nips and light brushes. Every kiss, every man before this has been nothing. Less than nothing. There is only Jake.

And while this should terrify me given the way he keeps running away, just for tonight, I refuse to be scared.

He pulls back just far enough that our foreheads touch. I love how heavily he's breathing, showing me he is every bit as affected as I am.

"Hi," he says.

"I think we're well past casual greetings."

I run my fingers up his neck to tangle them in his hair. He shudders under my touch, and his hands tighten on my hips.

"What are we doing, Jake?" I ask. "What is this?"

He nips at my bottom lip before whispering against them. "I'm done fighting."

"I don't know that I'd say we've been fighting—"

"No. I'm done fighting *this*. How I feel." His hand slides through my hair and to the back of my neck, his fingertips pressing into my skin in a way that feels possessive in the best way possible. "You," he says between heavy breaths, "are insufferable."

From anyone else, this would be an insult. But from Jake? It sounds like he has just told me I am the sexiest woman alive.

I LOVE it.

Laughter spills out of me, and he kisses me like he's trying to capture the sound. Like he's greedy for it. Greedy for me.

I pull back, but only a little, so my lips still brush his when I speak. "You have such a way with words, Mr. Fieldstone. Tell me more."

He opens his mouth to do what I ask or to kiss me—I'm honestly not sure and would be happy about either—when there's a crack. The whole railing lurches under me.

I let out a little squeal as Jake hoists me against his chest, stumbling back until he hits the wall with an *oomph*. As we watch, the whole wooden railing splits and falls to the sand below with a crash. It's only a few feet to the sand, not like I would have died or anything.

"You're always saving me," I murmur into Jake's neck.

"If you don't like it, stop needing to be saved."

I tilt my head back just a little, enough to see his eyes, almost black in the dim light. "I never said I didn't like it."

People are suddenly running from the back patio and spilling out from the side door. The bartender pushes out of the door next to us, followed by Naomi, Hunter, and another

211

guy who grins widely when he sees how Jake has me in a bridal hold.

A little embarrassed, I start to wiggle out of his arms, but Jake's grip tightens, and I give up. Might as well enjoy the sensation of his arms around me for as long as possible.

"You're not getting away now," he murmurs in my ear. And then, as he starts to back away from the crowd, he says to the bartender, "You should really get that checked out. Someone could get hurt."

Me, I think as Jake strides away with me snuggled to his chest. *I'm going to get hurt.*

But I can't bring myself to care.

NINETEEN

Lo

"SO, you don't hate living there too much?" Sadie is on speakerphone, and in the background, I can hear her fingers flying over a keyboard.

I choose my words carefully, leaning against the island in Gran's kitchen, which has no counter and no cabinet doors. The whole room smells of sawdust, and I love it.

"It's better than living with Mom and Craig, that's for sure. I get to the beach most days, and the people are really nice."

While those things are technically true, it's not the full truth. Or even partial truth.

"I'm glad you're surviving," Sadie says.

Surviving—ha! Oh, if she only knew.

But she doesn't know. And I'm not about to tell either of my sisters that I'm dating Gran's lawyer. The man neither

Merritt nor Sadie trusted from the outset—even if Sadie joked about his hotness. If they knew we were *actually* together ... it wouldn't go over so well. Merritt would probably be on the first plane down here to replace me. And I'm not about to do anything to risk what I have with Jake.

If my life were a movie, I'm at the part where time passes quickly, moment by delicious moment, all backed by some kind of upbeat soundtrack. I know it won't always be like this: waking up every morning with a smile, thinking of when I'll get to see Jake. I knock on the wall, getting a knock in return if he's not already out for a run. The man does love to run.

If he is already out when I wake up, he returns with coffee just the way I like it—with enough cream and sugar to bake a cake. We have breakfast on the porch if it's not already too muggy, or in one of our kitchens. Before Jake leaves for the office and I walk to the big house, we spend as much time as we can kissing.

We kiss like it's a currency about to be taken out of circulation and we need to spend every cent. Which ... is maybe a bad comparison since it already assumes this thing between us has an ending.

As optimistic as I am, I have a healthy dose of cynical realist living inside me watching everything with a narrow, assessing gaze. I have to beat her off with a stick sometimes.

Lately? I've done a lot of beating.

"I heard there was a tile setback," Sadie says.

"Just a tiny one."

"How tiny?"

I specifically told the tile guy NOT to give me an exact estimate on the delay. Because then I'd feel bad lying to my sisters about it. So, I literally do not know. "A week or two? I'm not sure. It's been ordered."

"There were no other, similar tiles?" Sadie asks.

Hunter chooses that moment to walk through. The look he gives me says *You could just choose something else for the kitchen backsplash.* He doesn't need to speak the words because after weeks of working with him, I've learned to decipher his beard twitches, his eyebrow shifts, and his silence.

"Sorry. Instagram has spoken."

"Maybe Instagram shouldn't be allowed to speak," Hunter mutters, lumbering off down the hall. I hear a wet saw start up near the main bathroom on the first floor.

I head outside to avoid the noise. And because Benedict King is on his way to approve the exterior choices. Sadie insisted on being "present," which I suspect was a direct order from Merritt.

"Do you really think it's wise to let your followers pick things out?" Sadie asks.

I close the front door behind me and sit down on the top step. It's already hot, but the ocean breeze makes it bearable.

"If it were just random Joe Schmoe Instagram, no. It would be stupid," I tell her. "But that's not my followers. I have big design firms and some really popular DIY and reno bloggers following along. It's been helpful, and the house will look stunning."

After my viral video featuring Jake (which he said I didn't need to delete after all), I had a massive influx of followers, all invested in seeing this whole house transform. Invested in wallpaper and tile choices. Invested in Steve the pelican, who will be safely relocated this afternoon by a wildlife rescue team. (Who also found me on Instagram.) Invested in Jake's occasional appearances, plus getting glimpses of Hunter the silent contractor—who has his own hashtag now.

The most shocking thing is that my new followers are invested in ME.

I've invited my followers to help me choose everything from paint colors to countertops to backsplash tile. I set up polls in Instagram stories and had followers voting and fighting in the comments. It might sound scary to let strangers help make design choices, but I narrow down the options first. And I've picked up a lot of design-savvy followers, including a few giant accounts of house flippers. I literally squealed when I got a dm from an HGTV personality telling me how much she loves my content.

It's made the whole thing more fun—for me, not Hunter—and I think the house will turn out even better. Eventually.

Once we get the plumbing issues worked out. And the roofing situation. And the electrical problems.

Add in delays with a lot of supplies, and this is shaping up to be an even bigger project than I imagined. But I totally love the way it's turned interactive ... and lucrative. I've been able to make quite a bit from affiliate links and have had legitimate brands reaching out to partner with me.

I don't mind the delays in the least. They mean putting off any thoughts about the future. Despite how happy I am with the *now*, I don't know what this means for what's *next*. Right now, the future is the big F-word in my life. Because the future means leaving the island. Leaving Gran's house. Leaving Jake.

Or, at least, it did. My original plan had been to stay with Mom and Craig for a bit while applying to other grad programs and finding some kind of job. Assuming I got in somewhere else, I'd get my master's and then my PhD.

But now, thinking about leaving makes my insides—and the rest of me—squirm.

It's not JUST Jake, though he's a big part. I feel a connection to the island as a whole. I stop by and see Ned every day, even for a few minutes. Saying hi, trying to teach Bard quotes from more diverse authors. When I get lunch at Harriet's and am greeted like I've always lived here. Frank gave me the best haircut of my life last week and caught me up on island gossip by way of TikTok.

I try to at least get my feet touching the sand, if not the surf, daily. My light brown hair looks sun-kissed and golden. My pale skin is a warm peach. My arms feel stronger from pulling up carpets and ripping out drywall.

I feel ... whole. More familiar with myself—who I am, who I want to be.

But that doesn't mean I'm not also full of question marks. Jake and I haven't defined things. Not exactly. There are a lot of assumptions, and I REALLY hope we're assuming the same things.

Namely, that I might want to stay and build a life here. With him.

"How's your work?" I ask.

"Boring as usual. Just saving the free world from cyberattacks. The usual. Oh—Merritt wanted to know about the pipes."

I groan. The way this panned out is: I email weekly reports to Merritt, Merritt complains to Sadie, and Sadie calls me. This was fine when things were moving forward at a fast clip. But now that they aren't, I can't lie about the delays.

"Hunter has a plumber coming out. Not a big deal. It's just old house stuff."

"It actually is a kind of big deal," Sadie says. "Even a small delay equals dollar signs. And we've had a lot."

"You sound like Merritt."

"Hey—I resent that. Just try to keep things moving, Lo."

"I can't control most of the delays."

Who knew all the pipes would need to be replaced? Or that a lot of the electrical wasn't up to code? Or that the roof was leaking? Hunter can do a lot of things, but we have to hire actual plumbers and electricians and roofers. Which means waiting on them to show up and do the work before we can move on.

"Yeah, well—you can control things like tile," Sadie says. "Pick a similar one that's in stock. Who cares what your followers like?"

I'm not going to get into a discussion that turns into an argument about why I'm making the choices I'm making. Honestly, the backsplash my followers chose is my favorite too.

Am I slightly more invested in the house than I should be? Possibly.

Am I going to apologize for this or change course? Nope.

"It's fine, Sadie. A tiny delay, all things considered. And it's not like all the work stopped. While we're waiting for one thing, we're doing another. I'm not concerned."

I'm more concerned with two other things. One—the way my sisters are going to flip when they find out I'm dating Jake. And two—the longer I stay, the less I want to leave. The more I can picture staying here, running the bed and breakfast.

With Jake.

Not that I've told him this. It's way too soon when we haven't firmed up a commitment to each other. That's like stage five clinger material.

I can imagine the conversation:

Hey, Jake. I know we talked about taking things slow and we haven't decided what this is between us, but I think I want to forget

about academics and stay on this island, running this bed and break-
fast with you. Whaddya say?

I picture him bolting so fast, a cloud of dust follows behind him.

So, yeah. Delays give me more time to talk to the important people in my life about the things I want and am terrified to say out loud. There's the whole state-and-manifest-it mindset, but I'm more of a conceal-don't-feel kind of person.

Which is why I haven't told my sisters about Jake. I tell myself it's because I don't want to jinx it when things are so new.

The thing is though ... they don't FEEL new. They feel like forever.

And I'm absolutely not about to say that to Sadie or Merritt.

Or Jake.

"Well, I'm glad you're not concerned, but I've got Merritt breathing down my neck, so—"

"Hello?" a deep voice calls out.

I get to my feet in time to see Benedict King hopping out of a golf cart. I know who he is, but we haven't officially met.

"Is that him?" Sadie asks. "Let's switch to video."

"Just a sec." I step down from the porch and extend a hand to Benedict. "I'm Lo. Great to officially meet you!"

He gives my hand a firm shake. "I've heard a lot about you from Jake, but it's great to officially meet you. Benedict King. Everyone calls me Ben."

"Really? Jake's only ever used your whole name."

Ben is Jake's closest friend, which I hope makes this process more of a formality. His worn boat shoes, board shorts, and polo with sunglasses tucked into the collar ease my worry. With light brown hair and an easy smile, Benedict seems totally chill. Chill with a side of money. Everything about his appearance is the kind of effortless that screams *expensive*.

Ben grins. "Jake also wears a tie when it's ninety-five degrees outside. He's formal to a fault. I promise he's the exception, not the rule."

This makes me smile. "He has a hard time not calling me Eloise, too."

I clear my throat, remembering my sister is on the line and hoping she didn't pick up on just how familiar this exchange made my relationship with Jake sound.

I wave my phone. "My sister is on the phone and wanted to video in for this."

"No problem."

I switch the call over to video, and Sadie's face fills the screen. I'm shocked to see her in full makeup with her hair curled.

"Why has he heard a lot about you from *Jake*?" she asks, suspicion dripping from her voice.

"Why are you dressed like you just got home from a club?"

That shuts her up. At least, for now.

Ben clears his throat. Rather than flipping the screen around, I turn the phone so they can see each other. At least, I'm hoping they can both see each other.

"Sadie, this is Benedict King. Ben—meet my sister, Sadie."

A slow smile creeps over Ben's face, making him look every bit the ladies' man he's rumored to be.

"Well, hello," he says in a smooth voice.

"Nice shirt, Benedict. Lo, you wanna tilt the camera a little so I can see Mr. Arnold's face?"

Ben's smile is gone, replaced with a furrowed brow as he tries to figure out what's wrong with his shirt. "My last name isn't Arnold," he says. "It's King."

I could explain that Sadie likes to mess with people but decide to just let it ride.

"There you are," Sadie says, clucking her tongue as I tilt the camera to get Ben's head in the frame. "Such a pretty face! I bet you get everything you want without any effort. Toss around a smile, a few stacks of cash ..."

I turn the phone back to me so I can glare at Sadie. "Hey, now! Let's keep things peaceful. Remember, Ben is here to approve things," I say through gritted teeth. "Be nice."

"That's okay," Ben says. He's playing it off like he's a good sport, but his cheeks and neck are red, and I can see his hands bunched into fists in his pockets. Clearly, her comments struck a chord.

"Shall we?" I ask. Jake is supposed to meet us, but he texted me that a meeting was running long.

Ben plucks the phone from my hand so he can talk directly to my sister. I guess he likes a challenge too.

Somehow, I become the third wheel to a video chat showdown between Sadie and Ben. I answer questions, but most of the discussion—read: fighting—is between them as we circle the house. Whether it's because he takes his job seriously or he's reacting to Sadie, beach chill Ben is gone. He may be dressed like a rich yacht club playboy, but now that his intensity is at full tilt, it rivals Merritt's.

"I don't care about your timelines," he almost shouts at the phone screen. "These paint colors aren't from the approved list, and we don't allow this kind of shingle."

Thankfully, nothing has been painted or shingled yet—I just have the samples set up on one side of the house, and I painted two shutters with samples my Instagram followers voted on this week.

"Jake should have given you a list of approved colors and

materials," Ben says, looking at me. "Did he fail to provide that?"

He did, but I immediately want to defend him. I have a vague memory of him saying he needed to get something to me, but that was back at our very first lunch. Embarrassment climbs its way up my chest.

"Uh, no." I scratch my leg where a mosquito has just bitten the heck out of me. I swear they're bigger here, like some kind of prehistoric insect that survived whatever killed the dinosaurs.

Ben's eyes flash with amusement for the first time since Sadie started giving him a hard time. "Ah, I see. You two have been too *busy* for discussions."

I'd like to hop inside the hole along the side of the porch, still open from when plumbers came this week to start work on the pipes. I give him a look I hope Sadie can't see. One that says ixnay on the akeJay.

"What does *that* mean?" Sadie demands. "And who are *they*?"

We've worked our way around the whole outside of the house and are back at the circular front drive where the wildlife rescue people have arrived for Steve.

"Hello!" a woman in full-on cargo attire calls. Her skin is a rich brown a few shades darker than her uniform, and her smile immediately puts me at ease. "I'm Mandy from Wildlife Services. This is my summer intern, Charles."

Charles on the other hand, is the picture of UNease, scanning the sky with wide eyes. He looks ready to hop back into the truck with his almost translucent skin, multiple earrings, and purple mohawk.

"We're here about the pelican," Mandy says.

"What pelican?" Sadie calls.

Ben says, "Shh! Let's see how this plays out."

I step forward, ignoring my sister and Ben. "I'm Lo. Thanks for coming. Steve—that's the pelican—is on the screened-in porch. You can follow me through the house."

I continue to pretend like I don't hear Sadie's remarks as we all walk into the house. When I shoot Ben a look, he only shrugs and turns the volume down. Down, but not low enough to quiet Sadie's shriek when Steve flies right into the house like he did the first day.

This time, I stay on my feet, but Ben trips over a box of tile samples, hitting the floor. Charles the mohawked intern dives into the fireplace—which has to hurt—and curls into a ball.

Steve flaps around the room a few times while Mandy tries to shoo him back toward the porch. I take the opportunity to rescue my phone from Ben. Sadie is laughing so hard, tears are rolling down her face, taking some of her makeup with them.

"Did you see that?" Sadie wheezes. "That raptor took out Cumberbatch."

"My name is Benedict *King*," Ben says from the floor, where he's examining his broken sunglasses.

"I cannot wait to tell Merritt about this. She will die," Sadie says.

"Please don't tell Merritt. Everything is under control." But she won't see it that way.

And maybe it's NOT so under control. Steve takes flight again, coming to perch on the new chandelier made out of dangling oyster shells.

"What's under control?"

Jake waltzes into the room, shooting me a smile which quickly fades as he takes in Ben on the floor, the intern singing "Kum-Ba-Yah" from inside the fireplace, and the massive bird on the chandelier.

"Let me catch you up," Ben says, getting to his feet. "There's a killer pelican in the house, and the outside choices don't meet my approval because you failed to provide your—"

Ben cuts himself off, eyes shooting straight to me before he says the word I know he was about to say. *Girlfriend.* He was about to call me Jake's girlfriend.

I'm grateful Ben seems to have picked up on my cues—and what is now almost panic—but I hope Jake doesn't. I don't want him to think I haven't told my sisters because I'm ashamed or embarrassed when neither sentiment is true.

Ben clears his throat. "You failed to provide *Lo* with the standard island requirements, so she'll need to update her choices, and I'll come out another day to approve."

Jake frowns, his eyes bouncing from Ben, to me, then back to Ben. "I thought I gave them to you. I'm sorry. That's totally my fault." Steve makes an extra loud squawk. "But I am not responsible for *that*."

"Don't worry, folks. We'll have Steve out of here in no time," Mandy says, and for once, I don't share her optimism.

Jake wraps an arm around my waist just as I remember I'm on a video call with Sadie. I flip the camera so it's facing the room, hoping my sister didn't see Jake's arm around me.

Hoping Jake didn't notice me trying to keep Sadie from finding out.

"Come here," Mandy calls in a soothing voice, and I assume she's talking to Steve until I see her reach out a hand to the intern.

Charles whimpers from the fireplace. His internship better be unpaid. With eyes on the bird, he climbs out carefully. But Steve must not like mohawks, because when Charles stands, the bird takes off again.

There's a moment of chaos as Steve circles the room, his

wings impossibly loud. As he heads right back toward the screened-in porch, he drops a deuce right on top of Ben's expensively casual haircut.

Sadie cackles from the phone. "I am SO telling Merritt about this."

TWENTY

Jake

LO'S STILL in her pajamas when she opens her front door
and pulls the coffee out of my hands without a word. I follow
her into her living room where she collapses onto the couch
and pulls her feet under her, her hands cradling her drink like
it's the only thing keeping her alive.

I sit down beside her. "Long night?"

She leans her head against the cushions and turns toward
me with a sleepy grin. "It's your fault. I stayed up late
finishing *One Hundred Years of Solitude.*"

Heat spreads through my chest. We've done this a few
times now. Recommended books back and forth. I never realized how much this would matter. Sharing this thing I love
with someone else. "It's amazing, right?"

She stretches her feet across my lap. "I loved it. And the
translation, too." She yawns before taking a long sip of her
coffee. "Did you run this morning?"

I move my hands to her feet and press my thumbs into her arch until she lets out a low moan that makes my gut tighten. It's still hard to believe I can touch her like this. And hard not to want more. "No running this morning." Though maybe I should have. Followed by a very long, very cold shower.

Lo wiggles her foot, as if asking for more, and I shift, angling my body so I'm facing her, my back leaning against the arm of the couch.

"Is Jake Fieldstone getting lazy?" she asks sleepily, her eyes half-closed. Her sweatshirt has slipped down over her bare shoulder, and it might be my complete undoing seeing her like this. Warm. Sleepy. Sexy. *Beautiful.*

"Or maybe you were just anxious to see your neighbor?"

She peeks an eye open and smiles, earning one from me. They come a lot easier when she's around. I think Lo likes the serious version of me as much as this one—the one where I feel loose and light and unbelievably happy.

"I skipped the run because it's already ninety degrees out, and it's barely eight a.m.," I say. "But I'm always anxious to see my neighbor."

She tosses an arm over her forehead. "Ugh. The heat. I don't remember it ever being this bad growing up."

"And we're just getting started," I say. "We haven't even hit July."

"Don't remind me."

I give her foot an extra squeeze. "Hey, speaking of July. I was wondering if you have plans for the fourth."

She sets her cup on the coffee table and sits up a little. "You mean, plans with the dozens and dozens of friends I've made here on Oakley?" she says dryly.

"People on Oakley love you. You could go anywhere you want on the fourth, and you'd be welcomed." I'm not exaggerating. Eloise has become the true darling of Oakley Island. I wouldn't be surprised if Frank has an entire playlist of videos on TikTok dedicated to singing her praises.

"Unfortunately for Oakley, I'd rather spend the fourth with my grumpy next-door neighbor," Lo says with an adorable smirk. "Assuming he hasn't gotten tired of me by then. The fourth is still ten whole days away."

At the rate things are going, the opposite might be true. I'm trying to take things slow, but she lives right next door. We're seeing each other every day, multiple times a day. Ten more days, and I might be completely gone for this woman. Two days.

Maybe I already am.

"Benedict is having a thing on his boat. Oakley has this enormous fireworks show out in the harbor, and they're always more fun to watch from the water. You want to go with me?"

"To watch fireworks with you from your billionaire best friend's enormous yacht? Um, yes. Yes, I do."

"I thought you might not want to hang out with Benedict after everything with the house. He can be a lot sometimes."

She quickly shakes her head. "He didn't feel like a lot. Just … passionate about his job? Honestly, most of the back and forth was between him and Sadie. She was on a video call the whole time."

I nod, a niggle of discomfort pushing through me at the thought of that video call. She tried to play it off, but it was obvious she's trying to keep our dating a secret from her sisters. When I mentioned this to Benedict, he couldn't confirm it but said he got the impression Lo didn't want Sadie to know about us.

I don't *really* care. But it still stings a little. I get her being worried about what her sisters will think. But why put it off? Unless she's thinking this isn't going anywhere.

If she sees an expiration date stamped on us, why tell her sisters at all?

It's an unreasonable worry. Lo hasn't given me any reason to think she's playing around. But I can't shake the feeling that she isn't just keeping secrets from her sisters. It feels like she's keeping something from me, too.

Lo glances at her watch before stretching her arms over her head. "I've got to get dressed. Hunter's meeting the plumber first thing this morning, and he wants me to be there." She leans over and kisses me with a familiarity and comfort that all but completely douses my worry. She lingers, her lips hovering over mine while her hand slides across my chest. "You are a very good way to start the morning," she says, her voice low.

I tip my head up and nip at her bottom lip, tugging her back for another kiss. It is a good way to start the morning, but it isn't enough. I want more of her. All of her. With me all the time.

"Want to come meet the plumber too?" she asks, her hands clasped behind my neck.

"I wish I could. I'm meeting Naomi and Liam for breakfast."

She frowns. "*Or* ... I could meet Naomi and Liam for breakfast, and you could help Hunter decide on the best toilet placement for the upstairs bathroom."

I kiss the tip of her nose. "Wish I could. But unofficial overlords actually have zero decision-making powers. It's in the paperwork and everything."

"You and your paperwork," she grumbles. She finally stands and moves away from the couch, her hand trailing across my chest as she goes. But then she's back again, leaning over my shoulder from behind and kissing me one last time. "But I'll see you later, right?"

I nod. Later today, and tomorrow and the day after that.

But I don't know how to stop my brain from tacking on to the end of that thought: *Every day until she's gone.*

I'VE SPENT SO MUCH of my free time with Lo the past two weeks that meeting Liam and Naomi for breakfast at the South Street Bakery feels strangely like coming up to the surface for air.

As though my sister has the ability to see exactly how I'm feeling, she gives me the smuggest grin possible as I walk up to the outdoor table where she and Liam are already seated. The bakery is a couple of blocks inland, so there isn't much breeze, and it's definitely too hot to be sitting outside. Only the enormous awning overhead and the fans positioned to blow cool air from the restaurant onto the patio make it bearable.

"Hey, kiddo." I pat Liam's shoulder and take the empty seat between him and Naomi, draping my suit jacket over the back of my chair.

Liam gives me a serious nod, like we're here for a meeting, not breakfast. "Hi, Uncle Jake."

"Long time, no see, brother," Naomi says, still smiling that smug grin.

"It hasn't been so long. I saw you ..." I trail off, trying to remember when I saw her, trying to remember what day of the week it even is.

"I last saw you with Lo out on the deck of The Round Up, and you two were—"

"Talking about very important client matters," I say.

Liam gives me a long look. "If you were kissing again, you can just say so. I was your wingman, remember?"

"Right," I say, clearing my throat and picking up my menu. "And you did a great job."

"Is she your girlfriend yet?" Liam asks.

"Yeah, Jake. Is she your girlfriend yet?"

Naomi swats the menu out of my hands. She's having way too much fun with this.

I heave a sigh, and Liam's brow furrows. "Mom says you need to lock that down."

"Does she, now?" I raise my brows at Naomi and her questionable topics of conversation.

"Here." Naomi pushes a drink my way. "I got you an iced coffee."

It's better than an apology, and I don't expect her to apologize anyway. This is how it is with us. I don't really mind, though I don't particularly want her talking to Liam about me needing to lock *anything* down.

"Were there no tables inside?" The iced coffee tastes amazing. But it also makes me very aware how hot it is out here. I'm already weighing the pros and cons of stripping off my button-down and eating breakfast in my t-shirt.

"Not a one. And a line out the door until just a few minutes ago. Looks like tourists, mostly. I think the world has finally figured out how fantastic our little island really is."

"Fantastic enough for you to move back?" I ask.

"And compete with all the tourists to get a decent coffee? I'm good."

This is the same song and dance we go through a few times a year. I get the reasons Naomi doesn't want to move back to Oakley. That doesn't mean I don't think she'd be better off if she did. "I could help more if you were closer."

"Are you offering to let me move in? Because I can't afford island rent, which means it's your place or Ned's, and I've had my fill of living above a bar, thank you very much."

I used to feel just like Naomi. Like life on Oakley would always be too small. But then I lived in Savannah, working at Margo's dad's firm, and my life felt constrictive for different reasons. The expectations, the pressure. I found myself longing for the simpler life Oakley would give me.

Now that I'm back, I can't imagine ever leaving.

The thought makes my stomach lurch. Lo and I haven't talked about it yet—it feels more like we're intentionally avoiding the topic—but we don't need to talk about what's already obvious. This island is just a pit stop for her. I can't— I won't—ask her to stay for me. I take another sip of my coffee.

"I wouldn't mind living with Ned," Liam says. "He taught me to tie proper knots. And I like Bard. If I can't have a dog, I'd be happy with a parrot."

"No pets," Naomi says.

I turn to face my sister. "If rent is the problem, I could—"

Naomi holds up a hand. "I know you could, but I don't want you to," she says, cutting me off. She gestures toward Liam with a tilt of her head. "And I'd rather not have seeds planted in places I don't want them to grow."

Liam breathes out a dramatic sigh. "She means she doesn't want you to get me excited about moving to Oakley if it isn't going to happen."

I chuckle. "We aren't getting anything past you, kiddo."

"You like your school in Savannah," Naomi says, tousling his hair. Liam immediately smooths it back in place. "And we aren't that far away."

232

Liam says nothing, carefully stacking the sugar packets, arranging them into neat piles by color. The waitress arrives, taking our orders and menus. A few SUVs with surfboards strapped to the top get into a honking match on the street, fighting over a parking spot. "Tourists," someone at the table behind us grumbles, the word carrying all the weight of a curse.

"Are you guys coming back for the fourth?" I ask, letting the subject drop.

"Not this year," Naomi answers. "Liam's school is doing a fundraiser thing at the park in Savannah. Selling drinks and popcorn for the fireworks there. I've somehow been roped into volunteering."

"*You* volunteered?"

Naomi's a good mom. A little less structured than I would be, probably, but she always has Liam's best interests at the forefront of her mind. Still. She isn't exactly the *volunteering* type. Never the one handing out juice boxes at the end of recess or whatever it is parent volunteers at schools do. It's just not her style.

"I know, I know," she says as she rolls her eyes. "But I'm telling you, she came at me with her high ponytail and her perky boobs and her clipboard, and I panicked."

I inhale some of my iced coffee at the mention of boobs. Naomi slaps me on the back—harder than necessary.

"She means Kelsey's mom. She's the PTA president," Liam adds. "What makes boobs perky?"

I bite my lip, stifling a laugh. "Yeah, Naomi. What makes them perky?" I eye her the same way she eyed me when Liam asked about Lo being my girlfriend.

"In the case of Kelsey's mom, about eight thousand dollars," she mutters. "Oh hey, look! It's our food. Who's hungry?"

Liam shoots his mother a look like he knows exactly why she's deflecting, but then there's a plate of gluten-free french toast in front of him, and he loses interest in anything but his food.

"Okay, for real, how are things with Lo?" Naomi's tone is serious enough that I feel like I owe her an honest answer.

"Good. Great, even."

"You really like her? Because I really want you to like her." Naomi leans forward, her expression earnest. "And I mean, after what she's been through, with the grad program not working out and losing her grandmother, maybe she *will* want to stay on Oakley, even if they do sell the house. Stranger things have happened, right?"

"Wait. Back up. What failed grad program?"

Naomi's eyes open wide, her fork freezing over her plate. "You don't know about that?"

A wave of hurt crashes into me. Naomi and Lo are friends. I like that they're friends. I don't like that Naomi knows something about her that I don't.

"I'm sure she was just embarrassed, Jake," Naomi says, clearly reading my expression. "That's the only reason she didn't tell you. It has to be."

"Embarrassed about what?"

She bites her lip. "I'm afraid she didn't tell you for a reason. It feels wrong to spill her secrets."

"You've already spilled it. All you need to do now is fill in the details."

Naomi takes a huge bite of her omelet, chewing slowly before she finally puts down her fork. "Fine. But only because I love you both. Lo was supposed to go to grad school. She applied to this really prestigious program in Washington State. At Greenwood U, actually. Mom taught there for a few years, right?"

"A visiting professorship."

"The point is, they've got this program that was tailor-made for Lo's interests, and she was really excited about going. She had the grades, did everything she was supposed to do, but then her undergrad advisor totally dropped the ball and didn't turn in his recommendation on time, so she didn't get in."

"That ... really sucks."

"Right? I mean, you should have heard her talk about the capstone project she did for her undergrad degree. She's freaking brilliant. There's no way she wouldn't have gotten in had she been given a fair shot."

"And they wouldn't give her one? Even after they found out it was her advisor that dropped the ball?"

Naomi shrugs. "They don't really care about stuff like that, do they? If you want to get in, you check all the boxes. That's mostly all college is anyway. Box-checking, box-checking, and more box-checking. The patriarchy."

"The patriarchy?"

"I feel like I can safely blame the patriarchy for most things."

Normally, Naomi's comment would spark a chuckle, or maybe a lively discussion of the patriarchy. My sister has that way about her, a way of making me joke around and enjoy conversations. Just like Lo.

But now, thoughts of Lo and her dreams—which I didn't fully know about and which are definitely not on this island—have my stomach clenching. A surge of protectiveness works its way through me. Lo has vaguely hinted that she thought about grad school a few times. But this is more than just thinking about it. She hoped for it. Planned for it. Banked on it happening. And now ... she's stuck here.

"I could call Mom," I say suddenly, my brain already working through what I would say.

"What, like, on purpose?" Naomi asks through a mouth full of fried potatoes. I can't fault her reaction. It isn't that we never talk to our mother. We do. Like clockwork. She calls the second Sunday of every month, first me, then Naomi. She asks all the questions she's supposed to ask, expresses (genuine? Naomi says yes, but I'm not convinced) interest in our answers, then fills us in on her most recent accomplishments.

This part of the conversation is always the longest. The lectures she's given. The introduction she was invited to write for a collection of obscure short stories no one outside of academia will ever read. The many, *many* accolades she's received for the endless, invaluable contributions she makes to her field of study. After the phone call ends, I'm positive she checks the "talk to the children" box on her to-do list and moves on to whatever comes next.

But all those accolades may actually help in this regard. "I could ask her if she'd be willing to help," I say, annoyed my sister isn't following along, though my brain is admittedly all over the place right now. "Mom taught at Greenwood. And she's published tons of stuff since then and turned into Harvard's favorite professor. She's *the* Elizabeth Fieldstone. I bet if she called Greenwood and asked them to give Eloise another shot, they'd listen."

"Really? Can they do that?"

"If the right people ask, I'm sure they can."

Naomi's still frowning, a deep crease running between her brows. "Well, yeah. But Jake, if they let Lo into the program, she'll ..." Her shoulders drop, and her words trail off, but I don't need her to say them to know what they were going to be.

If she gets in, she'll leave.

I breathe out a sigh. "I won't ask her to stay here for me, Naomi."

My sister gives me her most serious scowl. "What if she doesn't need you to ask? What if she stays just because she wants to?"

I'm already shaking my head before she finishes her sentence. "She might think she wants to *now*, but how long will that last? How long did it last for Mom?"

"Eloise is nothing like Mom."

Naomi is right about that. Their personalities couldn't be more different. But the things they have in common are the things most pertinent to this conversation. They're both outsiders, they both have career goals and aspirations that can't be met living on a tiny Southern island off the coast of Georgia, and they both had a choice taken away from them. Lo when her advisor screwed up, and Mom when she vacationed on Oakley, met Ned, and wound up pregnant with me.

"Lo deserves a choice," I say softly. "If I can give that back to her, I have to try."

"You're talking like there's only one grad school in the world, and Lo missed her only chance. If she wanted to, she could apply other places. Grad school is not a one-shot kind of deal."

"But you just said this was the program she really wanted."

"*Wanted.* Past tense. I have no idea what she wants now. Do you? Have you asked her?"

I grind my teeth together, frustrated at the turn our conversation has taken. But the path in front of me is crystal clear. I have the resources to make this happen. Well, to *possibly* make this happen. How can I do anything but try?

Naomi holds my gaze a long moment. "You'll do this even if it means losing her?"

I shrug. "If it means making her happy, then yes."

She scoffs, like she sees straight through me. "What about your happiness? Does that matter?"

I clench and unclench my jaw, then shove an enormous bite of breakfast burrito in my mouth because that's easier than answering her question.

Naomi nudges Liam. "Hey look. Uncle Jake is just like you. He also shoves food in his mouth when he doesn't want to answer a hard question."

Liam nods and mumbles through a mouthful of french toast, "It's bery eppective."

Naomi lifts a napkin from the center of the table and hands it to Liam. "Here. You've got syrup dripping down your chin." She looks at me and leans back in her seat, her arms folded across her chest. "I won't say it isn't sweet. That you're thinking of doing this for Lo. I can even believe you're motivated by a desire to put her happiness above your own. But you've been looking for reasons to push her away since she first showed up on Oakley, Jake. Why do you think that is?"

I don't answer because I'm not sure I can. But Naomi's on a roll. She doesn't really need me to answer when she gets like this.

"I think you know she's the real deal," she continues, tapping the table between us for emphasis. "And you're too scared to let it happen. The sooner she leaves, the less likely it is that you'll get hurt."

On that point, Naomi is wrong. I'm way past not getting hurt. I miss Eloise when she's five feet and one wall away. It would gut me for her to be all the way across the country.

"It may not even happen," I finally say, feeling a need to

diffuse the conversation. "I only said I was going to ask. Mom might not be able to help at all."

"Either way, promise to remember one thing."

I lift an eyebrow.

"*You* don't get to decide what makes Lo happy, Jake. *She does.*"

TWENTY-ONE

Lo

IF I HADN'T ALREADY GOTTEN over being mad at Benedict, his enormous yacht would make forgiveness easier.

"Just don't let him hear you call it that," Jake murmurs in my ear as we make our way up the dock.

"Why? It is a yacht, isn't it?"

The boat is massive. Gleaming white with *The Oakley* written on the side in navy cursive. The only thing not polished on it is the pirate flag flying from the mast, which makes me smile.

Is *mast* the right term? Clearly, I'm not up on my boat knowledge.

"It's definitely a yacht," Jake says, taking my arm as we start to walk up the narrow gangplank to board. "But rich people like to tone down their wealth."

"So, I should tell him it's a nice dinghy?"

Jake snorts, but before he can answer, Ben is there, taking my hand to help me on the not-yacht with a smile.

"Welcome, Lo. Jake."

"Thanks for having us on your ... uh, vessel. It—she?—is beautiful."

Jake and Ben do some kind of bro hug thing involving the kind of slapping that looks painful. It's a little strange seeing Jake interact with friends. He and I have grown close in the last few weeks, but there are still so many unknowns and unexplored sides to him. To us.

"I told her not to call it a yacht," Jake says. "Told her you'd take offense because rich people don't like to call a spade a spade."

Ben rolls his eyes at me over Jake's shoulder, then lets him go. "I'm not sure how you put up with this insufferable man, Lo. You're a saint."

"Thanks?"

"Nice shirt," Ben says, eyeing the Hawaiian print shirt I ordered and begged Jake to wear.

Honestly, I expected him to say no. And when he knocked on my door earlier wearing the turquoise and white button-down, I squealed and clapped my hands.

"Lo got it for me," Jake mutters, straightening the collar.

"It's good to see you in something other than a stuffy suit. Nicely done, Lo." Ben claps his hands, then rubs them together. "Come on. Feel free to look around. I'll give you the full tour later. We've got drinks being served by the pool up top when you're ready. In about half an hour, we'll take off."

I turn wide eyes on Jake. "Jake! This dinghy has a *pool!*"

"Ah, one more thing." Ben rubs the back of his neck, glancing at me and then back to Jake. "Margo is here."

My stomach clenches so hard, I almost double over from it. But Jake is watching, and I manage to do my best impres-

241

sion of a mannequin. Totally still. Maybe a little waxy and pale around the face.

"I'm sorry, man," Ben says. "I ran into her last time I was in Savannah, and she talked about how much she enjoyed last year. It just felt rude not to invite her."

Jake's hand tightens around my waist. I let myself fall against him, weighing out my need for comfort with my need to seem like this news does NOT bother me.

"I honestly didn't think she'd come," Ben continues. "I made a point to mention that you'd be here with Lo, but ... yeah. She came anyway."

"It's fine," Jake says, and I really hope he's right.

We linger after Ben heads back up. Jake presses a kiss to my cheek. I expect him to bring up Margo, but I'm relieved when instead, he says, "Go on—look around. I know you want to take some pictures."

Part of me wants to wait for the tour, but I can't resist exploring just a LITTLE. If that puts off having to see Margo? Bonus! I spend way too long exclaiming over details like the saltwater fish tank containing actual sharks and the entertainment room with a massive projector and deep, leather stadium seats.

"They recline with a button!" I gasp, and Jake takes a quick video of me making use of the motorized feature.

If the man ever wants to retire from law, he'd make a great personal assistant and videographer. He already knows me well enough to guess what I want videos of and is a master at finding the best light for photos.

He even pretends to be interested in what I post, though I can tell how much of a struggle it is for him to engage with social media of any kind. He may have a softer side, but the man is still one-hundred percent grump.

"Thanks for indulging me." I step up on my toes to give Jake a quick kiss on his jaw. "Am I annoying you yet?"

I learned well how annoying Instagramming everything can be for other people. Just ask my college friends. And for someone like Jake, older and more mature...

I do my best to shove an image of a smirking, very mature Margo from my mind.

"Never." Jake cages me in with his arms, my back flattened against a nearby wall. His eyes look almost silver in the dim light, and they're smoldering with heat. "I think you're adorable."

I wrinkle my nose. "Like a puppy?"

He shakes his head, then leans in, dragging his lips up my neck slowly. I can't hold back a shiver.

"Definitely not like a puppy."

My eyes fall closed. "It's just, when I think about things that are *adorable*, puppies come to mind. And children wearing matching outfits—"

"I *definitely* didn't mean like that."

"Then what *do* you mean, Mr. Fieldstone?"

Maybe we should be heading to the pool, not flirting down below. But the party upstairs will take us to Jake's ex, and right now, we're alone in a room on a freaking yacht.

Plus, pushing Jake to the point of losing control is my new favorite game.

"I mean, Miss Markham, precisely what I said. You are *adorable*. Which by definition means delightful and charming."

His mouth is warm on my collarbone, and I'm grateful my hula girl sundress has a sweetheart neckline. It gives his lips more room to graze. And graze he does, while I pretend he's not turning me into a melty puddle of goo.

"A walking dictionary, aren't you?" I tease.

243

"Yes. Need some synonyms?"

"That would make you a thesaurus. But yes. I'd love to hear more."

"You are beautiful." He punctuates the word with a kiss to my jaw. "Brilliant."

"You don't even know—"

"I *know*." A kiss just below my ear. Heat blooms through me, a ripple of desire, full and fragrant.

"Alluring," he says, and I think this must be Jake-speak for sexy because he pauses as if restraining himself. He's practically panting against my neck.

My stomach, once a no-fly zone for butterflies, is now a sanctuary for them, home to a whole host of flapping wings.

"Did you know a group of butterflies is called a kaleidoscope?" I ask.

Jake's arms move from the wall beside me to my waist. Suddenly, he spins me so my chest is against the wall and he's pressed against my back, trapping me. Not that I have even the faintest notion of trying to escape.

"Fascinating. Did you know that it's legal to get married by proxy in the state of Texas? In the case of an unavoidable absence, like military service, you can have a stand-in bride or groom."

"Tell me more."

He nuzzles my hair, and I smile when I hear him take a deep breath. Is he smelling me? The amount of pleasure this gives me must correlate to some cavewoman evolutionary throwback gene.

"The first law school was in Beirut in 450 BC," Jake says, his breath hot against my neck.

"Mmm. Is that right?"

He brushes my hair aside with his fingers and presses a kiss to the top of my spine. Have I ever been kissed there before? Based on my body's reaction—which is mind-numbing, toe-curling delight—I don't think so.

The guys I've dated in the past never spent time kissing me like Jake does. I had no idea how much I was missing. Jake treats kissing like it's a destination in and of itself, worthy of time and extensive exploration.

I am here. For. It.

Unless ... an evil and self-conscious part of my brain whispers as Jake's lips brush the shell of my ear. *Unless he's going so slowly because he thinks you're too young. That you can't handle more. Jake is a man. Surely you don't think he just kissed Margo.*

Talk about a quick way to ruin the mood.

I haven't given Margo half a thought since she warned me about Jake at the restaurant. Now I can't shake the mental image of Margo with her perfectly lip-stained lips pressed to Jake's. The fact she's here and the boat is pulling away from the dock makes me want to grab a life preserver and dive overboard.

But I'm not a coward. Maybe we haven't talked about why Jake and Margo didn't work, but they didn't. The end. Didn't he just make it clear with his words and lips that I'm his choice?

"We should probably head up," I say, trying to keep my voice light. No need to let Jake know about my sudden onset of insecurity. Because it does not exist.

He gives me a last, lingering kiss. Outside, I blink as my eyes adjust to the sun, sinking into the horizon but still bright.

"Wrong way, Magellan," Jake says, turning me away from the direction I was headed.

"I knew that. Wait!"

I pull him to a stop and take a selfie of the two of us. Not for Instagram. It's just for me. When we reach the top of the steps and the actual party, I stop and gasp.

Jake slides his arm around my waist. "You aren't going to leave me for Ben and his boat, are you?"

When he nips at my earlobe, I shiver. "Probably not."

He gives me a wicked look. "I might have to drag you below later just to make sure."

"Promises, promises." I stifle another gasp, bouncing on my toes. "There's a unicorn float!"

Money wouldn't motivate me to love someone, but I *am* halfway in love with this boat. The pool is set into the gleaming hardwood deck, an infinity edge showing off the choppy ocean beyond.

I've never been to a yacht party before, but this one is pretty much what I pictured. There are servers in crisp uniforms with trays of drinks and hors d'oeuvres for the guests. The men are dressed like Ben with that effortlessly expensive look, even the ones just wearing board shorts. Somehow, even their bathing suits look high class. The women are in bikinis and sundresses and all look like models or actresses. Maybe they *are* models and actresses.

Normally, I might feel a little self-conscious around so many rich, beautiful people, but the way Jake's hands and lips are constantly in contact with my skin washes away my doubts from earlier.

MOSTLY washes them away.

This isn't my scene, and these aren't my people, but I tell myself Jake *is* mine. Isn't he? Maybe we still haven't defined things between us, but the slow pace isn't reason for me to freak out. Especially not today.

I tell my doubts and questions to walk an invisible plank and swim back to shore. With*out* a life preserver.

There is no room on this not-yacht for doubts.

Especially not when there are still months of work left on Gran's house. I plan to stretch them as long as I can and enjoy every minute with Jake. We'll figure out what happens after that ... well, after that.

For today, I'm happy to accept a fruity frozen drink topped with a handful of maraschino cherries speared on a plastic toothpick shaped like a sword. I take a sip, trying to ignore Margo, whom I just spotted across the pool looking effortlessly posh and mature.

"Jake says you like sweet drinks," Ben says, nodding toward the beverage he just handed me. "I hope this isn't too much."

I take a second sip. If there's alcohol, I can't taste it, which is dangerous. Best go slow. I don't want to end the night falling overboard or needing Jake to carry me home again. Actually, I wouldn't mind the second so much. But I'd like to enjoy and remember it this time.

"It's perfect," I say. "Thank you. This is all amazing."

"So, no hard feelings about the house stuff?" Ben asks.

It's hard to remember that this is the same man who examined Gran's house with critical eyes. I wonder which is the real Ben—this smiling, easy-going beach bum kind of vibe or the man who was seriously intense about shingles.

Maybe both?

"Now that you've approved all my choices, it's fine. This makes a great apology."

"Oh, I wasn't apologizing." Ben smiles and takes a sip of his beer. "I'm very serious about my duties to uphold island standards. I blame Jake for not providing you with the lists of required colors and materials."

Jake groans and rocks back on his heels. "Yes, yes. It was all my fault. I've been distracted."

"I'm happy to see you with this kind of distraction," Ben

says. "I've never seen you smile this much in your life. I'm still getting used to this less prickly version of you."

"Don't get used to it," Jake says, glaring at Ben.

I think he meant that he's still going to be a grump, but those tiny doubts I tried to send back to shore are clutching the railing. *What if he means you'll soon be gone? What if he's already seeing the end when you're hoping this is a beginning?*

Ben provides an excellent distraction with his next statement.

"I was hoping you might bring your sister with you."

"Sadie?" After the way the two of them got into it on the video call, I'm shocked he's asking about her.

"I'm not sure when either of them will come back."

"That's too bad," Ben says.

I tip my drink in the direction of the pool. "Looks like you've got all the women you need."

A woman in a blindingly pink bikini sees us looking and waves. "Benjy, come swim!"

"Benjy?" Jake laughs. "Is this a new girlfriend?"

The lines tighten around Ben's mouth as he turns his back on the pool and takes a long swallow of beer. "No. And there are no girlfriends right now. Or women of any kind." When Jake raises one brow, Ben shakes his head. "They're just here for the party. Not for me. I actually don't know them."

"You don't know them?" I ask. "How are they here?" *And why is one of them calling you Benjy?*

"I've got to keep up appearances," Ben says, smiling as though his statement answers the question.

I get the sense Jake is holding back a remark he wants to say very badly, and Ben gives him a warning look before excusing himself to talk to one of the crew. And that's when Margo appears.

"Hey, Margo!" My voice sounds like I've just inhaled a balloon full of helium. I'm also inexplicably and enthusiastically waving.

She raises one perfectly manicured eyebrow. It's sculpted. Or threaded. Or whatever fancy women do to eyebrows. I find myself running a hand over mine and stop, fisting my hands at my sides.

"Hello, Jake. Eloise."

Margo's eyes slide away from me. They land and stay locked on Jake. I do my best not to grab him in some kind of proprietary way. Extending the claws, so to speak. Except my nails are pretty much bitten down to the quick from nerves. Better keep them to myself.

"Hello, Margo."

Jake's voice is cool, but not cold. I'd know. I've been on the receiving end of full-on frigid Jake.

Do I kind of wish he'd been Mr. Freeze? Yup.

Speaking of freezing, the conversation basically stops right there. Awkward doesn't begin to describe it. And between the three of us, I don't expect Margo to be the one to break the ice.

"Well, it's good to see you. Both—it's good to see you both," Margo says, and her smile almost looks genuine.

Is genuine with an edge of bitterness a thing?

"It's nice how you, um, match," Margo says, eyeing my dress and Jake's shirt.

Jake shifts, but his arm tightens around me. "Thank you."

I try to come up with something logical and rational and mature to say, but I can't. Instead, I just stand there, feeling like Jake's arm candy. But I happen to like candy, so ... yep. Call me candy.

"Well, this has been sufficiently awkward," Margo says. "Enjoy your night."

And then, she's gone. Leaving me feeling ... I don't even know. Like a maelstrom has erupted inside my belly while I'm pretending to be super chill?

"Should we swim?" Jake asks.

There's a nice breeze, but it's still July in the South. Which is to say: hot as the surface of the sun.

"I could be persuaded," I say. "I promise not to steal your clothes this time."

He tucks a strand of hair behind my ear. The look in his eyes turns my insides positively molten.

"I was kind of hoping for a replay. Maybe without the storm."

I give him a playful shove before we commandeer a set of lounge chairs, setting our things on them. I slip my dress over my head, channeling Merritt and her unwavering sense of confidence.

Jake seems to approve of my new bikini based on the way his gaze rakes over me. I rake right back, taking the opportunity once we're in the water to appreciate his tattoo and all those muscles.

"Running is responsible for all this?" I ask, smoothing a hand over his shoulder. I don't realize how much allure a nicely sculpted shoulder has until I get up close and personal with his. I give both of them an appreciative squeeze.

Jake's mouth curves into a smile. "No. I do weights a few times a week at Benedict's. He's got a home gym."

"Of course he does." I'm tempted to ask Jake more about Ben, more specifically about his *keeping up appearances* comment, but decide I'd rather keep my focus right here. "Tell me about your tattoo. It's a griffin, right?"

I swim around to his back, tracing over the whole design with my fingertips.

"I got it in my early twenties. A youthful decision."

My fingers freeze on the griffin's head. *I'm* in my early twenties. But Jake doesn't seem to realize the implications of what he's said.

"Does that mean you regret it?" I ask quietly. In my periphery, I see Margo slip into the pool wearing a sleek, black bikini.

"I wouldn't say that. I just might make another choice now that I'm older, more mature."

Again, *ouch*. He's talking about his tattoo, not me. But it's hard not to make the mental leap that maturity at twenty-one does not equal maturity at thirty-two.

The tattoo is large, taking up a good portion of his back, the wings curving over one shoulder and ending on part of his chest.

I press a finger to the griffin's eyes. "Well, I think it's beautiful."

"It's enormous."

"So what? It's fantastic."

He spins around to face me and wraps his arms around my waist. "We'll see if you feel the same way when *you're* thirty-two."

He's just being playful—I can tell he doesn't mean anything by it—but I still feel silly. Childish. My eyes dart to Margo, and I wonder how she felt about his tattoo.

"Enough talking," I say, leaning in for a kiss and pushing any thoughts of Margo away. "Someone promised earlier to make sure I was still his." And he better do it right now, because, with every passing moment, I'm feeling less and less sure.

"I THINK WATCHING fireworks from a hot tub on a yacht should be a mandatory life experience," I say, leaning against Jake's chest as another firework explodes overhead in a shower of green and blue.

Ben showed us the hot tub—located on a private deck off the main suite—during his tour and told us we were welcome to use it as long as we didn't tell anyone else. Now it's our own private little not-yacht oasis.

It's been a good way to end the night, which has been equal parts great and strangely weird. For whatever reason, I keep having to fight off nagging doubts and insecurities, most of them Margo-related. They're like gnats or mosquitoes, insistent and inescapable, despite my best efforts to shoo them away.

Margo has kept her distance, which I appreciate, but her presence alone has been enough to remind me of just how different we are. Coupled with Jake's turtle-slow pace when it comes to the physical nature of our relationship and his resistance to talk about anything that even resembles the future—I'm writing literal novels in my head detailing our eventual breakdown. Break-up? Can we break up if we've never officially declared ourselves a couple?

Margo called Jake a dinner plate, and he isn't *that*. But he's giving me more kisses than words to go on, and while I love his kisses, words of affirmation are my real currency. Today, I'm particularly feeling the lack.

Still, Jake's arm is around my shoulders, and we're watching a beautiful fireworks show from a private hot tub on the deck of an enormous yacht. I will not let my stupid insecurities ruin the magic.

"Mandatory yacht hot tub fireworks?" Jake asks. "As in, government-funded?"

"Sure. I can see lobbyists pushing for a bill. It could be a great tax write-off for the yacht owners. Plus, they could educate the masses on how it's not called a yacht."

Jake throws his head back and laughs at this, his cheeks glowing red as a screaming firework lights up the sky. I take a mental photograph since my phone is out of reach. Intentionally so—I've been afraid of dropping it in the pool or worse, completely overboard. So much water means so many possibilities.

Speaking of phones ... "You're ringing." I nudge Jake, who glances toward his phone but otherwise doesn't move.

"It's Naomi. Probably calling to wish me a happy fourth."

Is that a thing people do? I don't think I've ever called anyone to wish them anything but a merry Christmas. The phone stops ringing, then starts again immediately. Jake sighs, then stands, sending a wave of water over the lip of the hot tub.

"Better make sure she's okay," he says.

I watch the muscles in his back ripple as he walks to the lounge chair. I'm allowed to ogle, right?

Jake carefully dries his hands and face before picking up the phone and staring intently at the screen. He missed the second call too, but it starts to ring again.

"Naomi, this better be—"

Something about the way Jake's body goes rigid has me climbing out of the hot tub and touching his back. I can't hear the call, only the sound of Naomi's voice rising and falling. It sounds like she's crying. A knot of panic tightens in my chest.

"I'm on Ben's boat, but I'll be there as soon as I can."

As soon as he hangs up, he's in motion. Drying off, pulling his shirt over his head.

"Liam had an accident," he says, and my hands fly to my mouth.

"Is he—" I choke on the rest of my question.

Jake tries to force a small smile, but his expression is tight. "He'll be fine. But he's in the hospital. I need to find Ben so we can get back to the dock." Taking me by the shoulders, Jake presses a quick kiss to my lips. "I'll drop you off at the carriage house before I head to Savannah. Sorry to cut our night short."

"It's okay. I totally understand," I say, but Jake is already striding back through the suite, leaving me alone on this little deck.

I don't want to make the moment about me, because it's one hundred percent about Liam. Or maybe ninety-eight percent. Because the other two percent is stuck thinking I would have gone to the hospital with Jake had he thought to ask.

TWENTY-TWO

Jake

I MIGHT HAVE BROKEN a few laws and the sound barrier getting to the hospital in Savannah. And, of course, when I get to the emergency room, there's no sign of Naomi. A very bored receptionist tells me to wait, and I find myself sitting next to a guy who looks to be college age with a dish towel wrapped around his left hand. He's holding his phone with his right, uploading a video to TikTok. If the soundtrack playing in the background is any indication, the video is of whatever explosion caused his injury.

Liam is fine. He has to be fine. When she called, Naomi said he was awake and alert and asked about their insurance policy, which is about the most Liam thing ever. That has to be a good sign.

But hospital waiting rooms are much too good for overthinking and worrying.

I wish Lo were here. Benedict promised to get her home

safely, but now that I have time to think about it, I should have asked her to come with me.

Except, coming is the kind of thing she would do if we were a couple.

I can almost see Gennie shaking her head at me, telling me I'm an idiot because Eloise and I are clearly a couple. There's kissing and time spent together, memories made and things shared.

What I mean is that we aren't a *real* couple. The through-thick-and-thin, good-times-and-bad kind of couple. The serious, potentially forever kind of couple. That isn't us. It can't be us as long as our relationship has an expiration date.

And yet, Gennie's voice finally struggles to the surface despite me wanting to tamp it down. *Who do you want beside you when there's trouble?*

Lo. It's Lo.

She would have come, too. I even think she wanted to. The moment I got Naomi's call, I went into task mode, but when I picture her face before I left, I see a wistfulness there, a longing.

It's been happening a lot in the past week. The more time I spend with Lo, the more I feel her leaning in. *Settling.* She thinks she could be happy here. On Oakley long term. With *me* long term.

A part of me wants to believe that she could be, but a bigger part knows better. She's too young to truly know what she wants. It's the reason I've tried so hard to take things slow. Lo is an *all-in* kind of woman. If I took us there, she'd readily follow.

But would she regret it in ten years? It was that fear that drove me to finally call my mother about the program at Greenwood U. If Mom's enthusiasm is any indication, none of this will actually matter. Because Lo will be heading to grad school in a couple of months, just like she's always planned.

I shift in the plastic chair, which unfortunately draws the attention of the guy next to me. He looks surprised, as though he hasn't noticed me sitting here.

"Oh, hey," he says, doing a head jerk to move his blond bangs to one side. "Nice shirt."

I glance down, realizing I'm still in the ridiculous flowered shirt. No one but Eloise could have gotten me to put this on, and now I feel twitchy wearing it without her.

"Thanks."

He leans over, invading my space with his dish-toweled hand. "Would you mind—"

I don't get to hear whatever favor he was going to ask for, because Ned walks through the automatic doors just as the nurse calls TikTok guy back to triage. Ned flops into the now-vacant chair next to me with a groan, rubbing his bad knee.

"Any news?" he asks, and I shake my head.

"I texted Naomi to let her know I'm here, but I haven't heard back yet. She said earlier they were going to do some scans. My best guess is they're doing that. I'm surprised you closed the bar."

Maybe my criticism isn't too subtle. But I have never known Ned to close early. The bar is to my dad what academia is to my mom. Which is: something that takes precedence over everything else.

"I closed the bar when Naomi had appendicitis," Ned says matter-of-factly. "And when you got that infection after your wisdom teeth were taken out." He chuckles. "You were so drugged up, you couldn't even be trusted to pee by yourself."

I bristle, but he continues.

"But I didn't close." He pauses, glances at me, then away. "Lo is watching the bar."

I almost fall out of my chair. "Lo as in *Eloise*? *She* is watching the bar?"

"Is there another Lo?"

There isn't. Not a single person like her in the world. And that cheesy thought has me feeling all kinds of uncomfortable. But he seriously left her behind the bar?

"She couldn't handle two glasses of wine, but she's tending the entire bar? I find that a little hard to believe."

Ned sits up straighter and narrows his eyes. "She's spent some time there. I've shown her a few things."

Why do I get the impression he's downplaying? And why wouldn't Lo have said anything? And why does this irritate me so much?

A nurse walks in and calls, "Mr. Fieldstone?"

My stomach dips, and Ned and I both stand up, saying, "I'm Mr. Fieldstone" at the same time.

She barely blinks and motions us through a set of double doors.

After making our way through a maze of hallways, we find Liam in a curtained corner of the ER, propped up on a gurney, his arm wrapped in a thick cast and balanced on a pile of pillows. His eyes are open but heavy, and his face is pale. My stomach clenches with a new wave of worry. He looks more like a wax figure of Liam than himself.

But then his lips lift into the smile I know so well, and the knot of worry loosens the tiniest bit.

"Hi, Uncle Jake."

I move to the side of the bed while Naomi steps into Ned's arms. "Way to scare us all half to death, kid," I say, running a hand across his hair like I normally do, just more gently this time.

"I read a story once about a guy who had a brain injury

and afterward, he could play the piano even though he'd never played before. Weird, right?"

I roll my eyes with exaggerated flare. "Liam, if you want to learn how to play the piano, we'll get you lessons. You didn't have to go to all this trouble."

He laughs, then winces, and Naomi reaches a hand to his forehead. "Hey, watch with the giggling. We're avoiding any sudden movements, all right?" She shoots me a scolding look, but the light in her eyes says she's as happy as I am to see Liam acting and talking like himself.

I wrap an arm around her shoulder and pull her into a hug. "What's the latest report?"

"His arm is broken in two places," she answers, her eyes on Liam, "but both were clean breaks, and the doctor says it'll heal just fine. They want to keep him a few more hours for observation though."

"I'm concussed," Liam says sleepily.

"It's just a precaution," Naomi says. "They'll do another scan in the morning to make sure there's no swelling or internal bleeding to be concerned about, but so far, the doctors are pretty optimistic he's going to be just fine."

She smiles at Liam. If I didn't know her so well, I might have missed the slight tremor that punctuated the action. A surge of love and protectiveness for my little sister fills me. She's been doing the single-parent thing from the very beginning, and she's as tough as they come.

"I'm sure he will be," Ned says. "He's a Fieldstone. What's life without a concussion or two?"

"Nice shirt, by the way," Naomi says, snickering.

I pull at the collar. "Lo picked it out."

"Of course she did. That's not surprising. What's surprising is you actually wearing it." Naomi makes a whipping motion with her hand, adding in the sound effect for good measure.

Forget the love and protectiveness I was feeling. Would it be in poor taste to dump Liam's ice water on Naomi's head?

I catch Ned snickering behind his hand.

"Where is Lo?" Liam asks through a yawn.

I don't have an answer for that. Because apparently, she's slinging drinks in Ned's bar.

But if you'd asked her, she'd be here with you, Gennie's voice reminds me.

But then, would Ned have closed the bar without Lo stepping in? I'm not sure I want to know the answer.

"She's back on Oakley," I finally say, ignoring the way Naomi's gaze narrows at my words. "But she'll be so happy to hear you're okay." Liam nods sleepily, then yawns one more time, this one so big it starts a chain reaction, and suddenly, I'm exhausted down to my bones.

Half an hour later, they've moved Liam to an observation room in the pediatric wing, Naomi with him, and Ned and I are stationed in a different waiting room, this one empty except for the two of us. We're closing in on two in the morning now. Naomi tried to get us to leave, but as long as she's here, I want to be here too. The doctors wouldn't be keeping Liam if there wasn't some chance of him *not* being fine. It's hard enough she's here without Liam's father—not that I would wish that particular loser within a hundred miles of the hospital or anywhere else Naomi and Liam are. Any man who takes off after finding out he got his girlfriend pregnant doesn't deserve the privilege of being around.

But Naomi shouldn't have to do this alone. If all we do is wait, we'll wait together.

Ned feels the same way, apparently, because he rebuffed Naomi's attempts to get him home as thoroughly as I did.

After twenty minutes of waiting in mostly silence, I almost wish the guy with the exploded hand and his TikTok video were still sitting beside me. At least then we'd have a buffer.

Instead, my mother calls.

Ned watches me the entire time I update her on Liam's status, a weird look on his face that almost looks like ... happiness? Or pride, maybe? It's obvious he's glad I'm talking to her, which I don't really understand. I'm not so much of an ogre that I wouldn't want Liam's grandmother to be updated. Am I?

I think of Naomi's acceptance of Ned's presence at the hospital. She didn't seem surprised he was here, so maybe Gennie's right, and I really am too hard on everybody.

"Listen, while I've got you," Mom says, "I heard back from my associate at Greenwood."

My breath catches, and my heart immediately starts pounding. "Already? That didn't take long." I'm desperate to know what Mom found out, but I'm not sure I want to have this conversation here, in front of Ned. With Liam in a hospital bed down the hall. "Actually, Mom, I'm not sure now is the time—"

"Nonsense," she says dismissively. "Liam is going to be fine. And this will only take a moment. Yeses are generally like that."

"It takes a moment to sink in. "They said yes?"

"Of course, I'm sure my recommendation carried some weight, but apparently they reevaluated her application and were impressed enough to make room for her."

"This fall?"

Mom pauses. "That *is* what you wanted, isn't it?"

It's exactly what I want. And the last thing I want. How can it be both at the same time?

"Anyway, I have the number of the woman Eloise is supposed to call. Dr. Banerjee is a brilliant woman and a good friend. I'll stick it all in an email, but you'd better get the information to her as soon as possible. They're offering her a graduate assistantship, and she'll need to respond about whether she wants it as soon as possible."

I end the call, still unsure how to process the information Mom just gave me. I am both grateful for the distraction because I can't do anything for Liam but wait, and annoyed by the distraction because even though I'm just waiting, shouldn't all my thoughts and worry be for him?

"What was that about?" Ned asks.

"Nothing. Just giving Mom an update on Liam."

"Sure. Then you talked about something else. What's happening this fall?"

I don't want to talk about my relationship with Lo with Ned. Not in the middle of the night. Not when I'm still so conflicted about everything. I lean forward, propping my elbows on my knees, and drop my head into my hands, massaging my fingers over my scalp. "Nothing. Just ... news about a program Eloise is interested in."

Ned nods knowingly. "And your mother knows something about it? I guess that makes sense. The two of them are a lot alike."

I lift my eyes to his.

"Lo," he adds, as if I need the clarification. "And your mother."

"Are they?"

"Oh sure. The way Lo dotes on the bird, teaching him lines of poetry, going on about literature and all that." He smiles, his eyes crinkling at the corners. "Every time she walks into the bar, Bard has started saying, 'She walks in beauty, like the night.'"

"Lord Byron?"

"So Lo says. You know I don't have an ear for things like that."

"You make it sound like Lo is there all the time. At the bar."

He shrugs. "A few times a week, at least. I told her if she was going to teach the bird lines of sappy poetry, she had to let me teach her how to bartend. She isn't half-bad."

Lo has been learning how to bartend. Spending time with Ned. She's mentioned the parrot a few times. But I've somehow missed just how frequently she's been there. I have a feeling the problem isn't that she's been keeping it from me. But maybe I haven't been listening, too intent on ignoring anything that might make Lo seem like a long-term part of Oakley Island.

"She's a quick thinker. Fast on her feet," Ned says. "And all she's gotta do is smile, and any man on all of Oakley would be eating out of her palm."

I shift in my seat, suddenly uncomfortable with that thought. I don't want anyone anywhere near Lo's palms. Or any other part of her. The sense that she belongs to me, that I would stop at nothing to keep her safe, settles over me. It's not unlike what I feel for Liam and Naomi. A different flavor of the same bone-deep feeling.

You know what it is, Jake. Name it. Embrace it.

I chuckle to myself as Gennie's voice sounds in my head. I have to wonder if she talks to her granddaughter as frequently as she talks to me, or if she only shows up inside *my* subconscious.

I do know what the feeling is.

But swift on the heels of Gennie's optimism—*my* optimism?—is a foreboding sense of dread.

I want Lo to stay. But I can't *ask* her to stay. Especially not now.

"Even that's like your mother," Ned continues, oblivious to the battle raging inside me. "They're kind in the same way." Ned's eyes turn distant, like he's back in time to when Mom still lived on Oakley.

I can't suppress the scoff that rises to the surface. Kindness? To her professor friends, maybe. Her students. But not to the rest of us.

Ned's eyes narrow. "Your mother *was* kind, Jake. *Is* kind. She always has been."

My jaw tightens. "Was it kind when she left?"

Ned shakes his head sadly. "Don't do that, son."

"What, point out the truth? She *left*, Dad. Left all of us. That wasn't *kind*."

His gaze holds mine for a long moment. There's an undeniable sadness lurking behind his eyes, but his words are steady. "I don't fault her for leaving, Jake," he calmly says. "It wasn't a decision she made lightly, and I understood why she had to do it."

"How can you not fault her? You raised us alone. *Living above a bar.* It took half of Oakley to keep us in school and eating vegetables, and—"

"And you turned out pretty well, didn't you? She always knew you would. We both did. Oakley does that for people."

I can't argue over the benefits of growing up on Oakley Island. But how does Ned seem so at peace about this? We don't talk about Mom. I always figured it was because whatever pain she inflicted on Naomi and me when she left was only half as bad as what she brought on Ned. He never brings her up, so we don't either. At least not with him.

But there is no malice in his voice now. Not even a trace

of bitterness. He just looks ... tired. Maybe even a little wistful.

"I still don't understand."

He leans back in his chair, his arms propped behind his head. "It isn't that complicated. Beth was never meant for a life on Oakley Island. She had plans. Dreams. But then she spent a summer here, we fell in love, and two weeks before she left town, she found out she was pregnant with you."

I nod along. This part of the story I know. Ned came clean when, while working on an eighth-grade genealogy project for school, I found a copy of his and Mom's marriage certificate and did the math. They'd only been married two months when I was born.

"Would she have stayed if she hadn't been pregnant?"

"It was never her plan to stay."

"But you fell in love." Now I'm the one who sounds wistful, even if I do know better.

"Love doesn't always make sense, Jake." He grunts. "And it doesn't always work out. We tried for a while. Your mother hung up her plans to get a Ph.D., and we built a life on the island. For a while, I even believed it would stick. But ..." He shrugs. "She wasn't ever truly happy. Honestly, I'm surprised she hung on as long as she did."

I shake my head. "How are you so unaffected by this?"

Ned raises an eyebrow and smiles. "It's been twenty-five years. I wasn't always unaffected, but you know what they say. Time heals all wounds and whatnot." He drops a heavy hand on my shoulder blade. "If you want to be healed, anyway."

I'm not sure what to make of our conversation-turned-confessional. On the one hand, I understand the importance of pursuing your dreams. I'm an attorney instead of a bartender because I pursued mine, even when it wasn't what other people wanted for me. Except for Gennie, everyone imagined me running the bar with Ned. The only reason I'm back in good graces with the town is because I decided to bring my practice back to Oakley instead of staying in Savannah like everyone expected.

But Mom didn't have to be as uninvolved as she has been. She could have visited more. We could have spent summers with her. Things could have been different.

Except, I'm not sure I truly would have wanted them to be. I had a good childhood. A good life on Oakley. I can't be happy about the choices Mom made. I maybe *can* acknowledge that I shouldn't be so hard on her. I can own that she loves us. That in her own way, she's always wanted what's best for us.

You could also forgive her, Jake.

I roll my eyes at Gennie this time. I've made a lot of progress in the last twenty minutes. I'm liable to pull a muscle if I make any more concessions.

"Hey," Naomi says, appearing in the waiting room doorway. "What's going on in here?"

I stand up. "Nothing. Just talking. How's Liam?"

"Asleep, thankfully."

"Is it okay for him to be asleep?" Ned asks. "I thought you were supposed to stay awake when you have a concussion."

"I asked the same question, but I guess protocol has changed. The doctor says it's easier to heal when you're asleep."

"Can *you* sleep?" I ask. "I can go and sit with Liam for a bit if you think you can."

She yawns. "I might could try. Are you sure you don't mind?"

"Come on," Ned says, sitting down on the long, padded

266

bench pushed up against the wall. He pats his leg. "Not the greatest pillow, but it's better than nothing." She points me in the direction of Liam's room, then collapses onto the bench next to Ned. I leave them there, my own mind and heart stretched tight. Ned maybe did okay raising a family without Mom beside him. And Naomi is making it work too.

But it isn't what I want.

I can't leave Naomi when I'm half of her entire support system, but I also can't expect Lo to give up her dreams for a life she never signed up for. She's only here because she has to be.

Just like Mom.

I won't sign up for this. I won't doom myself to repeating my father's history.

Lo has her ticket off of Oakley Island, and I have to make sure she takes it.

TWENTY-THREE

Lo

WHEN I GLANCE up to see Jake walking in, I fumble a pint glass and slosh beer over the side. Which ... is not my best showing. But I've been waiting to hear from him since last night, and all my texts have gone unread. Yes—there have been a lot of texts.

Because I'm worried. Not because I'm clingy and still fighting hurt that Jake didn't invite me to the hospital or even update me via text. I know it's one more pressure he didn't need, dealing with my dumb feelings, but it's hard to swallow them down.

I care about Liam too. And Naomi. Heck, I care way too much about Jake's whole family. I even like the dumb bird, even if he does seem averse to learning Toni Morrison or Maya Angelou. I figure he knows enough quotes from dead white guys and needs to branch out.

The point is, I'm hurt and trying not to be hurt, or at least trying not to *show* that I'm hurt now that Jake is finally here.

Jake's gray eyes narrow on my hands and the spilled beer. I want to tell him it was my first mistake—a tiny lie—but the words don't reach my lips before he's on the other side of the bar next to me. So close I can smell his aftershave.

Well, that's just not playing fair! Every man has to know the effect those scents have on women!

My hand shakes, and a little more beer sloshes over the side.

Jake takes the pint glass from my hand and sets it aside, grabbing a fresh one and pouring a perfect beer. Not too much of the foamy head, which is my biggest issue. I can't quite get the angle of the glass right, no matter how many times Ned has tried to teach me.

"How's Liam?" I ask as Jake hands the customer his beer with a nod.

"He's okay. Concussion and a broken arm. They kept him overnight for observation, but he's back at home now."

Tension I didn't even realize I was carrying releases on a shaky exhale. I want to hug Jake, to wrap my arms around his waist and press my cheek to his solid chest right where the griffin's feathers extend. I'm aching to reconnect with him, to dispel the hurt and the lingering tendrils of self-conscious-ness from last night on the boat. But Jake's body language is like a neon sign flashing *Stay Out!*

"I texted."

He winces. "I know. I—reception wasn't great in the hospital, and I was just ... trying to be there for Naomi."

His words do little to dispel the hurt. I expected radio silence from Ned. He only carries a flip phone and won't send texts to save his life. But Jake couldn't have texted one quick message to let me know Liam was okay?

The strangest sensation washes over me. An awareness that this is somehow the beginning of the end. Jake didn't reach out to me because he wasn't *thinking* of me. Because I don't mean to him what he means to me.

I force a smile. "Good. Is Naomi freaking out? Is she the kind of person who freaks out? I feel like she'd be super calm and totally on top of things, but I guess I haven't seen her in an emergency situation yet. Merritt and Sadie are the calm ones in my family. I'm the one who gets all keyed up."

Jake raises one dark brow, his expression lifting in a way that almost looks like a smile. "Like right now?"

A tiny tendril of the tension in my gut loosens, even as I swallow down a passive-aggressive remark. He could have texted me any time to give me an update. That might have kept me from getting all *keyed up*. But I'm not going to be that person.

I give him a light smack on the shoulder. "Shut up! I've just been worried!"

Jake absentmindedly starts cleaning up the messes I've left behind the bar. A few lemon rinds and balled-up napkins, a mixed drink I made incorrectly that someone sent back, and a soaked bar towel I dropped in the sink.

My cheeks flush, and I grab the bar towel. "I can do that."

Jake glances at his hands, as though just realizing what he's doing. "Right."

For a moment, I scurry around like a tornado of tidiness. The last thing I want is Jake thinking I've been a disaster behind the bar. Nothing has caught fire (yet), and I only had the one drink sent back. I think overall, I've done well holding down the fort. Er, ship.

"'Love is the song of the bird and also the cry of parched earth,'" Bard the bird squawks, and I almost drop a glass.

"Bard!" I gasp. "You did it!"

Jake frowns. "What's the quote from? Did you teach him that?"

I can't help my pleased smile. "I did, and it's from an indigenous poet. He needs some diversity. I've been working on him, but he's been stubborn. Or at least, pretending to be stubborn. Have you been holding out on me, Bard?"

He dances a little in his cage, and I drop an apple slice into his bowl. He gobbles it up with a snap of his dark beak. I'm still not brave enough to hand-feed him. Ned says he's not known to bite, but I enjoy my fingers too much to risk it.

"You're spoiling him," Jake says, but his tone isn't irritated. He sounds more ... impressed.

"I'm *training* him."

Jake looks like he's about to say something else, but I jump in. "Ned should be back in a couple of hours," I say, immediately regretting the hope in my voice. Like I'm desperate to spend time with Jake. Only, I'm starting to feel like I *am* desperate. Like if I let him out of my sight, I'll only be expediting the loss looming over us. "He only needed to sleep a little while after last night," I add.

Jake leans against the bar and folds his arms, his gray gaze intense. "Ned told me you were here last night. So he could go to the hospital." His words feel as much like an accusation as a statement. But his expression reminds me of when we first met—totally unreadable.

I shrug. "Last night was easier. The rest of his staff was here to keep me from messing anything up. Luckily, it's been pretty slow today."

Jake glances around the mostly empty bar. When his gaze flicks back to me, there's a fire behind his eyes that wasn't there before. He looks like he wants me. *Needs me.* Or else like he wants to tear me limb from limb, but option A is less terrifying, so I'm choosing to believe that one.

I take a step toward him.

Maybe all my doubting is just exhaustion. It's been a long twenty-four hours. First the yacht and Margo and all my insecurities bobbing to the surface. Then worrying about Liam, wondering why Jake didn't think to ask me to come to the hospital. Then trying to take care of things here. Pretending to be a bartender when I'm anything but.

That has to be it. Exhaustion and me just being paranoid.

If it's only exhaustion, why didn't he call you?

Doubt weasels its way back into my thoughts, and I clench my fists in frustration.

It would help if I knew what Jake was thinking. But I don't want to push. The last thing I want is for him to think I'm jumping ahead or getting too clingy or—the absolute worst in this particular scenario—not being mature about all this. But he's bound to have had so much more experience, life experience and otherwise. I feel like he needs to set the tone.

Even if I'm dying to know what, precisely, that tone is.

"It isn't a big deal, Jake." I smooth a hand down my ponytail. "Once Ben took me home, I couldn't help wondering if Ned was able to get away, so I walked over and offered to help."

"Apparently, you walk over a lot."

I bite the inside of my cheek. "I like your dad. And the bar." When he doesn't speak, standing there like a very hot, possibly very angry statue, I ask, "Are you ... mad?"

"You shouldn't be here."

My heart sinks.

Forcing a smile the same way I force down my hurt, I turn away, grabbing a couple of dirty glasses from behind the counter. I start toward the swinging kitchen door without

272

giving Jake so much as a side-eye. If he's going to be like this, he gets NO eye.

"Well, I am. I don't get your issues with your dad. If you don't want to tell me, fine. But I like him. And I wanted to help, so I did."

I kick open the swinging door with perhaps a bit too much force and have to use my hip to stop it from crashing back into me. Then I disappear into the kitchen, fighting back tears trying to fall for reasons I can't quite understand.

It feels like Jake and I are dancing around an argument. Like the words we're saying are all up on the surface while whatever emotion I'm feeling—that we're *both* feeling—is hidden underneath. The push and pull, the back and forth of knowing and not knowing, trusting and doubting. It's too much.

Honestly, I just want to go to bed. Hibernate for four days and have this conversation when I'm fully rested, fully caffeinated, and not so … *keyed up* about things.

I'm about to return to the front and suggest we take a break and revisit the subject tomorrow, maybe over dinner or a nice, calming walk on the beach, when Jake barrels through the door. His arms slide around my waist, and he tugs me into his body.

Well, okay then.

I make a little *oof* as our chests collide, but then my greedy hands move up his back, gripping the collar of his shirt.

This. This is what I needed.

I allow my eyes to close as I burrow my cheek into his chest. He presses his nose to my hair, and suddenly, the world is right again, spinning on its axis just as it should be.

What was I so worried about? Why was I feeling insecure?

This man. His arms. His solid—though sometimes grumpy—presence. He's all I need.

"Why?" he asks, his voice rough and low.

It takes me a sec to backtrack and remember our conversation. "Why am I helping your dad?"

He takes me by the shoulders, gently pushing me back just far enough he can meet my eyes. His expression looks almost tortured, and my chest constricts.

"It should be me," he says, and only then do I realize he was never angry with *me* at all.

He's angry with *himself*, the kind of anger fueled by guilt. I don't know much about the tension between Ned and Jake, only that it seems to grieve both of them, and they both seem unable—or unwilling?—to repair the cracks.

I swallow. "He loves you."

I love you, I think.

As though my thought was somehow projected out loud, Jake's gaze softens. It does not cool though. Instead, as his gray eyes trace a path from my eyes to my lips, the heat becomes languid and slow—melted taffy, sweet and warm and thick. He leans closer.

"You are not making this easy," Jake says.

I don't have time to wonder what he means before his lips find mine.

We have kissed what seems like countless times. But this kiss is different. *Charged.* He isn't just kissing me, he is devouring me, tasting me, decimating me.

It takes my lips a moment to catch up, but then I'm giving back as much as I get.

This kiss is more than the sum of us. It is a living thing of its own, dragging us along while we try to keep up, hold on, not get swept completely away.

On second thought, sweep me away. I'm happy to be lost

274

here with him. *In* him.

Jake's hands are in my hair, lightly tugging and holding me in place. Mine are just as greedy, my fingers yanking at his shirt like I'm trying to remove it from his body. Which, honestly, I wouldn't mind. I'm in the mood to explore that tattoo of his again, to study it with my fingers and then with my lips.

But then Jake pulls back, breaking the kiss and stepping away from me with a frustrated growl. His hands are on his hips, and he swears under his breath before he steps back to me. His hands gentle, one cupping my head while the other falls to my waist, holding me against him as we both breathe like two sprinters who've just competed in the hundred-yard dash.

His words come back to me. *You're not making this easy.*

Is he frustrated because he didn't want to kiss me? Because he wants more, and we're currently standing in the kitchen of his father's pirate-themed bar?

I'm sure somewhere in his tiny bird brain, Bard has a quote for this exact moment.

"Lo, I need to tell you something. I've done something for you," Jake says.

The delight shooting through me could be harnessed as an alternative energy source. I'm shocked my skin isn't glowing.

"You did?" I'm practically bouncing on my toes, and Jake gives me a crooked grin, though not before a flash of something else crosses over his expression. Doubt? Fear? Or was it more resignation?

He leads me out of the kitchen and over to a table beside the bar. He slides out a chair, waiting for me to sit before dropping into the seat across from me. This feels so formal. So...official.

"You know my mother is a university professor," he begins, his hands clasped in a way that reminds me of our first meeting all those weeks ago when we first learned of Gran's will.

We've talked about his mother. Briefly. But I quickly got the sense she isn't Jake's favorite topic of conversation. I nod slowly. "Her analysis on feminism in nineteenth-century literature was required reading in one of my literature classes."

"That sounds like something Mom would write." He reaches for my hand. "A few years back, she did a visiting professorship at Greenwood University. She was there for three semesters."

My heart rate starts to climb. "Okay," I squeak out.

Jake smiles, and my heart drops to the floor like it knows what's coming before the rest of me does. "I called in a favor," Jake says. "Asked Mom to make a few calls. If you haven't already gotten word, a spot opened up in the Greenwood Master's program this fall. It's yours if you want it."

This fall. The program I have always dreamed of attending has a spot for me this fall. That's practically now.

Except … *how?* I never told Jake about my failed attempt at grad school. "Naomi told you?" I say, remembering that afternoon in the closet when I told her about my fizzled dreams.

Jake nods. "But I wish I'd heard from you. Why didn't you tell me?"

I shrug. "Because it's embarrassing. I literally pinned my entire future on one program, then crashed and burned. You have your life figured out, Jake. And I'm …" *Numb.* Right now, I'm numb.

"But that isn't true. Not anymore."

I shake my head. "I appreciate the offer, Jake, but they

rejected my application. I don't want them to change their minds out of pity. Or because your mother asked them to."

He's holding both of my hands now, his expression earnest. "Lo, it wasn't your fault you didn't get in. Had they had your complete application, you would have. All my mother did was ask them to give you a fair shot. Pity doesn't have anything to do with this."

"Even if that's true, if they took the spot from someone else—"

"They didn't. Someone dropped out, and a spot opened up. That's all this is."

Jake leans back, dropping his hands into his lap. The distance seems fitting because this thing he did for me is going to put an entire continent between us.

Why am I not rejoicing? Why am I not squealing and jumping up and down and throwing my hands around his neck to thank him?

Jake seems to be wondering the same thing as his brows draw low over his eyes. "I thought you'd be excited. Isn't this what you wanted?"

It suddenly occurs to me why I'm trying to (kindly) reject Jake's offer. It *is* what I wanted—emphasis on the past tense. What I want, present tense, is the man currently trying to send me across the country.

"It is," I say, though I hardly sound convincing. "Or it was anyway. But Jake, I can't leave Oakley." *I can't leave you.* "The renovation has to continue, and it won't if I'm not here. My sisters have lives. Jobs. Plus, I can't afford Greenwood's program. I was hoping to scholarship, to get an assistantship, maybe, but this late in the game—"

"There *is* an assistantship. That's the best part. It's with Dr. Banerjee herself—Mom says she's really important—and it will fully cover your tuition. You'll only have to worry about living expenses."

"Dr. Banerjee?" It's more than I ever would have hoped for back when I was applying to the program.

"You have to be there by the fifteenth of this month, earlier if you can swing it, but Mom says she's excited to have you on her team."

The fifteenth of this month. That's barely over a week away. Ten days and I'll be *gone*.

"And I already talked to your sisters," Jake continues, clearly oblivious. "They're both on board. Merritt's going to come down for a little while, and Sadie has some vacation time saved up she's willing to use. They want this for you." He swallows. "We all do."

They all do.

Even Jake.

Hot shame washes over me. My doubt, my fears, they really *were* justified.

While I've been busy falling in love, Jake has been busy arranging my departure. Sure we've kissed. Spent time together. But we've had exactly zero talks about any kind of future together, about the status of our relationship.

Because there *is* no relationship.

"I guess you thought of everything," I finally say, managing a weak smile. He thought of everything, and he's perfectly fine saying goodbye to me in ten freaking days.

I stand and push away from the table. "You can handle things here, right? If I go? I should probably start to pack."

Jake frowns even as he nods. "Yes, but ... Lo, what's wrong? Why aren't you happy?"

I shake my head and turn away. I don't want to have this conversation here. I don't want to have it at all because my feelings are obviously bigger than his, and there's no way he isn't going to notice. Tears are already streaming down my face, but if I don't get out of here soon, those tears are going to turn into full-on ugly crying. Huge guffaws. Painful hiccups. So. Much. Snot. Why can't I cry in a pretty way instead of turning into a splotchy, snotty monster?

"Eloise," he says. "Please."

I turn, my foot bouncing in nervous agitation. He wants to do this here? *Fine.* "What about us?" I hate how much hope is in my voice.

He says nothing, just clenches his jaw, his brow furrowed. His expression tells me everything I need to know.

"Right. Got it. There is no us. This has all just been for fun."

"That's not what I said," he says simply, his eyes still cast downward.

"But it's written all over your face. What was that? Back in the kitchen?" I snap, my sadness shifting into fury. "Why did you kiss me like that?"

His shoulders drop the slightest bit. He feels *guilty.* Guilty for kissing me. Because he already knew he was saying good-bye. "I shouldn't have—I just got caught up in the moment. I don't want to hurt you, Lo."

I scoff. "So you thought kissing me like your life literally depended on it then sending me packing would be no big deal?"

"I'm not sending you packing. I did this *for you.* Because you've always dreamed of this program."

I take a shaky breath. "What if dreams change?"

A man at the bar loudly clears his throat—he must have slipped in without us noticing—and Jake hurries over to serve him.

We shouldn't be doing this here.

But then, it somehow feels fitting in a full-circle kind of

way. This is where it all started, after all.

Jake is back in less than a minute, but now he has the bag I stashed behind the bar in his hand. He tugs me toward the door. "I didn't handle this the way I should have," he says. "Go get some rest. I'll come over later, and we can talk about this."

I take my bag, but he isn't getting off that easy. I shake my head. "Just answer my question."

He sighs, his hands propped on his hips. He is so stupidly, painfully handsome, it makes my tears fall even faster. "The world is so big, Lo. And you've seen so little of it. You may think you want this now, but you're too young to —" He runs a hand across the back of his neck. "I just think you'll regret not taking the opportunity while you can."

I sniff. What will he regret? Me? This? Everything? I can't keep myself from asking my next question. "What if I said I was in love with you?"

His eyes spark to life, and for one single moment, I feel like I'm seeing the real Jake. His *real* emotions. But then he shutters closed, his eyelids dropping and his hands balling into fists. When he opens his eyes again, his expression is cold and flat. "I'd tell you I'm not worth it. You don't belong on Oakley, Eloise. You don't belong with me."

Well. Not much room for doubt there.

"Just so we're clear—you're the one sending me away here, Jake."

He shakes his head dismissively. "You were always going to leave."

I give him a quick, decisive nod before shouldering my bag and pushing out the door. I'm grateful most of my tears hold on until my back is to him.

He's right—I was always going to leave.

I just hoped he'd give me a reason to stay.

TWENTY-FOUR

Lo

TURNS OUT, when you've got academic royalty greasing the wheels, it only takes four days to upend your life, pack up your meager belongings, and fly across the country to start as an assistant in the position of your dreams.

Whoopee.

If I don't sound grateful, I am. This is everything I wanted … before Jake.

And the irony of it is—I wouldn't be here without him, and now I'm here and don't want to be.

Though I'm not sure I want to be on Oakley Island either. Not after the awkwardness between Jake and me those last few days before I left. I think he was hurt I wasn't more grateful for the favor he called in, and I *know* I was hurt at being pushed away. But still. He all but completely avoided me.

No more kitchen kisses. No more coffee on the front

porch. My time on the island was bookended by the grumpy, distant version of a man I thought I knew.

Don't even get me started on Merritt. I'm not sure how she was able to take off work for an extended period. She almost tore my head off when I asked a few questions, and she provided zero answers. So, yeah—in the end, leaving was much easier than I thought it would be.

"These are reproductions of the letters between Willa Fremont and her editor, who later became her husband." Dr. Banerjee slides a folder across the desk to me, then folds her dusky brown hands, blinking her golden eyes my way. "Such a beautiful story, isn't it?"

I stare down at the folder, a faint smile on my lips. I hope Dr. Banerjee can't see the bitterness just under its surface. "It is."

Is it absolutely the worst thing ever to be assigned this part to research—a blossoming love story when my own just imploded? Though, to be fair, mine was never really a love story. More like a girlish crush.

"The letters have long been admired," Dr. Banerjee continues, "but I'd like to dig deeper and study them relative to the work Fremont was producing at the time she was receiving them. It's not quite so straightforward, though, as she rarely published poems immediately after she wrote them. It will take some effort to reconstruct an accurate time-line of her drafting and publishing, then layer the dates of the letters on top of that.

A few months ago, I'd have been like an overexcited golden retriever off leash and chasing down a tossed tennis ball to be tasked with this assignment.

The most I can do now is nod.

"What's my timeline?"

"We've got a month before I need to present. So, maybe a

week or so? Maybe two? That should give me time to sift through what you find and work it into my existing research."

"Cool." I shake my head. "I mean, I'll get right on it."

I'm almost to my office door when Dr. Banerjee calls my name. "Eloise."

I squeeze my eyes shut for a moment, thinking of Jake, thinking of Gran. I almost correct Dr. Banerjee, telling her to call me Lo. But the masochist in me wants the punishment. I want the reminder of how naive I can be.

I turn back, tucking the folder against my chest. "Yes?"

"Is everything okay? That is to say, are *you* okay?"

Why wouldn't I be? My heart's just been cranked through a meat grinder, pulverized beyond recognition. But I'm totally fine. No big deal.

"I know you suffered a loss recently," she says.

You can say that again.

Though I'm not sure you can lose something you never had. And Jake was never really mine.

"Were you close with your grandmother?"

It takes a moment for the words to take shape, to become clear. Dr. Banerjee thinks I'm upset because I'm mourning my grandmother. *Not* a fledgling relationship with a man who clearly has a stunted emotional maturity.

"I'll be fine, Dr. Banerjee. Thank you for checking on me."

"If there's anything I can do to help you settle in, please do let me know."

Her smile is sad, and I hate how nice she's being. Dr. Banerjee is the type of woman I aspire to be: brilliant, confident, and compassionate. So many academics are so caught up in the research and the cerebral stuff, that they struggle with personal connections.

Funnily enough, at this moment, I could use a tiny bit *less* compassion.

I walk out of Dr. Banerjee's office, walking slowly across the campus I've always dreamed of calling my own. The temperature is cooler here in Washington, the air less humid. But none of the trees have Spanish moss dangling from them. And there are no pelicans waiting for a handout, no sound of the waves crashing against the shore. No faint scent of salt on the air. I've never been so homesick for a place I never actually called home. The homesickness is followed by a sharp, visceral longing for my gran.

I make it to the tiny studio apartment I have all to myself and shut myself inside where my grief over losing Gran mixes with my grief over losing Jake and hits me full force.

I crumple to the ground, papers scattering around me, and stay there until I've run out of tears.

The first letter from Jake arrives the next day.

I stare at his handwriting, which I'd know anywhere, even though I only saw the blocky script a few times. There is no return address, not that I need one. The stationery I recognize as well—it's from the box I found in Gran's closet.

My throat feels tight, and my eyes burn.

For a solid minute, I stare at my full name—Eloise Markham—before sliding the envelope unopened into a drawer in my desk.

TWENTY-FIVE

Jake

I MISSED Eloise the minute she crossed the bridge off of Oakley Island.

But missing her was expected. A normal reaction.

I planned to let myself wallow for a few days until the *missing her* faded.

But there was no fading of anything. Instead, my sadness sharpened into a fine point. Settling deep in my gut, it became a throbbing, gaping wound constantly reminding me of what I gave up.

Because I *did* give her up. She made it perfectly clear just how unhappy she was with me when she left. And she had every right to be.

Work is pretty low key right now, which is good because I'm spending most of my afternoons at Ned's—an intentional move of self-preservation because as much as I want to bathe my emotions in scotch, Ned won't let me overdo it.

The downside is that being at Ned's also reminds me of Eloise. Bard the Bird has been spouting new quotes every day, most of which I've had to google to identify.

One from Willa Fremont about undid me, especially coming from the parrot's mouth. Beak. Whatever.

"To love you well is to say goodbye," he squawked.

Bard is particularly stuck on this one.

The first time he said it, I nodded, thinking of how I'd done just that. I'd said goodbye because it was the best thing for Lo.

But the longer I'm without her, the worse I feel. And the more I suspect that everything I did was a colossal mistake rooted in my own fear.

Not sending Lo to grad school. I stand by my conviction that she would have regretted giving up on her dream.

But maybe I didn't have to end things. Maybe I didn't have to push her away.

Ned slides a glass of water across the bar and takes my empty scotch glass. "I'll trade ya."

Bard chooses this moment to return to Shakespeare. "A coward dies a thousand times before his death," he squawks.

My eyes jump to Ned's, and he chuckles. "Don't look at me. I didn't tell him to say it."

The truth is, I don't need Bard to call me a coward to feel like one. But when Liam got hurt, and then Ned started comparing Lo to Mom, and grad school for Lo became an actual possibility, all of my worries and doubts compounded, and I freaked out.

"You can still fix this," Ned says, his sad smile partially hidden beneath his mustache.

"Like you did with Mom?" Perhaps not fair, but I'm not feeling particularly rational.

Ned shakes his head rather than rising to the fight the

way I want him to. "Your mother never lied to me about what she wanted. I always knew where she stood. Same goes for her. We tried to make the best of our circumstances." He shrugs. "What's best turned out to be separating."

Best for whom? I want to ask. Ned, when I really look at him, still carries a sadness I can now recognize firsthand. I wouldn't wish it on anyone.

"Good talk, Ned. Thanks for the encouragement."

"You're missing the point. I knew from the beginning what your mother wanted. But have you asked Lo what she wants? Did you even give her the chance to have an opinion?"

I'm barely holding back a sharp retort I know he doesn't deserve when a few customers walk in, giving me a brief reprieve—a moment to let Ned's words settle.

And ... he's right.

I didn't ask. I assumed.

Because assuming was easier than risking the loss I believed was inevitable.

Because I thought I knew what was best for Lo.

Because I was afraid she would settle and then change her mind.

Naomi's words from breakfast all those weeks ago come slamming back. *You don't get to decide what makes Lo happy, Jake. She does.*

Lo tried to decide. And I wouldn't let her. And now she's thousands of miles away, living a dream that doesn't include me.

The little bit of clarity that comes from acknowledging my mistake is strangely cathartic. I don't hurt any less. If anything, I feel worse. But I'm too logical a person not to appreciate understanding the source of my pain.

I swallow down the ice water and leave money on the bar.

Just before I walk away, I grab a dry cocktail napkin and scrawl, *Thanks, Dad. You were right.*

"SO, YOU AND MY SISTER?"

My head snaps up from where I'm stretching on the carriage house's front steps after my morning run. Merritt sits on one of the chairs—*Lo's* chair—eyeing me over her cup of coffee. This no-makeup, messy-haired version of Merritt reminds me of Lo, though I haven't seen much resemblance between them until now.

"What do you mean?"

Merritt rolls her eyes. Blue, but not the brilliant turquoise Lo has. "I mean, when did you and Lo get together? And what happened before she left?"

"I don't—"

"I'm not an idiot. First, Lo is miserable. I could see it before she left, and in the few times we've talked, she sounds like a total sad sack. Second, you look the same. Third, you keep casting these longing eyes at my side of the carriage house." She takes a sip of coffee. "If you don't want to talk to me about it, fine. She clearly doesn't either. Just figured I'd offer. Maybe I could give you some insight."

Could she, though? Lo made no secret of the fact that she hasn't been very close to either of her sisters, especially not Merritt, who not very long ago tried to get me to spy on Lo.

"Sadie would probably do better at this," Merritt says, as though she's got a direct line to my thoughts. "Still, Lo and I may not be close, but I'm observant. I know her better than almost anyone."

I sink down on the top step and unlace my running shoes. "I think I made a mistake."

Merritt hums but says nothing.

"Okay, I *know* I made a mistake."

"And what are you going to do about it?"

"*Should* I do something about it? I mean, she's doing what she dreamed of doing. She's there and I'm here. It seems like the best thing for Lo is to let her move on."

I almost choke on the last few words, and Merritt shakes her head.

"If you're really asking yourself if you *should* do something about it, then you don't know my sister as well as I thought. And you definitely don't deserve her."

With a last look that could cause a whole garden to wither and die, Merritt leaves me on the porch.

I'm torn. On the one hand, I want to buy the next flight out of Savannah, show up on Lo's doorstep, and beg her to forgive me. On the other ... what if it's too late? What if Merritt's wrong, and Lo isn't miserable? What if she's already moved on with her life, and getting off of Oakley was all she needed to realize the island—*that I*—was temporary? A blip. An insignificant journal entry she'll laugh about in ten years.

But living in fear is what got me here in the first place.

I push into my half of the carriage house feeling more and more certain that I have to do something. Merritt's words replay in my brain. *You don't know Lo as well as I thought.*

I *do* know her. So, what would matter to Lo?

Authenticity. *Words.*

I won't ask her to come back. But I will tell her how I feel. I just have to figure out how.

———

IT'S LIAM, of all people, who finally gives me the winning idea.

"Could I write Lo a letter?" he asks, looking up from his mac and cheese, cheeks puffed out like a gluttonous chipmunk.

My fork freezes halfway to my mouth. Because why didn't I think of this? I didn't want to text. I'm awkward on the phone and unlikely to win anyone back. But letters ... the very thing I know Lo is studying.

I set down my fork. "Of course." I clear my throat. "What would you like to say?"

"That's private," he says, giving me a stern look. "Unless I need help with spelling. But I probably won't." He takes another bite, talking through it. "Have you written to her yet?"

I shake my head. "No."

Liam blinks, then blinks again. Balancing his fork on his plate, he folds his hands on the table, looking the way I imagine I do when meeting with a client. "Why not?"

Knowing his aversion to lies, I am as honest as I can be with an eight-year-old. "I didn't think of it. But I think I probably should write to her."

He raises one eyebrow, and again, I'm so reminded of myself that it's almost scary. "Just *probably*?"

I think of the big box of stationery Lo unearthed in one of Gennie's upstairs closets, and a wave of excitement rolls through me. She went on and on about how sad it was that nobody ever writes letters anymore. She probably took all of Gennie's stationery with her, and I won't have anything half as nice, but the words are what truly matters. "Why don't I find us some letter-writing materials once we clear the table?"

290

Liam nods and goes back to his macaroni. "I can help if you need me to."

It's a perfect idea, even if the idea of putting my feelings on paper, of being as honest with Lo as I've started to be with myself, makes my throat tighten.

"Thanks, kiddo," I say. "I'm going to need all the help I can get."

TWENTY-SIX

Lo

ELEVEN LETTERS.

ELEVEN.

Arriving every day or every other day, sometimes two at once. There's even one from Liam that I apologetically stuffed into the same desk drawer with all the others. I just ... couldn't.

For days, my heart has beaten a dangerously erratic rhythm every time I open my mailbox. Clutching in disappointment when there's nothing from Jake, swooping down to my toes every time there is.

I'm fine. *Everything is fine.*

I've kept the letters shoved in the drawer this whole time, trying to ignore my awareness of them.

Which is, of course, impossible. They're like my own less gothic and murdery version of *A Tell Tale Heart*.

"Fine! You win!" I yell, like they are living things, not pieces of paper covered in Jake's masculine scrawl.

I jerk the drawer open and pull out the letters, tearing them all open at once in what feels like a fit of romantic rage.

Is that a thing? It is now.

I spread the letters over the top of my comforter, arranging them in the order they arrived. And then I start to read.

It's like I've been granted access to all the parts of himself Jake has kept hidden. All the unspoken words, all the things I wondered about are laid out in a completely Jake way. I make my very best attempt not to let my tears fall on the pages. I don't want to risk ruining the ink. Most of my tears end up dripping into my smile.

The words aren't flowery, which would have felt fake coming from him, but they are absolutely romantic in a very Jake Fieldstone way. They are raw and honest, practical and to the point.

The point being: Jake still wants me. He regrets pushing me away, and though he wanted to do what was best for me, he knows he should have asked me what I wanted. He confessed that he made a big mistake and that he was afraid.

Jake—admitting he was afraid.

Is it bad that I feel happy hearing he's every bit as miserable as I am? Is it bad I want to grab my bag and hop on the first plane back to Georgia?

"I wouldn't say it's *bad*. Just ill-advised. Maybe a bit impractical," Naomi offers, because yes—I called Jake's sister to ask for advice.

Not *because* she's Jake's sister. More because I can't think of anyone else to talk to about what to do. I still haven't told my sisters about how I got involved with Gran's lawyer. One of Jake's letters confirms that Merritt has figured us out, and that is as good a reason as any *not* to call Merritt or Sadie. They would make the conversation about them, and what I really needed was to have a conversation about Jake.

"Right. Definitely impractical," I say.

For a LOT of reasons. The assistantship will help me through school, but money is tight. And now that my Instagram content is back to general lifestyle stuff and not renovating Gran's house, I've lost steam.

The only sponsors reaching out are looking for content related to design and house flipping, and I can no longer give it to them. Grad school is great, but it effectively killed my fledgling influencer career and the side income that came along with it.

"What do you want to do, Lo?" Naomi asks, not even a hint of what *she* wants me to do in her voice.

And there's the big question. What DO I want?

"I want it all," I say, pulling my feet up and curling them under me. "I don't want to give up my goals and plans for a guy."

Even Jake. Even after the letters. While he shared how he's feeling, he also didn't ask me to come back. He didn't ask me to *take* him back. He made no promises, only confessions and apologies.

Naomi seems to sense that I'm still processing. Or maybe she's just busy getting Liam ready for bed. A moment ago, they had a very serious discussion about why fluoride is needed in toothpaste when it's also in the water we drink.

"The thing is, I'm not sure my goals and dreams are still the same as they were," I say.

I've thrown myself deeply into the work Dr. Banerjee gave me. And while it is fascinating, and I am still interested, I can't stop thinking about Gran's house and whether Merritt will stick with my wallpaper choices for the various bathrooms or if she'll wait for the backordered tile. Jake's letters included just enough information to make me realize how much I'm missing. He says Merritt is mostly deferring to Hunter, but for how long? Merritt is not the deferring type. Whatever she's going through, it won't last forever, and then she'll be back to her controlling, micromanaging ways.

I'm twitchy with the thought of going back to find Gran's bed and breakfast totally sanitized and without personality, as practical and stark as my oldest sister.

Not to mention the general worry I feel for Merritt. What's going on with her anyway?

But more than all of that, I miss knowing Jake is on the other side of the wall. I miss our early morning coffees and starting my day with one of his kisses and ending the same way. We barely got started, and yet, from the very beginning, from that first heated kiss on the crumbling balcony at *The Round Up*, I've known there's something big between us.

I wasn't sure until the letters that he feels the same way.

And now that I DO know how he feels ...

"It's okay for dreams to shift," Naomi says. "For them to expand to make room for another person."

"You sound like you're speaking from experience."

"I am," she says. "Though not in the romantic sense. My whole world expanded when Liam arrived. It's not quite the same, I know. But I don't regret the things I had to give up to fit him into my life and to fit myself into his. Sometimes, dreams get deferred. Sometimes they get lost or we're forced to let go, to make other choices."

I think about Naomi's words all night long, letting them roll around like the rough stones inside the rock tumbler I got for my ninth birthday. Only, the tumbler's motor burned out before it smoothed out the rocks the way they did in all the commercials.

The next morning, my brain feels like that burned-out motor when I stop by Dr. Banerjee's office. For reasons I can't explain, I have Jake's letters bundled up inside my laptop bag.

Dr. Banerjee closes her laptop and gives me her full attention. "How are you doing, Eloise?"

"I'm making good progress. I think I'm about halfway through the letters and ..."

I trail off as she shakes her head. "I don't mean the research. Though I'm quite glad you're enjoying the work. I meant how are *you*?"

Bursting into tears in front of my mentor and boss isn't how I imagined this going. But lately, I've been finding my best-laid plans seem to crash and burn on impact. And I shouldn't be surprised, really. The past three months have been punctuated with *a lot* of unexpected crying spells.

Unable to speak because of the hiccuping, awful noises coming out of me, I grab the stack of Jake's letters from my bag and thrust them across the desk.

Dr. Banerjee locates a box of tissues before she picks up the letters. I blow my nose with a gooselike honk while I watch her. She scans the first letter, then the second. At the third, she sighs heavily, and I prepare myself to hear that I'm too young to fall in love, too bright to give up my future in academics for a lawyer living on a small island she's probably never heard of.

Instead, Dr. Banerjee asks, "Do you know why I took you on as my assistant?"

"Nepotism?" I answer, only half-joking.

She laughs, then covers her mouth. "Sorry. But no. Not because Dr. Fieldstone vouched for you. It was your essay."

"My essay?" I snag another tissue from the box, just so I have something to do with my hands.

"Do you remember what you wrote?"

Honestly, I don't. When I shake my head, her smile lifts.

"You wrote about the way letters and words and relationships can steer and impact our paths, shaping our future into something wholly different." Dr. Banerjee taps the letters on the desk. "It seems perhaps you're living out your research."

It's so obvious, I can't believe I didn't make the connection myself. Which tells me just how far off my game I am.

I sniff. "I'm not sure what I'm doing. Or what the letters mean."

Studying me for a moment, Dr. Banerjee leans back in her chair. Her eyes are so impossibly kind that fresh tears sting my eyes. "But they mean something to you."

They mean EVERYTHING.

I manage to nod. It suddenly occurs to me the significance of Jake sending letters. He didn't text. He didn't email or call. He sat down with pen and paper and wrote me *love letters.*

Because he knew they would mean more to me than anything else.

Because he knows *me.*

"I've always been someone who thinks outside the box," Dr. Banerjee says after a moment. "And I think I have an idea."

FROM THE LETTERS

Dear Lo,

There is something intimidating about sitting down to write a woman who is, at this very moment, studying some of the greatest love letters the literary world has ever seen. I've read a few of the letters Willa Fremont's editor wrote, the one or two that are available online, and I cannot even hope to compare.

I'm too logical to be brilliant with words, but I can tell you the truth. I owe you that much. And I hope my meager attempt will resonate in some small way.

Eloise. Lo. I do not regret asking my mother to help nudge Dr. Banerjee into accepting you into the Greenwood program. Mom tells me you're brilliant—that Dr. Banerjee cannot stop talking about your insight and understanding. You were meant for this. I know that.

But I was wrong in thinking that a graduate program is ALL you are meant for. Life is so much more than what we do or where we study. It's about people. About relationships.

It's about love. You've always known that, I think. It was me who was too scared to admit it.

I was wrong to send you away, Lo. To believe that we couldn't find a way to be together while pursuing our dreams. I was afraid of losing you and somehow thought that pushing you away would make your leaving easier to accept. Because I was positive you would leave. If not for this grad program, then for another one. Another life. A bigger one.

But old scars made me think that way. It wasn't fair to tie those scars to you.

Can you forgive me? I was wrong. I was scared. I will never not regret this mistake. Love, Jake

---

Dear Lo,

I thought you might be interested to know that Steve has settled into her new home and is really thriving. Did I mention Steve is a *she*? She even has a boyfriend, so her future is looking very promising.

Liam sends his love and wanted me to double check that you received his first letter. He also helped me formulate a list of all the things we love about you, and I thought I'd share it, unedited.

1. You have unparalleled fashion sense. Even if I am allergic to pineapples.
2. You light up the room with your optimism and enthusiasm for basically everything.
3. You make people feel good when you talk to them. You listen with your entire body, like what people say really matters to you.

4. You are an incredible kisser. Best I've ever experienced. (Liam wants you to know he did not contribute to this one, and he thinks I'm gross.)
5. You are very good at being unapologetically you. Not many women have that kind of confidence at twenty-one.
6. I see your eyes every time I close mine, and I don't think there's anything more beautiful.
7. You make me want to be better. Nicer. Humbler. Less ... grumpy.

Love, Jake

Dear Lo,

I watched a movie last night that made me think of you.

The next morning, I went on a run, and the sun rising over the ocean made me think of you.

That afternoon, I met with a client who wore a pineapple pin on his lapel. Of course, I thought of you.

I sense a pattern developing.

Luckily, I really like thinking of you, so I can't say I mind that I see you everywhere, in everything.

Love, Jake

Dear Lo,

I have news! Merritt actually smiled at me today. She was also rolling her eyes, but I'm still counting this as an accomplishment. You Markham women are tough nuts to crack. (Just between you and me, her smile pales in comparison to yours.) Now that she's figured out about us—did I tell you she figured out about us?—I feel as though I need to convince her I'm a decent guy.

I get the sense Merritt has been through something recently. She's lost the edge she had when we first met, and she's letting a lot of the decisions I expected her to be very invested in fall to Hunter. And don't worry—Hunter is honoring every request you made. Your fingerprints are all over this place, Lo. As they should be. I'm positive your grandmother would approve.

Love, Jake

PS. Mom tells me she's still hearing wonderful things about you from Dr. Banerjee. I can't say I'm surprised. I'm so glad you're thriving. Academically, anyway. Is it bad if the tiniest part of me hopes you might be missing me too?

———

Dear Lo,

Last night, I had a dream that you were in my arms, asleep beside me. Your hand was curled against my chest, your head rested on my shoulder, and your entire body was pressed against mine. It was so real, so vivid, that when I woke up, the pain of your absence was as visceral as it was intense.

I don't know how to stop wondering if I've missed my chance. If I will ever have the privilege of waking up beside you. It seems like a happiness I don't deserve, but I crave it all the same.

Bard has been quoting quite a bit of Willa Fremont: "To love you well is to let you go." This one always hits the hardest. I don't want to let you go. And yet, I know if that's what's required for you to be happy, I will put your happiness over mine every single time.

Hearts are messy, complicated things. I'm trying to do better at listening to mine. To believe that happiness is something I might actually deserve. Your grandmother once told me I wouldn't believe the way the world opens up when a person decides to love.

I think I finally understand what she meant.

Love, Jake

Dear Miss Markham,

Uncle Jake says I have to call you that. He says it's polite. I say it sounds silly. Anyway. He's not helping me with the rest of the letter unless I need spelling help.

How's Olympia?

We miss you. I miss you a little because you're nice, but Jake misses you the most. I know because he's being weird. He stopped shaving and looks dirty. Mom calls it lumberjack chic, whatever that means.

I think you need to come back. Uncle Jake says we can't ask you to come back, but I'm not letting him read this. Come back. Please. I don't like Uncle Jake's beard. And he's in a really bad mood all the time. More than usual.

If this is love, I'm never doing it.

-Liam

TWENTY-SEVEN

Jake

IT'S BEEN THIRTY-SEVEN DAYS, five hours, and twenty-three minutes since I last saw Eloise. But who's counting? Definitely not me. That would be way too sad. And a giant cliche. But I still know the exact times because of Liam.

Liam is counting, and he reminds me every time I see him.

"Aren't you a little young for this kind of math?" I ask on Sunday afternoon when Naomi drops him off at my place so she can go on a lunch date with an accountant she met online.

"I'm almost *nine*, Uncle Jake," Liam answers defensively.

"An almost nine-year-old who knows how to program a countdown app on his mother's phone," Naomi adds.

Liam smirks and rolls his eyes, looking way too old to be *almost nine*.

"He's going to be so fun when he's seventeen," I say.

"He will be," Naomi says. "He's going to be independent and honest and smart and resourceful."

I raise an eyebrow.

"I'm manifesting, Jake. Telling the universe what I want and hoping it delivers. Don't ruin this for me." She nudges me with her shoulder. "How are you holding up?"

I shrug. There is an unsent letter on my kitchen table. It's been three days since I sent the last one, and I'm struggling to make myself send another. I still haven't heard anything back. Not a text. Not a phone call. Not a return letter.

That last one has surprised me the most. As much as Lo loves the romance of letter writing, I hoped she'd write back.

Maybe it is actually over. Maybe the letters—my words, my heart bleeding on the page—weren't enough.

"It's going to be okay, Jake," Naomi says.

I push my hands into my pockets. "I don't want to just be okay," I say simply. I lift my eyes to my sister's. "I want her back."

Naomi's expression softens. "I know you do. And maybe you'll still get her back."

"Please don't give me false hope. It's probably time I get past this. I forced her to move on, now I need to do the same thing."

She studies me for a long moment. "What if I just give you *hope*? Nothing false about it?"

I narrow my eyes, and her lips lift. She isn't quite smiling, but her eyes are dancing like she knows something. "What are you trying to say?"

"I'm saying I've got to go, or I'm going to be late." She darts through the living room and kisses Liam's forehead. "See ya, kid. Don't be trouble for your uncle."

"Naomi." I follow her to the porch, but she's already down the steps and climbing into her car.

"I'll be back in a couple of hours. Byeeeeeee," she calls before she slams her car door closed and speeds off.

I cannot settle down. If not for Liam, I'd probably go for a run to burn off the nervous energy Naomi's revelation—*can it be called a revelation when I don't actually know what she was telling me?*—has done to me.

I'm determined to get answers out of her when she picks Liam up, but it's like her radar has picked this up because she doesn't even come inside. She honks from the car, and Liam races out and climbs into the backseat like he's in on the secret.

"Naomi!" I call as she spins out of the driveway, but she only lifts her hand out the window in a backward wave.

I wait exactly thirty-two minutes—that's how long it takes her to drive home—and text her.

Jake: What are you not telling me? And do I need to drive over there to make you say more?
Naomi: You're funny like this. All desperate and stuff.
Jake: NAOMI.
Naomi: I've already said too much. Just try and relax, okay? Things are going to work out.
Naomi: AND DO NOT TEXT ME ABOUT THIS AGAIN. I've got to get Liam ready for bed, and you're being very annoying.

I sigh and toss my phone onto the couch. She's said too much? That means Naomi knows something.

I'm going to need to go on that run after all.

Five miles and half a shower later, a knock sounds on my

front door. If not for the seeds Naomi planted in my brain earlier, I might have ignored the knock. Assumed it was a random Amazon delivery, or Merritt wanting me to pass yet another question along to Hunter.

But Lo is on my brain. She's also impacting every part of my nervous system, which goes into hyperdrive at the sound of a second knock. I can't stop the hope that surges through my chest. I want her to be standing on my porch more desperately than I have ever wanted anything in my life.

I am still dripping wet, only a towel wrapped around my waist, when I swing the door open.

Lo smiles, her eyes raking over my body, lingering on my tattoo. I've never been more glad to have spent the money on such an elaborate spread of ink.

I will my heart to slow down.

Lo is here. On my porch.

I've hoped for this, and now that she's here, I don't know what to do.

Her gaze slides up to mine, the turquoise eyes I've been dreaming about sparkling. "Why am I so good at catching you with your pants off?"

Hitching my towel a little higher, I lean against the door jamb. I'll never admit this, but I need the support. "If I recall, you've been pantsless yourself a few times."

"Just the once," she shoots back. "How was I to know the ocean would be so mean?"

I smile and give my head a little shake. "You're back?"

She bites her lip. "I am."

I could stand here forever. Drinking her in. Watching the way the porch light is tossing shadows across her face, highlighting her cheekbones, catching on the pale blue of her eyes.

But then a mosquito buzzes around my chest, and Eloise reaches out to slap it, her fingers colliding with my skin. She wipes the dead mosquito away with a wince, her fingers returning to the spot like her touch alone will be enough to erase the bite.

"Sorry. I just didn't want you to get—"

Her words trail off when I close my palm over hers, pressing her fingers flat against my chest. "Thank you," I say gently. "Do you want to come inside? It's late. This is the hour flying cockroaches come out."

"Oh, good grief," she says, stepping toward me. "You had to mention the roaches, didn't you?"

I tug her into my living room, her body colliding with mine, and I'm suddenly *very* aware that I am only wearing a towel. I close the door behind us and take a giant step back. "I'll be right back. Don't go anywhere. Please," I add, and she smiles at the word.

"I promise."

I rush to my room and throw on some clothes, barely pausing long enough to put on some deodorant and run my fingers through my hair. When I make it back to the front room, Eloise is standing by my kitchen table, the unsent letter in her hand.

Now that I've officially uncorked my bottled-up emotions, I can't seem to stop the flow. Maybe I don't want to.

Maybe I won't *have* to.

Lo turns to face me. "Were you going to send it?"

I wrap a hand around the back of my neck. I will only be honest with her about this. "I ... hadn't decided yet."

"You were going to give up?"

"Maybe more like I was going to respect your choice and not become insufferably annoying?"

She smiles as she runs a finger along the edges of the

envelope in her hands. "You might be insufferable, but you could never be annoying. Can I read it now?"

I shake my head, and her face falls.

"You can. Of course you can. Just—not yet." I motion my head to the couch. "Can we talk first?"

She settles onto the couch beside me, the letter still in her hands. I want her to read it. But I'm feeling ... buzzy. On edge. I don't know why she's here or how long she plans to stay, and I feel like I need to modify my expectations accordingly before we have the *I love you* conversation.

Because that's what's written in the last letter. That somewhere along the way, I fell in love with her. Only I was too much of a coward to own it. I wasn't brave like she was. *Is.* She has to be brave if she's sitting across from me right now.

"How long—" my voice catches, and I clear my throat. "How long are you in town?"

She shrugs. "Forever, probably."

My eyes widen. "But your program—"

"Isn't the most important thing," she says, cutting me off.

"But I don't want you to—"

"I know, I know. You don't want me to give it up for you. It's important to you that I live my dreams. Blah, blah, blah. But that's why I'm here, Jake. I love my program. But only half as much as I'd love it if I got to also love you."

She scoots a little closer and reaches for my hands. "I didn't drop out. I'm still enrolled, still working with Dr. Banerjee. Greenwood has a low-residency option for my grad program, and it only took a little bit of paperwork to switch me over. I'll spend six weeks on campus twice a year, but otherwise, I can do everything from here. *And* Dr. Banerjee is willing to let me continue my research remotely during the weeks I'm on Oakley."

My hands start to tremble, and she squeezes them a little tighter.

"So, you're here to stay."

She nods. "At least until the middle of August when I'll have to head back for my first residency. But I'll be back by the end of September."

This feels too good to be true. She's here, and she isn't leaving. At least not permanently. But she's also not compromising her dreams for me.

"I don't know what to say."

She nudges my knee. "You could say you're happy. Naomi says you've been moping around here making everyone miserable. And you might need to talk with Liam when he's a bit older. He sent me a letter saying he never wanted to fall in love because it just brings misery."

I choke out a laugh. "I'll make a note to have a conversation with him in a few years." I pause. "But it's true. I have been miserable."

"But you aren't anymore?" She bites her lip, looking hopeful.

"I'm definitely *less* miserable."

Her head tilts, the curve of her lips and her husky voice sending out flirty vibes. "Any ideas on how you could be *not* miserable?"

"I do have a few ideas." My gaze drops to her lips.

"If there's one thing I love, Mr. Fieldstone, it's *ideas*."

That's all the invitation I need. I lean in and kiss her, my hands lifting to curve around either side of her face. The moment our mouths touch, it's a key sliding into a lock. Her arms wrap around my neck as she slides into my lap, and we are lost in a frenzy of kisses and touches.

I cannot get her close enough. I crave her like she is the air in my lungs, the blood pumping through my veins.

Eloise is essential.

She pulls back, her forehead resting against mine, her chest heaving, her fingers tangling in the back of my hair.

"'And the sunlight clasps the earth,'" I whisper softly. "'And the moonbeams kiss the sea...'"

Her lips lift in a smile. "'What are all these kissings worth if thou kiss not me?'" She shakes her head. "How long have you had Percy Bysshe Shelley in your back pocket?"

I shrug. "A while. Bard taught me. But I get the credit for the timing. That was all me. Impressed?"

"By you? Always."

I reach for the letter that slipped out of her lap when she slipped into mine and hand it to her. "Here. You can read this now."

Her expression brightens as she breaks the seal and pulls out a letter, the shortest one I've written so far. "Can I read it out loud?"

I nod, and she clears her throat. "Dear Lo," she reads. "I always believed that love was not a reliable thing. That it will fail us more than it doesn't. That it will cause more harm than good. More heartache. More pain." Her eyes lift to mine for a brief moment before dropping back to the page. She licks her lips. "Then I met you. And discovered that even if I never see you again, I still wouldn't wish away the opportunity to have fallen in love with you. Because in loving you, I have finally found my true self."

Her hands fall to her lap, and her eyes close.

My hands tighten where they're sitting at her waist. "It's stupid," I say softly. "Cheesy."

She leans forward and presses a lingering kiss to my lips, her cheeks damp with tears. "It isn't stupid or cheesy. It's perfect."

"I love you, Lo," I say, a thrill shooting through me. It's the first time I've said it out loud.

Lo kisses me, her lips lingering as she whispers against my mouth. "I love you too."

Hours later, after countless kisses, a DoorDash delivery of dinner we'd both forgotten to eat, and a movie we only pretend to watch, we doze on the couch, Lo's body pressed against mine, her head resting on my chest.

"I really do think I'll be happy on Oakley, Jake," she says sleepily. "I love it here. And not just because you're here. In a lot of ways, it feels like this town was made for someone like me."

"Someone like you?"

She sits up a little, propping her chin on my chest so she can look at me. "Sure. It's the reason I love Instagram so much. I love being a part of a community. But Oakley is even better. Everyone looks out for each other." She pokes me in the ribs and grins. "You're frowning, but I love how much they all love you."

"It's not half as much as they love you," I say, catching her poking fingers and threading them through mine. "Have you seen Frank's 'Eloise' playlist on his TikTok?"

Her eyebrows shoot up. "Do I *want* to see his Eloise playlist?"

"No. No, you do not," I say dryly. "Suffice it to say, Frank is your number one fan."

"Come on, Jake. At least arm wrestle him for the title."

I shrug. "Nah. I was hoping for something a little more official."

She bites her lip, her eyes dancing. "Something like … boyfriend?"

"How about overlord instead?"

Her laugh vibrates against me, moving through my chest.

To have her here, happy, in my arms, is more than I've let myself hope for the past few weeks. But now that she's here, there's no going back. But the permanence doesn't feel over-whelming. It just feels *right*. Like I've finally found where I belong.

And it's right here in Eloise Markham's arms.

EPILOGUE

Lo

I'LL NEVER GET USED to Ben's yacht. Jake breathes a heavy sigh when I keep stopping to take pictures. But I see the smile in his eyes. When I strike a little bit of a sexier pose and tell him, "This one is just for you," the smile moves from his eyes to his mouth. I'm wearing my pineapple dress at his request. With a cardigan over top since technically, it's a summer dress.

It's New Year's, and it might be cold, but the pool on the top deck is heated. Because that's what you get on a *dinghy* like this. I've got my suit on under the dress, and I'm more than ready to join our friends up top. This time, there is not a model or potential model on board. Both my sisters are here, which feels like a miracle, plus Naomi and Liam, and some other friends we've made over the past few months.

"Come on," I say, tugging on Jake's hand. "Everyone's waiting."

But Jake isn't letting himself be tugged. Instead, he pulls me into his arms, wrapping one around my waist as he leads me in the opposite direction.

"No pit stops, Mr. Fieldstone."

He kisses the spot on my jaw he *knows* makes me give into just about anything. "Just a small one."

"Jake ..." Another kiss has my eyes fluttering closed. "Ugh, fine."

He pulls back and shoots me the kind of grin that still makes my stomach twist and spin. "Come on," he says, tugging me toward Ben's master bedroom. "You'll like this detour. I promise."

Thankfully, Jake pulls me right through the bedroom— I'm not about to have THAT kind of detour on Ben's yacht with everyone upstairs—and out onto the small deck where we spent the fourth of July in the hot tub.

The moment the door opens to the deck, I gasp. Because it does NOT look like it did in July. Fairy lights are strung overhead, and candles are everywhere. I mean, EVERYWHERE.

Jake knows me well enough to know I'm fighting off worries about fire hazards because he leans close and whispers, "All candles are firmly secured to the deck. I made sure."

"Thank you," I say, noting the bottle of champagne chilling next to a bottle of fizzy apple cider—because I'm still not much of a drinker. "But what is this?"

I get my answer when I glance over to see Jake down on one knee, looking up at me with his fathomless gray eyes.

"This," Jake says, holding out a small ring box, "is a proposal, Miss Markham."

I eye the box but am not about to throw it open. That's tacky. Even if I'm dying to see what Jake chose.

"And what, pray tell, are you proposing, Mr. Fieldstone?"

He opens the box, and I gasp. "I am proposing a life full of days spent arguing. Laughing. Talking. Teaching birds literature and swimming without losing our clothes."

At that moment, fireworks start shooting off from the top deck, the scream of a rocket going up making me gasp.

"Of fireworks—that Ben set off too early." Jake mutters the last part. "This will be really awkward now if you say no. But it is my sincerest hope, Eloise Markham, that you will let me make you officially, legally, contractually, fully mine."

I'm having trouble locating a coherent thought. Or moving my limbs. Jake has struck me dumb and paralyzed me with his words. And with the ring. The stone I recognized immediately as Gran's. It's a beautiful, round-cut emerald, but the setting is new—an intricate gold band that wraps and swirls around the stone.

Jake lifts the ring, and it glitters in the light as more fireworks go off above our heads. A cheer accompanies this one, and Jake is right—it would be SUPER awkward if I said no right now. Not that I ever would. He could have proposed months ago, back before I left for my first residency at Greenwood, and I still would have said yes. He could have proposed any of the times I came home to visit or when he came to visit me, and I would have been absolutely ready with a yes.

I've even—embarrassingly—practiced my acceptance, so anxious I've been for this moment.

And now he actually has proposed, and I can't say a thing.

"Would you believe your grandmother had this set aside? She gave it to Ned in her will. I didn't know what it was because she sealed it in an envelope with a note saying *when* —not *if*—we wound up together, Ned was to give me the ring so I could use the stone and choose a setting for you."

I can't help but laugh through the happy tears filling my eyes. "She was such a meddler, wasn't she?"

"She was. But it's nice to know I have her stamp of approval." He shifts a little, starting to look the slightest bit worried. "That is, if you'll marry me."

Though it feels a little cheesy, I kneel down right in front of Jake and cup his stubbled jaw in my hands. "It's not just a yes. It is an unequivocal, absolute yes, yes, YES."

I know he had to know I'd say yes, but relief still crosses his features, and it's completely adorable. "You will?" he asks, like he's just been told he chose the winning lotto numbers.

"I will. Though I think I'm supposed to wait until the actual vows to say that part." I pause, letting my fingertips rove over the familiar planes of his face. "But, um, do you think we could not wait so long for that part?"

"As in, you can't wait for me to put a ring on it?"

"Yes. I think I've waited enough."

His lips quirk, and I let my fingers trace his bottom lip.

"I'm all for a quick engagement. But just so we're clear, we've been together for five months. For most people, that wouldn't be considered waiting very long."

"Oh, Mr. Fieldstone." I press a chaste but lingering kiss to his lips because I just can't wait any longer. "I thought you knew by now that I am not most people."

Jake lifts my hand and slides the ring on my finger. The fit is perfect, and I swear, I can almost hear Gran laughing in delight. I also swear I see a familiar-looking pelican swooping low overhead, but I MUST be imagining that part.

"No, Miss Markham. You are not like any other woman in this world. You are you. Maddeningly impulsive. Hopelessly romantic. And completely perfect as you are."

And then, with fireworks bursting overhead, his ring on

my finger, and his hands wrapped firmly around my waist, Jake seals his words with a kiss to rival all the other kisses we've shared. Because this one holds the promise of *forever*.

THE END

BONUS EPILOGUE

Merritt

SOME PEOPLE SAY *best-laid plans* like it's a bad thing. As though making plans is a surefire way to ensure that they fail.

Up until three weeks ago, I'd have disagreed. Strongly.

Now ... I'm not so sure.

The way my life colossally imploded, it seems like all my carefully crafted plans actually conspired against me, resulting in an even bigger disaster.

My career? Toast. Not just toast, but bread blackened to the kind of unrecognizable crisp worthy of setting off the smoke detectors.

My personal life, which solely consisted of one now-ex boyfriend? Makes burnt toast look like a Michelin-star-rated dinner.

Well played, life. Well played.

Beside me in the passenger seat, Lo shifts, toying with

her phone. Looking for messages, if I'm not mistaken. Probably from our lawyer. The awkwardness between them since I arrived yesterday is the kind that only comes from an ended relationship.

Lo doesn't want to tell me? Fine. I legitimately can't be mad. I didn't tell either of my sisters why I was *really* able to come take Lo's place. The three of us don't share a lot of our lives. We're more like a loose braid, coming undone at the end. If I stopped to think about it, I might get sad, so I don't.

"You got the document I sent?" Lo asks.

"As previously stated twice now, yes."

To be honest, I was shocked by my youngest sister's thoroughness in documenting all paint colors, tile names, flooring options, and wallpaper choices for Gran's house, neatly organized room by room. Not that I'm going to stick to what she suggested. But if it helps her feel better about leaving ...

"And, also again, I promise I'll do my best to stick to your suggestions."

Lo nods, but when I glance over as we pull up to the airport, I see the corners of her mouth pull down like she doesn't believe me.

Smart girl.

I park, get out, and offer her a stiff hug, more than a little surprised when she clutches my shirt, not letting go. Now we're locked in the kind of embarrassing public display I try to avoid.

I start to pat her on the back, wondering how to extricate myself, when she pulls back with a sniff. Flashing me a brief smile that looks about ready to crumble, she turns to grab her bags.

I return to the driver's side but stand there until she

reaches the doors and turns back. "And be nice to the contractor."

She looks about ready to have a breakdown and is warning me about the contractor?

"I'm always nice." She gives me a look, and I huff a breath. "I'm always pleasant and professional."

It must be enough, because Lo nods, her hands tightening on the bags. "Good. Hunter can come across as quiet and gruff, but he's a big softie underneath. Don't break him."

With a wave, Lo disappears inside the airport, the doors whooshing closed behind her. I stand by my door until a car behind me honks and the airport security guy blows his whistle, urging me on with a wave of his hand.

Hunter. A name like a chorus to a song you can't get out of your head. It's been playing behind my eyes for years, no matter what I did in an attempt to silence it. Memories, like old film, flash through my mind. Sand rough palms, laughter, the scent of salt, not quite as sharp as the taste of it on skin. Promises made, then broken. Deep brown eyes flashing with hurt, then anger, then something even worse.

What are the odds there's another Hunter on Oakley Island—another Hunter who is gruff and quiet but a softie underneath?

Given my current state of best-laid and totally un-made plans? Absolutely zero.

Don't break him, Lo said.

Too late. But what no one knows is he broke me right back.

A NOTE FROM EMMA & JENNY

Hey, lovely readers!!! We are SO glad you found and read this little book. We hope you love Eloise and Jake (and Liam and Naomi and Ned and ... well, everyone) as much as we do. We absolutely fell in love with them while writing.

I (Emma) have to confess that I'm not the best at working with others. Supporting other authors? Yep. Encouraging other people? Totally!

But working closely like this sometimes brings out my stubborn, difficult, control freaky side. So I was nervous. Jenny and I were already critique partners and this seemed like a perfect partnership to bring in some income between our solo releases.

It didn't quite happen as fast as we thought (let's blame summer for that), but we are still on speaking terms and still like each other!!! (You do still like me, right, Jenny?) This summer, we were also supposed to meet in person but dumb covid prevented that. So, we wrote a whole book while being online friends. Sweet!!!

A fun thing happened while we collaborated on this. By

the time we got to final edits, reading back through the book, I often wasn't sure what I wrote and what Jenny wrote. We hope this was a seamless read for you as well, melding our styles and capitalizing on our strengths.

It does take a village, and we're grateful to the early readers who helped us realize we accidentally murdered Jake Fieldstone by having him eat pineapple after telling Lo he was allergic in Chapter One. (Okay, exaggeration since he doesn't make the allergy so serious, but it sounds more fun to say we killed him off.)

Thank you also to the people who obsessively watched our Instagram teasers and searched for clues in the hashtags. #yallaretheverybest

---

Jenny here, and YES, Emma, I still like you! Honestly, I'm not sure I've ever laughed my way through creating a novel more than we did through this one. It's been so much fun, and I can't wait to write more! (But seriously, we have to meet in person. And soon.)

We're already in the brainstorming stages of Merritt and Hunter's story, and of course, we can't leave Sadie out, so her book three will follow shortly after. Early readers have let us know they also think Naomi deserves a happily-ever-after, and we really like happily-ever-afters, so we hope we can also make that happen!

To all of you who read and support and cheer us on, thank you! You make this job so much fun. We absolutely could not do what we do without all of you!

All the heart-eye emojis,
Emma & Jenny

ABOUT EMMA

Emma St. Clair is a *USA Today* bestselling author of over twenty books. She loves sweet love stories and characters with a lot of sass. Her stories range from rom-com to women's fiction and all will have humor, heart, and nothing that's going to make you need to hide your Kindle from the kids. ;)

She lives in Houston with her husband, five kids, two covid-decision cats, and a Great Dane who does not make a very good babysitter. She earned her MFA in fiction at University of North Carolina at Greensboro writing literary fiction, but for now is focused on LOLs and HEAs.

Let's connect!

Newsletter signup: http://emmastclair.com/romcomemail

Instagram: https://instagram.com/kikimojo

Facebook Reader Group: https://www.facebook.com/groups/emmastclair/

Facebook Page: https://www.facebook.com/thesaintemma

BookBub: https://www.bookbub.com/authors/emma-st-clair

Website: http://emmastclair.com

ABOUT JENNY

Jenny Proctor grew up in the mountains of North Carolina, a place she still believes is one of the loveliest on earth. She lives a few hours south of the mountains now, in the Lowcountry of South Carolina. Mild winters and of course, the beach, are lovely compromises for having had to leave the mountains.

Ages ago, she studied English at Brigham Young University. She works full time as an author and as an editor, specializing in romance, through Midnight Owl Editors.

Jenny and her husband, Josh, have six children, and almost as many pets. They love to hike and camp as a family and take long walks through the neighborhood. But Jenny also loves curling up with a good book, watching movies, and eating food that, when she's lucky, she didn't have to cook herself. You can learn more about Jenny and her books at www.jennyproctor.com.

Let's connect!

Newsletter Sign Up: https://subscribepage.io/S933oF

Instagram: www.instagram.com/jennyproctorbooks

Facebook: www.facebook.com/jennyproctorbooks

Facebook Fan Group: www.facebook.com/groups/jennyproctorbooks

Bookbub: https://www.bookbub.com/authors/jenny-proctor

Website: www.jennyproctor.com